Readers love *Riding Shotgun* by AMY LANE

"...an amazing, complex, time-sensitive thriller. Wow! With all that going for it, I have a new favorite story—definitely on my list of 'best of 2024,' for sure."

—Rainbow Book Reviews

"It's a quick, fun story with lots of action and some hot sex. And a HEA that satisfies."

—Sparkling Book Reviews

"Every attack left me at the edge of my seat. I can't wait to see whose story will be next..."

—Paranormal Romance Guild

By Amy Lane (CONT)

Published by DSP Publications

ALL THAT HEAVEN WILL ALLOW
All the Rules of Heaven

LUCK MECHANICS
The Rising Tide • A Salt Bitter Sea

PRINCETON ROYALS
Riding Shotgun • Running Scared

TALKER
Talker • Talker's Redemption
Talker's Graduation
The Talker Collection Anthology

WINTER BALL
Winter Ball • Summer Lessons
Fall Through Spring

GREEN'S HILL
The Green's Hill Novellas

LITTLE GODDESS
Vulnerable
Wounded, Vol. 1 • Wounded, Vol. 2
Bound, Vol. 1 • Bound, Vol. 2
Rampant, Vol. 1 • Rampant, Vol. 2
Quickening, Vol. 1
Quickening, Vol. 2
Green's Hill Werewolves, Vol. 1
Green's Hill Werewolves, Vol. 2

Published by Harmony Ink Press

BITTER MOON SAGA
Triane's Son Rising
Triane's Son Learning
Triane's Son Fighting
Triane's Son Reigning

Published by DREAMSPINNER PRESS
www.dreamspinnerpress.com

RUNNING SCARED

AMY LANE

Published by
DREAMSPINNER PRESS

8219 Woodville Hwy #1245
Woodville, FL 32362 USA
www.dreamspinnerpress.com

This is a work of fiction. Names, characters, places, and incidents either are the product of author imagination or are used fictitiously, and any resemblance to actual persons, living or dead, business establishments, events, or locales is entirely coincidental.

Running Scared
© 2025 Amy Lane

Cover Art
© 2025 L.C. Chase
http://www.lcchase.com
Cover content is for illustrative purposes only and any person depicted on the cover is a model.

Trade Paperback ISBN: 978-1-64108-847-3
Digital ISBN: 978-1-64108-846-6
Trade Paperback published August 2025
v. 1.0

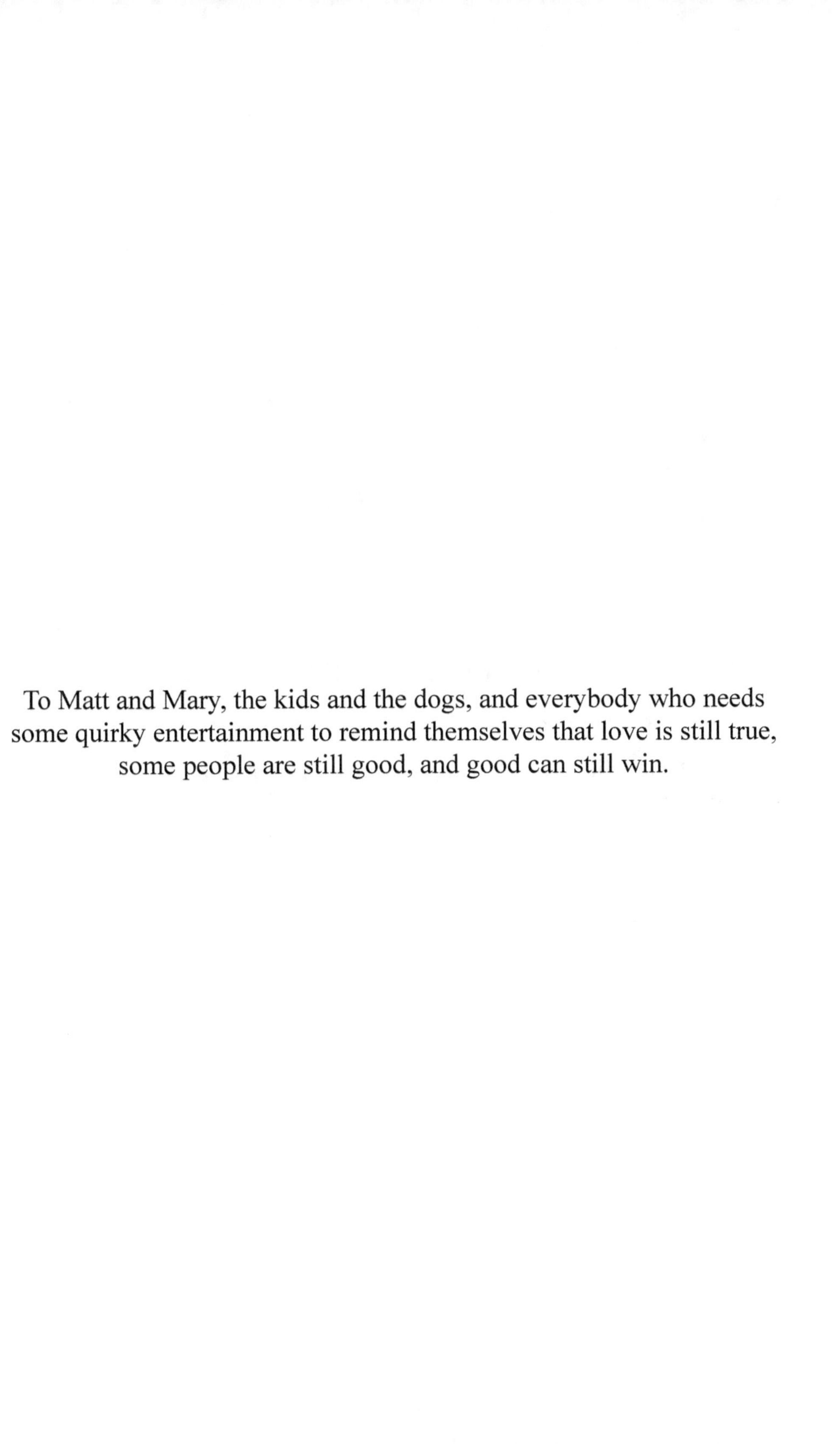

To Matt and Mary, the kids and the dogs, and everybody who needs some quirky entertainment to remind themselves that love is still true, some people are still good, and good can still win.

Author's Note

It's fiction, like, you know, *Wizard of Oz* or *Chronicles of Narnia*. Fiction.

WHAT IS THAT AND WHAT IS IT DOING

"EIGHT YEARS to get through med school," Bailey Dodge muttered through a bite of donut, "three years of residency, two as an attending, and this is my life."

The potential human traffic jam that was Outskirts General Hospital seethed around him as he struggled into his lab coat and tried to remember if he'd brushed his teeth that morning. The myth of the well-off doctor growing fat and avuncular in family practice was drifting further and further away with every minute spent in this hellhole.

But Bailey couldn't seem to quit the ER.

He'd tried. When the hospital had made cutbacks, he'd tried. When threatened—both in job and in freedom—for administering lifesaving care to pregnant women, he'd tried. When three of his interns had been forced to quit because they felt the same way but they hadn't had tenure, he'd tried.

But there were people here—good people. Nurses, janitors, orderlies, who seemed to depend on him to run in, lab coat flapping, to try to make sense of the terrible chaos of human tragedy that was life in a busy ER.

But God, he was tired. His head ached from lack of sleep, his feet ached from being on them for so long, his *body* ached because, well, he hadn't been touched in *forever*. But there'd been a pileup out by Manor, and Outskirts General got all that action rather than nearby—but still twenty minutes or so away—Austin.

"What do we got, Sarree," he asked Sarah Wilson, his charge nurse. She'd been the one to catch the call from dispatch, alerting them to incoming ambulances and pulling him out of his nap in the intern's cot room because he was shorthanded and working a double.

"Sorry to get you for this, Bail," she said crisply, but yes, genuinely apologetic. "It sounded like a complete goat rodeo, but there's apparently only a few injuries, two of them minor. They're in the open cubicles, each with their own G-man attached.

"G-man?" Bailey asked, eyebrows up.

"Part of some weird smuggling thing?" She sounded genuinely baffled. "All I know is that there was a showdown between semitrucks, and the only reason it wasn't an absolute bloodbath is that your guy in Room 3A can—and I'm quoting two state troopers *and* the G-men here—'really fuckin' drive.'"

Bailey stared at Sarree in surprise. A sturdy Black woman with the mind of a military general, Sarree Wilson could be warm with her family, and he'd seen her crack a rare smile when he'd worked *really* hard for one, but she was raised church right, and almost never, *ever* swore.

"Really?" he asked.

"Do I *look* like I'm kidding?" she demanded. "Here I was, rousing *you* from a much-needed sleep and calling for a stock up on bandages and blood, when half the state troopers in Austin stalk in, G-men on their tails, and they are absolutely gobsmacked. And the guy in 3A doesn't have a spot of blood on him."

"What's he got?"

She grimaced. "We took him for X-rays and a CT, but it's looking like a whole lot of soft-tissue damage and bruising. Apparently his semi *should* have jackknifed and gone over, but this guy pulled every muscle in his body keeping it upright."

"Damn," Bailey said. "Sounds impressive."

"It was," said a crisp voice with the faintest—oh so faint—of California accents. "I would appreciate it if…." The voice faltered for a moment as Bailey made contact with a startling pair of brownish-hazel eyes. There was a deep breath as Bailey tried to restart his heart, and the G-man—he had to be, although he was wearing khakis and a collared shirt—in front of him resumed talking.

"I would appreciate it if you took special care of him," said the surprisingly young agent. "On top of being brave and, yes, sparing your ER a lot of bloody casualties, he is also my brother, and while he's a pain in my ass, my parents would be most upset if his head popped off because he stalwartly refused to tell us it hurt."

Bailey found his lips curving into a surprised smile. "One of those," he said, with a nod of understanding. The young G-man was just… just so beautiful, it was hard to remember he was talking like a professional. The last time he'd been nearly stunned into submission by nice eyes and a stoic demeanor it had been….

Oh, he couldn't think about that. No, no, he couldn't.

"It is said," the agent intoned with some disgruntled dignity, "that we are a lot alike. I have no idea if it's true, but we are *drowned* in family who insist upon it." He stuck out his hand. "Special Agent Dean Royal. My brother Val is your patient. Right this way."

And then the handsome little shit—and he *was* handsome, with dark hair doing the clean-cut G-man thing and a balanced, well-proportioned nose and chin, as well as cheekbones to *die* for—actually gestured to Bailey to follow him *in Bailey's own hospital.*

The absolute gall of the man would have had Bailey stuttering, only Sarree had just handed him Val Royal's X-Rays and CT scan, and Bailey actually had a job to do.

"How's it look?" Special Agent Royal asked, unabashedly peering over Bailey's shoulder.

Bailey yanked his hand away, bemused by all this… *chutzpah* as well as unsettled by that much closeness. "It *looks* like your brother's business," he said shortly. "Have you never heard of HIPAA laws?"

Dean Royal grunted. "Yes, I have heard of HIPAA, but now that you've heard of the Royal family, you will understand why none of that applies. While you go talk to Val, I need to go report to my mother, and if I don't have some specifics and stats, she will *fly from Bakersfield* to make sure her baby is okay. My parents are not rich, and if that's an unnecessary trip, I would prefer she not make it." He rolled his eyes, seeming a little embarrassed. "Besides, it appears as though my asshole brother has finally met an equal asshole, and he might actually get *laid* and become *less* of an asshole, but only if he *is not dying.*"

Bailey blinked. "Wow, you weren't kidding about your family, were you?"

"No. I never exaggerate," Dean Royal said, without the faintest touch of humor. "I have *never* exaggerated, and I am not exaggerating about this."

Next to him, Sarree made a sound like a cat strangling on its own tongue, and Bailey wondered if she'd fallen in love a little.

"Well, it's good to know where I stand," Bailey said. "How about you go in there and let me take a check on his charts—"

"What do they say?" said two men who had apparently just appeared, like magic, down the bustling corridors of the ER. The one who spoke, a little grayer, a little taller than his slighter, more-humble companion, had a swagger to his shoulders that Bailey might have appreciated on any day a pugnacious G-man hadn't just chewed him out for not violating HIPAA laws.

"They say give me a minute with his charts!" Bailey protested. "Good Lord, did I go down for my power nap and wake up in a Marvel movie? I haven't even spoken with the patient yet!"

The two men grimaced, and Bailey waved his hand at the entire testosterone posse that was overwhelming his little hospital. "Go away!" he all but begged. "But I will tell you that if the injuries are what I think they are, it might be better to keep your friend here for observation—"

"Son," said the older man, "I've *been* in a hospital bed. If all he's got is soft-tissue damage and a concussion, I might be able to give him a better night's rest in a nice hotel than here. I can bring him back in the morning if you like."

Outskirts was a small hospital, but it was also a busy one. Freeing up a bed in the ER with no danger to the patient was no small offer.

"Let me look at his charts," Bailey said with a sigh. "I might take you up on that, but first I have to *see what's doing.* Now go talk to him, but my God, no yelling. If he appears overwhelmed or about to puke, everybody back up or they're going to get it on their shoes. Now go."

Everybody went except Special Agent Hottie.

"Was I not talking to all three of you?" he asked, declining to mention that Dean Royal's sweat and heat was working like an aphrodisiac in the cool of the antiseptic hospital.

Lean lips quirked up in a smile of pure arrogance. "No," he said. "I don't think you were."

Bailey let out a sigh and pointed. "Stand over there," he said, all the authority he could muster in his voice. Dean raised a lazy eyebrow, but he went.

And Bailey wondered if he could kickstart his brain again now that his libido had been freed of Special Agent Royal's distracting presence.

"That young man smells as good as he looks," Sarree said, with the same tone of voice she used in assessing the extent of wound irrigation.

"Oh my God, so it's not just me?" Bailey muttered, taking a glance at Val Royal's charts. Every doctor so far had noted that the patient would need rest, a warm bath, a soft bed, and some muscle relaxants, as well as dark and quiet. Bailey had slept in hospitals for a long time now as a doctor, and he was under no illusions as to how restful they were as an institution.

"No, sir," Sarree said, in answer to Bailey's earlier question. "But I don't think I'm the man's type."

Bailey glanced up and saw that Dean Royal was studying Bailey with interest, a glint of amusement and something else… something glowing and, oh hell, *hot* in his eyes.

"He's sort of an asshole," Bailey muttered, making a notation next to the drug recommendations and then pulling out his prescription pad. "It's a shame he's my type."

Sarree gave a brief cackle. "A shame?"

Bailey gave her a beleaguered glare. "The man is based in California, he's here for his injured brother, and *I* have to work tonight, remember?"

She harrumphed. "I don't think you're giving that young man enough credit. I'm thinking with that glint in his eyes, he could overcome any obstacle you put in his way."

Bailey gave the man in question a sideways glance, and to his horror, he made eye contact, the kind that clung.

Oh, those hazel eyes did not get any less appealing when they were staring at Bailey like they were trying to devour his *soul*.

Sarree cleared her throat, and Bailey jerked his attention back to the matter at hand. Okay, then, all things considered, if Junior G-Man here could promise his brother would get some rest and someplace comfortable to stay, and somebody to bring him back the next day for a follow-up, he was pretty sure that would be a better bet than a night in the hospital.

He glanced up at Dean Royal sourly. "Okay, then," he said. "Let me actually *see* the patient. Then I can buzz the pharmacy to start his prescriptions, and we'll see what we can do."

A HALF hour later, after one more visit with the grumpy but cooperative Val Royal, Bailey stepped out of the rather crowded room and took a breath. The ER had settled down to the late-afternoon quiet stage, and he wondered if he could hit Sarree up for that two hours of sleep he so desperately needed.

Without conscious thought, his imagination summoned up an arresting pair of hazel eyes. Val's eyes had been darker, he thought randomly, and the face a little more square. The man had been handsome and well-built, but something about Junior G-Man's swagger seemed to be yanking Bailey's chain.

As though conjured by thought alone, the man himself was suddenly at Bailey's elbow.

"Thank you," he said. "He'll do much better with McCauley taking care of him."

"Are they an item?" Bailey asked and then fought the temptation to kick himself. For fuck's sake, this was *Texas*, and you just did not ask another man if his brother was gay.

Dean Royal didn't seem put off in the least. "Here's hoping," he said with feeling. "Val's a grumpy bastard. He needs some softening."

Bailey started down the hall, relieved when Sarree nodded at him, pointed at the clock, and held up three fingers.

Bailey blinked. "Three?" he asked out loud.

"Not a minute less," she told him.

"*You* are definitely on the Christmas card list," he told her, and his reward was the faintest crack of a smile.

"So what do *I* have to do to get added to the Christmas card list?" Dean Royal asked at his elbow, and Bailey realized the man had followed him quietly as he headed for "the crib"—the spare room full of cots where doctors on call or pulling doubles went to catch a few winks.

"Let me sleep?" Bailey offered, suddenly disconcerted.

"*Let* you sleep or *help* you sleep?" Dean asked, his voice falling to a purr.

Bailey's eyes popped *way* open. For a moment all he felt was outrage. "I am *not* that easy!" he protested as he took the last left down the corridor that led to the crib.

Dean cocked his head. "I didn't say you were easy," he evaded. "I said I could help you sleep."

"Yeah, but you didn't mean with Reiki, did you?" Bailey demanded, and he saw the corners of Dean's mouth turn up right before he pounced.

One minute he was standing at the door to the small bunkroom, his hand on the handle, glaring at Dean Royal in irritation, and the next, Dean was pressing him back against the door, hand fumbling for the handle, his mouth so hot on Bailey's that he thought he was going to explode.

The door opened, and they tumbled into the room. Bailey had enough presence of mind to glance around and make sure it was empty while Dean threw the bolt, and then Bailey was being kissed back against the bunk bed until he couldn't move, even to sit on the lower bunk.

Dean's hands were busy at the waist of his scrubs, and it turned out Bailey didn't have to sit down. Dean squatted in front of him, dropped Bailey's drawers, and….

"Oh God," Bailey gasped.

Dean was licking him, pulling his mostly hard member into a hot, skilled mouth, and Bailey saw fireworks as he grew *fully* hard and Dean kept sucking. His hair was too short for Bailey to get a grip on it, so mostly all he could do was cradle Dean Royal's skull and try to form words.

The words weren't going well, but the blowjob was *spectacular.*

"Oh God," Bailey gasped again, pulling his hand up to his mouth so he could groan into it without making too much noise. Dean was *really* good, his mouth and tongue moving on his head, his hand gripping the shaft and pumping. Not too hard—that was a mistake sometimes when passion erupted—but just hard enough.

Hard enough to make Bailey want more, to want to be lying, vulnerable, pants down, ass up, as this man plundered his body.

He wasn't aware of spreading his thighs, but he must have, because he felt Dean's spit-slickened finger probing, and God, that was all she wrote. Bailey grabbed the frame of the bunk bed with one hand and moaned into the other as his cock spat come and Dean Royal swallowed it down.

There was a heartbeat of silence, and Bailey stared down at Dean in shock. For his part, Dean gazed up Bailey's body, a sort of irresistible smirk on his face as he wiped himself off on the inside of Bailey's briefs.

"Uhm…," Bailey managed behind his hand, and then Dean stood, pulled his hand off his mouth, and kissed him, gentler this time, nuzzling Bailey's neck and his ears, making reassuring humming sounds in the back of his throat.

"Uhm…," Bailey tried again.

"Do you have a card?" Dean asked, and Bailey blinked hard, trying to parse that.

"What?"

"Never mind." Dean dipped his fingers into the pocket of Bailey's scrub top and pulled out one of the cards Bailey carried to paperclip to pretty much everything—paperwork, receipts, drug prescriptions. "Is this your work cell or your home cell?"

"Work cell."

"What's your personal?"

Bailey rattled off his home cell number on automatic, and Dean pulled one of Bailey's own ever-present pens from the same pocket from whence came the card and wrote it down quickly.

"Good boy," Dean murmured, putting the pen back and thrusting the card into his pocket.

"Why'd I just do that?" Bailey asked, a terrible lassitude stealing over him because *that's what happened* when you hadn't slept for forty-eight hours and somebody sucked your brains out of your dick like it was a straw.

Dean patted his cheek gently. "So next time I'm in Texas," he said softly. "You can return the favor."

"Next time—"

Dean dropped quickly to the floor to pull up Bailey's scrubs and tuck him in, giving his cock a loving little kiss before it was all tidied and put away. Then with a little push in the right place, he had Bailey sitting down on the lower bunk before he swung Bailey's legs sideways and onto the bunk, leaving Bailey no choice but to put his head down on the pillow.

With a last fussy movement, Dean Royal pulled the afghan some intern had crocheted and left in the crib for her colleagues over Bailey's shoulders and tucked him in.

"You need your sleep, Dr. Dodge," Bailey's own Junior G-Man whispered. "But I sure am grateful for a quickie in the crib."

With that he kissed Bailey's cheek and then… *nuzzled* his temple.

"I'm HIV Negative," Bailey mumbled, probably a day late and a dollar fucking short.

"I'm on a prophylactic protocol," Dean told him with a little pat on his hip. "But it was sweet of you to think about it."

Bailey's eyes were at half-mast, but he still managed to say, "Are you really coming back to Texas?"

"Yeah." Dean smoothed his fingers through the hair at Bailey's temple. "I know a really hot doctor here, and I'd like to know him better."

And then he was gone, and Bailey fell asleep so fast that when he woke up, he wondered if it was a dream.

It wasn't until he stumbled back onto the ER floor, a giant mug of coffee in his hand, that he thought to check his phone.

You haven't seen the last of me, Dr. Dodge.

Bailey smiled, knowing the anonymous texter had to be Dean Royal but absolutely positive what had happened in the crib was just a really amazing interlude, never to be repeated again.

THREE WEEKS later, while stumbling up the stairs to his apartment after another double shift, he found Dean sitting on his hardbound suitcase, leaning against the wall in the foyer next to his door, his arm in a sling and his eyes closed as though in sleep.

As Bailey careened to a halt in front of his own damned apartment, those amazing hazel eyes opened, and Dean gave that dead sexy smirk that Bailey couldn't believe turned his key.

"Dean?"

"Heya, Dr. Dodge. Aren't you going to invite me in?"

"Did you get *shot*?" Bailey asked, a little bit of panic skittering through his blood.

"Cool your jets. It's only a sprain." Dean accepted his hand up, and Bailey unlocked his door and paused.

"How did you even find me?" he asked, as though this had just occurred to him.

Dean rolled his eyes. "FBI," he said, and Bailey grimaced.

"Yeah. Dumb question. Come in."

Dean did, sparing a glance around, taking in the cream-colored couch and the cream-colored cat and the ebony paneled tables, bookshelves, and dining set—and the bright ocean and wheat field blown-up photographs on his walls to give the small area a feeling of space, as well as green-and-rose-colored throws on the couch.

"Nice," he said, with a tilt of his head that indicated he meant it. "What's the cat's name?"

"Abominable," Bailey said, sparing a pat for the animal, who spared less than a glance for Bailey. "Bumble for short."

Dean let out a surprising bark of laughter, and Bailey spent a moment staring at the smooth column of his throat and the momentary relaxation of a face that always seemed to be held stiffly at attention.

"Dean," he said after the laugh faded, "what are you doing here?"

Dean held up his good hand and cupped Bailey's cheek with it. "You," he purred, that suddenly sexually dominant side popping out again, "owe me something, Dr. Bailey Dodge. I've come to collect."

His mouth on Bailey's was a little less surprising this time, but no less commanding. Bailey fell into the kiss without a net and allowed Dean to push him back toward the bedroom.

They'd have to talk this time, right? This couldn't be a relationship already, could it? They needed to discuss what they were doing, how this was happening, what sort of affair this was, didn't they?

People didn't just have sex whenever one person was in town, right?

Right?

A Royal Meeting of the Minds

Laure: Okay, guys, sibling text meeting.

Val: Why am I here?

Sal: Because you need to stop having sex with your new boyfriend. You'll dehydrate, princess. Don't you know how to pace yourself?

Val: Well, it's not like I've been training for sex like it was an Olympic event like *some* people. Laure, why isn't Dean on this thread?

Reg: *Omg is he dead?*

Val, Sal, Laure, and Prock: NO!

Laure: *Omg*, what has so traumatized you that your go-to for a meeting is that somebody has to be *dead*?

Chance: You guys, he worries. Be nice.

Laure: Sorry, sweetie—it throws us off our game, that's all. I just wanted to ask everybody if they knew who Dean was seeing.

Sal: As far as I know, he's still having a passionate affair with the stick up his ass.

Prock: Didn't you name it once? Back when Dean was in the academy?

Sal: Phil. I called it Phil because it was apparently the only thing that could ever Phil Dean with joy.

Reg: Ouch.

Chance: Wait, isn't that Fill?

Sal: Oh God, Sunshine, I just cannot with you! Somebody pinch his little cheeks!

Prock: He's at Mom's house for summer vacation. When we're done here, I'll have Mom do it.

Sal: Prock, your only shortcoming as a brother is that you never dumped ants on Dean when he was a kid.

Prock: You keep saying that. Why didn't *you* do it?

Sal: Because a five-year age difference made me too old to do it, but you were only two and a half years older, so you were fine.

Prock: Didn't feel right. What can I say? Dean would have been hurt, but what's worse, he wouldn't have said a word, and then we'd feel *worse*, and then he'd win. The only way to win with Dean is not to play.

Reg: Chance, I get the feeling we were *really lucky* to be the youngest two. The top five apparently had to survive the Hunger Games to get to adulthood.

Chance: I didn't read those books. Will I get that reference if I watch the movies instead?

Laure: Seriously, Chance, you need to hang out with Russell and Shaw more often. My kids know their movies.

Reg: I feel like college was wasted on him.

Prock: *People!* Can we focus here? Laure had a question!

Reg: I think it's perfectly clear that we have no idea who Dean is seeing. Why are we having a sibling meeting about this again?

Laure: Because I asked Dean's partner if he was inviting anybody to the family picnic, and Marcus said no, but Dean would if he could pull his head out of his ass. I was curious, that's all.

Sal: I too am now curious. Not that the tightass would ever tell *us*, but I feel as though somebody here might know if Dean was seeing anybody. Who's closest to him?

Laure: Val.

Prock: Val.

Chance: Val.

Reg: Val.

Val: What in the furry *hell*? Everybody knows Laure is my ride or die!

Laure: I'm still your ride or die, big brother, but you and Dean were always the most alike. You knew he was getting his degree in law enforcement and aiming for Quantico before any of us. If Dean was seeing anybody, you'd know.

Sal: She's right. So who's he seeing?

Chance: Reg, you're my ride or die, right?

Reg: Of course, little brother. I wouldn't leave you hanging.

Chance: Thanks. Why isn't Val answering?

Laure: Val?

Prock: Val?

Chance: Val?

Sal: Prince Fucking Valiant, where in the *hell* did you go?

Laure: You guys, this can only mean one thing.

Prock: That asshole knows, and he isn't telling us?

Sal: Wow, Laure, so much for your ride or die.

Laure: Don't worry—this ride or die has a secret weapon.

Chance: *Omg— You guys!* Who told Mom to come out and smack my ass? I was *in the pool,* and suddenly I have to help Dad clean the garage! And my ass hurts!

Laure: I wouldn't do that.

Prock: Dude, no.

Reg: Of course not!

Sal: He was bothering me. That kid needs a *job*.

Prock: Another reason I wouldn't dump ants on Dean. Sal, you prissy bitch, you can't leave the baby alone?

Sal: No, and you guys shouldn't either. We're depriving those two of some of the best times of their lives.

Reg: Just wait until one of us draws you for Christmas, Sal. I may be quiet, but I have plans.

Laure: You guys, does *anybody* know who Dean is dating?

Sal: Princess, if we did, I think it's perfectly obvious I wouldn't have resorted to child abuse by proxy to entertain myself.

Laure: You all suck.

Prock: Except me. I'm the straight one, remember?

Laure: Fuck you all. If there is a Goddess, I'll be reborn into a family of Amazons. Peace *out*.

Sal: She'd lead that army into glorious battle too.

Prock: But we'd miss her cooking. Reg, you need to ask Dean who he's dating.

Reg: Why me?

Prock: Trust me. Not making the rest of us hate you is your superpower. You get the info from Dean, and then we can chill Laure the fuck out and she won't stop cooking for us.

Reg: That is actually a threat. Fine. I'll get back to you losers.

Chance: We're still on for a movie tonight, right?

Reg: Course. I'd invite Sal, but he lives three hundred miles away.

Sal: *clutches heart* Now that you've made me regret my life choices, I have a business to run.

Prock: That was genius. You both hit him where he lived and told him he was loved. Reg, don't ever doubt your superpowers, they're golden. I gotta run. I too have a business to run.

Chance: Reg, you'll always be my ride or die, right?
Reg: Until you fall in love, baby brother.
Chance: Screw that. Forever.
Reg: Sure.

ROYALLY BUSTED

DEAN WRAPPED his arms a little tighter around Bailey's long, lean body and sighed.

God, he was delicious.

Three months ago when Dean had first met him, in the ER tending to Val, Dean had thought he was cute. Then he watched him be competent and compassionate and kind to Dean's brother, and Dean had thought he was more than that. He was *worthy*.

And then—and this was the true miracle—Dean had seen him be *funny*.

Dean himself was *not* funny. He knew this. He took everything too seriously, too literally to be funny. Humor relied on different levels of meaning, and Dean's specialty, the thing he was *really* good at, was drawing a straight line between ideas.

This was harder when you were working with two levels of meaning, so Dean often didn't bother.

But he did appreciate it when somebody was naturally funny. Sal, his older brother, was naturally funny. Laure, his sister, was also pretty quick on the draw. Their mother was a *riot*, and Dean would make no apologies for thinking she was the greatest woman of all time.

But Dean was not funny, and when Bailey had made him laugh, he had been… charmed.

And then Dean had analyzed Bailey's long frame, his narrow face, his square jaw and graceful brow, and he'd been… well, more than charmed.

Smitten.

He'd expected their brief interlude in the bunkroom at the hospital to be all he needed, but, well, he'd needed more, so he'd taken Bailey's card, and since then any excuse to fly to Austin—including two days off in a row—had gotten him on a plane.

It didn't hurt that he and his partner at the Bureau had been working a case involving the Russian mafia and a nearby cartel south of Austin that threatened to become a bloodbath—he and Marcus practically had their own suite at a nearby Holiday Inn Express. After his injury wrestling cattle (and hearing an earful from Marcus via text about how they were *never* hiding in a cattle truck again; he didn't care if there was a sign from God saying "Bad guys hid their stuff *here*!"), Dean had spent a week in Bailey's apartment, bringing takeout, petting the cat, watching TV with Bailey, falling asleep in his arms. No, it wasn't ideal—Bailey hadn't known he was coming and hadn't known how long he'd been there, but for a week they'd lived almost like a normal couple, and Dean had found it....

Comforting.

Amazing.

He and Marcus had gone into the field at the end of the week, as soon as his injury had healed, and the first night they'd been stuck in a shitty hotel room in Tijuana, doing surveillance on the Russian mobsters trying to sell tech to an absolutely monstrous cartel, Dean had thought of Bailey coming home to a note that read, *Don't forget me. Back soon.*

And he'd felt the absurd urge to cry.

He hadn't cried since the sixth grade, when Val had kicked his ass for telling Chance that Santa Claus wasn't real.

Chance had cried, and Reg—who didn't get mad at *anybody*—had yelled at Dean for being cruel, and Dean had tried to explain that it was ultimately much kinder to realize the lie and misinformation now than it would be to get to the second grade and have all the kids laugh at him.

Chance had cried harder, and Dean had actually welcomed Val paddling him with a shoe.

It hadn't hurt—or it had, but Dean bore pain stoically, even in the sixth grade—but Val's words had all but ripped him open.

"You may think you're above us, Dean Royal, because you're smarter than us, but you remember that those two kids have as much right to believe in goodness and kindness and magic as anybody. Of *course* they would have figured it out sooner or later, but Chance just spent a *week* petitioning Santa to get you your own tablet because he knows you're trying to move into high school next year, and now you broke his heart."

And that, of all things, broke Dean's.

He'd started crying, and then Val had hugged him tight, and then Chance and Reg had run into the room and begged Val not to hurt him, and Dean had cried harder, and, well, his proudest, most masculine moment it had not been.

And in this cramped stucco hotel room, with an ambient temperature of about 90 degrees making Marcus's foot odor even stenchier and a burrito grabbed from a local taqueria about to make its presence known in a bad way, Dean had felt that same absurd sense of letdown.

On paper, cutting out of Bailey's apartment as soon as he got Marcus's text and leaving a note had seemed like the right thing to do.

In practice, it might have been much crueler than Dean had intended.

Of course, that night the Russian mobsters had taken out an office of the cartel as Dean and Marcus watched in horror, and the resulting flight through Tijuana and across the border near San Diego and then debrief to their section chief had taken two weeks.

They'd been left with a single lead about the movements of the Russian mob and a confidential informant who had come out of the woodwork somewhere up north and asked only to be moved to Austin so he could work as a doctor in a nearby hospital.

And Dean had arrived at Bailey's apartment to a predictably frosty reception.

Bailey had said something like "Dean, we have to talk," and Dean had been so afraid that meant "Dean, you can't come here anymore," he'd promptly seduced Bailey until his eyes rolled back in his head and he forgot his own name.

Dean was good at that. He was well aware it was all he brought to the table.

There had been no more "we have to talk" noises, but Dean had noticed that when he'd showed up on the doorstep since then, the look in Bailey's eyes was a sort of hurt joy. Yes, he was happy to see Dean, but he knew that maybe not tomorrow, and maybe not the day after, but pretty soon Dean would be going again.

Dean didn't know what to do with that.

His one play was to fuck away the pain, and he wasn't sure how long that would last.

But right now, Bailey was warm and pliant in his arms, and the harsh sunlight of an Austin, Texas, summer was trying to penetrate the heavy white drapes across the bedroom windows, and all Dean wanted to do was keep smelling the sweat and sunshine at the nape of Bailey's neck.

"You always smell so good here," he mumbled, nuzzling that spot right there. "Why?"

"Baby shampoo," Bailey mumbled back. "Makes my hair shiny."

Dean laughed then, wide-awake and very surprised. "God, you're funny," he said, his voice full of admiration, and to his horror the look Bailey turned back over his shoulder wasn't happy or pleased—it was injured.

It was practically bleeding.

"What?" Dean asked, legitimately surprised. "What was that look?"

Bailey just shook his head. "I've got a shift in two hours," he said instead. "I need to shower and do some laundry or I won't have anything when I get back."

"I should be able to do that for you," Dean said promptly. He honestly didn't mind being at the apartment when Bailey had to work. It may not have been *his* home, but it was *somebody's* home, and Dean's nerves, used to being stretched taut, appreciated the difference between that and a hotel bed.

To his dismay Bailey shook his head. "No," he said, sounding miserable. "You can't promise that, and I'm visiting my dad in Fort Stockton tomorrow, so I need the clothes. Let me out of bed."

Dean did, surprised at the defeated tone of his voice, at the sadness in his eyes—at the whole way this once-wonderful morning had gone.

"Bailey, what's wrong?"

"I told you," Bailey said, keeping his face averted. "I'm visiting my dad tomorrow. He's cooking dinner. I do this once a month. You can't be surprised."

"I'm not," Dean said, baffled. "But why… why do you make it sound like dinner with your father is the end of the world?"

"Because you haven't asked once to meet him," Bailey returned, anger burning in his voice along with the unhappiness. "And I get it. I'm just… just a drive-by piece of ass to you, but… but I keep hoping that someday I can at least introduce you to my father as a friend, and it just hit me, in bed a minute ago, that that's not going to happen. You are *never* going to want to be introduced to my father, and I… I mean, don't get me wrong, the sex is *great*, but that's all it's ever going to be to you and…." His voice dropped, the anger draining out. "I thought I could do that, but it turns out I can't."

Dean blinked at him, scrambling. "You want me to come meet your father?" he landed on, and Bailey rolled his eyes in disgust and stalked into the bathroom.

Dean tumbled out of the sheets, pausing to make the bed because he hated an unmade bed, made sure the phones were in the charger and Bailey's picture of his old boyfriend who had passed away was straight, as was only respectful, and then followed him in.

"It's not only sex!" he cried over the pounding of the water.

Bailey ripped the shower curtain back and stared at him. "It took you five minutes, and that's all you could come up with?"

Dean scowled at him, stripping off his clothes.

"You are *not* coming in here!" Bailey protested.

"Of course I am. I need a shower, and we're having a discussion, and this only makes sense." And Bailey's skin seemed to feed something in Dean that he usually needed a week at his parents' house to get. That humming sense of well-being that his family could give him—if he relaxed enough to let it—seemed to fill Dean up with only a few touches from Bailey. Even the random ones, like to his hair as they sat at the TV, or across his back as Dean was making dinner. But he didn't have words for that.

Still, Bailey was staring at him (or squinting at him through the spray) in outrage as Dean entered the giant glass cubicle, which as far as Dean could tell was the only reason Bailey was paying such outrageous rent for this apartment.

Yes, Dean had looked up the cost of rent here when he'd looked up the address the first time. Was he not supposed to?

"God," Bailey muttered, turning to the spray at last. "You really can't take a hint."

"No," Dean said, reaching around him and making sure their bodies slicked together as he did so. "I'm very mildly on the autism spectrum, so taking a hint is not my strong suit."

Bailey gaped. "You... you never mentioned that before." Then he shook his head, scattering droplets of water *everywhere*. "Not that it should surprise me. You haven't mentioned *anything* before!"

He was charging up his mad again, Dean thought, once again at a loss.

"What were you hinting?" he asked, partly to derail Bailey's mad, and partly to try to get a footing on why this thing, this unnamed, amazing thing that he and Bailey had been doing for the last three months might be going to suddenly disappear.

He didn't want it to disappear.

In fact he was realizing with a bit of panic that he absolutely needed that thing *right here*.

"That I wanted you to meet my father!" Bailey burst out.

"That might be hard," Dean said. "I'm expecting to get called into the office later today. I will still have time to do your laundry, though."

"*See*?" Bailey cried, making no sense at all. "I didn't *know* that, and it would be *nice* to know that. It would be nice to have some warning when you're going to show up—"

"Oh!" Dean said happily. "That's easy. Whenever my case takes me here or I have a weekend off."

Bailey scrubbed at his face with his hands, and Dean helpfully put a washcloth and his soap bag in his hands so he could do that more efficiently.

Bailey stared at the objects and then started to use them absent-mindedly, shaking his head and muttering to himself. It was hard to hear above the spray, but it sounded like he was saying, "*Such* useful information," and "It would have been great to know that from the start!"

"The autism?" Dean asked, to make sure. "It wasn't assessed until college, when we were studying metacognition and ways people absorb information. I replied to a test question that I had to very carefully organize information or I couldn't connect motivation to result—for example, unless I explained to myself why it was important to pass English, I would simply not do the homework because it seemed frivolous. Once I could explain to myself that English was about communication, which is obviously my weak point, I actually enjoyed my classes. I learn with very specific guidelines and communicate very literally. Why would it be a problem?"

"It wouldn't," Bailey said shortly, "unless your lack of communication was *hurting my feelings*, and I assumed you were doing it because you *didn't care*."

That pulled Dean back. "But I do care if I'm hurting your feelings," he said, dismayed. "I'm sorry. What would you like to communicate about to help me fix that?"

Bailey let out a groan. "Dean, I can't do this in the shower. I can't do it on the way to work. And if you're not going to be here when I get back, I don't know why I should bother at all. I *care* about you, but I am obviously the last thing on your priority list—"

"That's not true!" Dean protested, his dismay morphing into panic. "I had to bring my plants to the office in Sacramento because they would die because I spent so much time in Austin. I *miss* my plants. My brother Reg was going to help me pick out a kitten, and I had to put that off, and his feelings were hurt, but I am spending all my time in Austin, and it wouldn't be fair to the kitten. You *are* on my priority list!"

He stood there, naked and dripping—he hadn't soaped up at all—and Bailey finished soaping his pits and then handed the bag to him, along with the washcloth.

"I didn't know that," he said softly.

"I didn't know you needed to," Dean said, hoping this could be the end of it.

"I did," Bailey said with a sigh.

Dean couldn't be sure, but he thought maybe—just maybe—he could make a move now. He got close enough to wrap his arms around Bailey's shoulders and pull him back against Dean's chest. "Are there other things you need to know?" he asked, thinking that a list might be nice. He and Marcus lived off lists when they worked together.

"So many things," Bailey said with a little laugh. "But right now… for once, I don't want to talk. This is nice."

Dean let out a sigh, enjoying Bailey's body again, some of his morning reforming around him with the peace he desperately needed.

"I'm glad," he said. "I don't want to talk about the kitten. It makes me sad." He hated to admit it, but he *missed* his family. Every last interfering one of them had a solid, immutable piece of his heart.

"How many brothers do you have?" Bailey asked. "Just the two?"

It occurred to Dean that *this* might be the kind of information Bailey had been talking about when he insisted they communicate.

"Five," he said shortly. "And one sister."

Bailey stiffened in his arms. "*Five?*"

"Why is *that* freaking you out?" Dean asked, truly at a loss.

Bailey snorted and went back to letting Dean soap him up. "That's a big family, Dean. You didn't mention them."

"Did you think all the time I spend on my phone is for work? Marcus has his own family to bother."

"Marcus isn't your brother?"

Dean blinked, and it occurred to him that if Bailey didn't know *this* at least, he may perhaps have kept his life too much to himself.

"Marcus is my *partner*," he said. "With the Bureau. His last name is Cabrillo. We work cases together."

Bailey was quiet for a long moment. "I can't figure out if that's better or worse," he muttered. "How is it I didn't know that?" Then he straightened up and glared at Dean. "Oh yeah. Because you didn't *tell* me that!"

With that he stepped carefully out of the shower and out of Dean's arms and began to towel off while Dean soaped his hair.

"It's not my fault you didn't ask," he said, mostly to himself.

The ripping back of the shower curtain came as a surprise. "I'm sorry?"

"You didn't ask," Dean told him crossly, closing his eyes so he could rinse his hair. He finished, shook his head, and stepped out, then reached around Bailey's angry body to grab the last dry towel.

"I didn't… I didn't…."

"I asked," Dean said. "You were very forthcoming. You told me about your father, how your mother passed when you were in high school, how hard medical school was, how much debt you still have." He smiled a little, wistfully. "How much you love your cat, and how you leave the television on sometimes or have the neighbor boy come in and make sure he's okay and feed him when you're working doubles. How your dad calls and talks to him, and you know that because your recorder tapes him singing. I told Val about your dad singing Gordon Lightfoot to the cat—he said that was encouraging."

"You told your brother about me?" There was something desperately hopeful then about Bailey's voice.

"Yes," Dean said.

"Anybody else?"

And he hated to shut that eagerness down, but he didn't lie, prevaricate, or exaggerate.

"Only Val. Val doesn't get nosy. He takes what I tell him in stride." In the name of honestly, Dean felt like he should add, "Mostly he just grunts."

"Great, there's two of you," Bailey muttered and then shook himself and, to Dean's immense relief, smiled a little. "Okay. It's not exactly an invitation home to meet the parents, but I'll take it. It's progress. Dry off and I'll make you breakfast." His face fell again. "Do you really have to leave today?" he asked wistfully.

And—perhaps for the first time—Dean felt apologetic about answering the demands of his job. "We have to catch a flight to the Chihuahuan Desert today. We have a *very* exciting development in our case."

Bailey just stared at him. "The Chihuahuan Desert. That's romantic."

Dean knew he was being sarcastic, but he didn't play sarcasm games. "In fact it's not. There are some lovely places in Mexico and South America, but unless you're an ecologist or botanist interested in three quarters of the world's species of cacti, there's not much to recommend it." He wrinkled his nose. "It's really hot in July, for one thing."

Bailey raised his eyebrows, and that soft smile appeared, the one that Dean was starting to treasure. "Poor baby," he said, moving close enough to kiss Dean's cheek. "I'll have to make you something really good for breakfast."

Dean smiled back, savoring the feeling of their skin, warm and clean, in the steamy heat of the bathroom. "Maybe we could stop for breakfast on the way to the hospital."

Bailey's eyebrows went up. "You're taking me to the hospital now?"

"Yeah," Dean said softly, going in to kiss him again.

Bailey let out a soft sigh of surrender, and Dean fell into his sweetness all over again. Oh, this was good. Yes, it was probably addicting, but Dean? He was already an addict, and he had zero regrets.

Dean felt Bailey open, as he always did, and captured his breaths in his heart, like he had from the very beginning. He devoured, stroked, lubed, and thrust with the same certainty he'd always used, but as he buried himself in his lover's body, for the first time in an active, healthy sex life, a little voice in his head was saying this—the lovemaking, the sex—was not enough, and a little voice in his heart was begging him to open for more.

A Left Turn to Hell

"Oh shit!" Bailey said as Dean pulled his rental car to the front of Outskirts General. "I forgot my ID!"

"Will they let you in without it?"

Bailey wrinkled his nose. "Yeah, I can get a visitor's ID on my way in. It just, you know, looks flaky."

Dean's mouth twisted into a smile that, for Dean, was almost *goofy*. "Well, I *did* almost make you late."

Bailey knew his own smile was just a little bit shy. "It was… memorable," he said primly. Oh God was it. Was it *ever*. True, he hadn't had sex in nearly four years before Dean had seduced him in that crib, but this morning, after pulling off little pieces of Dean's armor, it felt like the sex had gotten… better. Not that it had been bad before, but it had been like having sex with a tidal wave. Sure, it was exciting, and it rolled you over and over again inside it, but it was like some huge natural *event*.

This morning Bailey had felt the human being inside him as Dean had thrust. Instead of being completely blinded by *wooolf, damn*, he'd been tingling with the distinctly personal sensation of being touched. Small things—Dean's fingers breaching him, lubricating him, making sure he was ready—struck him as suddenly considerate. Dean always *had* been considerate, but Bailey was starting to see the attention to detail now. Things that had always seemed too smooth to be mechanical but too mindless to be thoughtful now assumed a special significance.

Dean hadn't just been "having sex," he'd been "executing an operation" on Bailey's body, with forethought and gentleness. Something about the way Dean had said, "It's all in how I assimilate information," had struck a chord.

Dean had been collecting little pieces of Bailey's life and forming a pattern—because he cared about *Bailey*.

Bailey had expected those conversations to happen naturally, spontaneously, as they had with… just in general. But that wasn't how Dean operated.

Now, in the car after a long, interesting conversation about Dean's family, during which Dean had answered questions freely and without reservation as though Bailey could have been asking them *this whole time*, Bailey kept remembering a moment, his back arched, his head tilted back in climax, and Dean's gentle fingertips drifting along his hairline, under his cheekbone, along his jaw.

Such a tender gesture from a man Bailey had begun to suspect of using him for booty calls.

That morning after their shower, their talk, that *terrible* wistful expression on Dean's face when he'd talked about getting a kitten with his brother, none of that had been about booty calls.

"Was it?" Dean asked now, obviously teasing. "Was it memorable?"

"Val, Laure, Sal, Prock, you, Reg, and Chance," he rattled off. "*I was not top ten of my med school class for nothing.*"

"And your father's name is Connor," Dean said lazily, probably to prove he was smarter, "and his dog's name is Cathy, which is an odd name for a dog, but she's a golden retriever, and you said it's short for Catherine the Great."

Bailey shook he head as Dean came to a stop. "It's not fair. I told you that *weeks* ago, and you still remember it."

He paused, one hand on his door handle as Dean leaned across the console of the sedan to give him a kiss. One hand came up to brush Bailey's nose, and Dean pulled back and said, "You have seventeen freckles across your nose and cheeks, but that might be just because it's summer, and your nose peels even if you never go out in the sun."

Bailey covered his nose, feeling the closeness of Dean's regard pierce him to the bone. Forget "under his skin," Dean Royal had deftly become a part of Bailey's soul.

"God, you're a pain in the ass," he said, his breath sighing from his chest as he said it, like a swoon.

"I am not," Dean replied earnestly. "I am *very* considerate with the lubricant and stretching, and your ass should feel invigorated."

Bailey's laughter was partly a gurgle of embarrassment and partly a hoot of genuine glee, because thirty-something doctor or not, that joke never seemed to get old.

And then Dean smiled, letting Bailey know it had been a fully *intentioned* joke, and Bailey loved him more.

Dean's lips brushed against his, and Dean said, "I'll try to remember to text you before—"

"Between!" Bailey warned, because they'd spoken about this at length too.

"Between," Dean repeated obediently. "*Between* visits."

Bailey smiled at him warmly, trying to ignore the word, the big word, the L-word, the big L-word that he'd just used in his head.

"I'll look forward to your next one," he said softly. "Be safe, G-man."

"Get some sleep, Dr. Dodge," Dean said, every bit as sober.

And with that Bailey had to leave, forcing himself into the dedicated heat of the Austin summer, two minutes shy of 11:00 a.m. He waved at Dean's rental for a moment, almost positive he saw Dean's hand come up in response as he exited the roundabout, and Bailey had no choice but to go in.

Sarree, of course, gave him an absolute ration about forgetting his ID, but Bailey was sort of on cloud nine, so he blithely let her rant at him while he checked his charts, drank his third cup of coffee (only his third), and set about his rounds, Sarree at his side.

Right before he entered the first patient's room, Sarree stopped him.

"Wait," she ordered, and he came to a military halt while she eyeballed him intently. "You are entirely too happy." She scowled at him for a moment, and then her expression lightened. "Oh my God—he's here!"

Bailey felt heat in his cheeks, and his seventeen freckles probably stood out in stark relief.

"Well not any*more*," he muttered. "He's probably on his way home to Sacramento as we speak. But yeah. He got in two days ago, just in time for my day off, and…." He shrugged, unable to keep the smile from his face. "It was nice," he said, as demurely as he could.

She let out a bark of laughter. "Nice? I see stubble burn on your neck, my fair Irish friend—you had yourself a *time*."

Bailey had to glance away, mostly to contain his smile. "He told me about his family," he all but whispered. "And there's a *lot* of them. And… and he opened up about why he's so closemouthed and… and he…." It sounded stupid when he said it.

"Let you know you were important?" she asked kindly.

"*Yes!*" he told her, his grin absolutely unstoppable. "God, Sarree, it's just… just the nicest thing to have someone in your life who cares like that. I haven't felt like this since…."

And it hit him then that after all his complaining to *Dean* about what *Dean* hadn't been saying, *Bailey* had been keeping one very big thing to himself.

"Since Emmett," she said, catching his eyes.

Bailey nodded. "I… I haven't told him about Emmett yet," he admitted.

"It was an awful, awful time," Sarree said, and he heard *her* voice choking up, and he squeezed her arm in response.

None of them talked about it. It was such a terrible chapter of American history *period*, and for those who'd been on the front lines, who had lost people on the front lines, it had been so much worse. Every day—*every day*—it hadn't been a question of who but of how many. And the statistics, over 11,000 deaths in Texas alone, didn't account for people who had died in their homes unattended, or who died of complications after the initial fever and cough had passed.

Didn't account for Emmett Coyle, who had wrestled with the disease for two weeks, come back two weeks later, and dropped dead of a cardiac embolism during his second shift, an event that a young man who took stellar care of himself would ordinarily not have suffered.

It had been COVID. Bailey knew it, Emmett's family had known it, the entire ER had known it—but he'd never been a "COVID statistic" because the bureaucracy didn't work that way.

It didn't matter—not really. But the few ER employees who'd been able to wrangle two hours out of the day had been the only ones at the funeral. They'd stood in the pouring September rain, maskless so they wouldn't get waterboarded, and said goodbye to as good a doctor, as good a friend, as good a man, as they'd ever known.

And Bailey's lover, the man he'd planned to marry and who'd told his whole family he was marrying Bailey. They'd been planning on that spring.

Bailey, his heart tattered and useless, had seen his lover put in the ground… and had gone back to work that same day.

Because there *was* nobody else who could do it.

And Bailey had already suffered his own monthlong battle with the deadly disease.

He'd been secretly hoping *he'd* drop dead too.

He obviously hadn't, and he and Sarree and the other survivors of Outskirts General ER, 2020–21, had continued to forge the sort of bond psychologists usually only found in foxholes after world wars.

Absolutely inescapable. They'd fought together; they weren't going fucking *anywhere*.

Except Bailey's dad was getting a little older, and Fort Stockton was farther away than Bailey liked, and the house his father lived in was falling down, and his only company was his dog. Bailey's dad, who was a widower, had helped Bailey through med school working as a plumber and electrician and had always had Bailey's back—*always*—and had called him every single morning after Emmett had passed away. Bailey suspected his dad had even gotten Cathy the golden retriever so he could text Bailey pictures of the dog being positively adorable when they weren't able to visit and Bailey needed something, anything, to smile about.

Bailey's dad deserved more than an impersonal retirement home, but he hated the city, and Bailey could see a moment of reckoning coming that he didn't want to face.

And what COVID hadn't been able to do, the Dobbs decision *had* done. Many of the die-hard ER staff had begun to peel away a little at a time, many of them going places where they couldn't get incarcerated for doing their jobs.

Bailey suspected the only reason *Sarree* hadn't retired was because she worried about Bailey, and it occurred to him that she might be rooting for Bailey to find a mate here because then she'd know he'd be okay.

"I...." Oh, how embarrassing. "I got all huffy with him today," Bailey told her. "Because, well, he's great at getting *me* to talk, but he's terrible at talking himself, and I accused him of being secretive, but...."

"You haven't told him?" Sarree demanded.

Bailey winced. "I-I didn't realize what a mess I still was," he said at last.

"Baby," she said softly, "you should tell him. It doesn't make you a bad person if you don't, but it will probably hurt his feelings."

Trust Sarree to put it into perspective. Not unforgivable, but definitely addressable.

"Thanks, Sarree," he said. "I.... Thank you."

"My husband has a little cottage on the Gulf of *Mexico*," she said dreamily. "All the kids will be out next year and in college. He's making plans to add a craft room with natural sunlight and to buy me one of those expensive quilting machines for a retirement present." She gave his cheek a light pat. "I might start looking up sales."

And with that she pivoted on her heel, and together they headed toward their patients. Bailey was left under no illusions that Sarree's dreams rested on his narrow shoulders, and he owed it to her to meet any obstacle head-on.

Even the damage to his own heart.

THEIR MORNING passed relatively quickly. They did rounds, Bailey prescribed treatments, recommended discharges or admissions depending on the case, and triaged anything serious, such as broken bones or cuts that would need stitches, or in the case of a young construction worker who had fallen off his ladder, both, plus surgery.

He and Sarree made an effective team—he made the stat decisions, she directed the troops—and together they worked their way through the morning. At around two, when he normally would have taken his break, he realized he was being run off his *ass*.

"Oh my *God*," he muttered to Sarree. "Where the fuck is Vlade?"

Vlade Karkov was a new attending, recently transferred from somewhere up north. Neither Sarree *nor* Bailey knew him well—but then, he'd done his job crisply, efficiently, and without any particular emotion too. While it was true that the Outskirt's ER was sort of a family, they tried to be a welcoming one, especially because they wanted to *keep* people there and not lose them to states that weren't trying to kill pregnant women on general principles.

They had *tried* to be friendly—they really had.

But Vlade had rebuffed their attempts and generally kept to himself, a thin-faced, severe-looking man in his early thirties with dark hair and a sour mouth, Bailey wasn't sure if Vlade didn't like gay people in general or Bailey in particular, but he always seemed to save an especially vile sneer for Bailey.

"Probably at the proctologist's," Sarree said grimly. "Lord knows, he needs that stick removed stat."

Bailey grunted and rolled his eyes. "Agreed, but I could have sworn I saw him clock in."

The computer where people logged in to their shifts was back by the crib, next to the vending machines with the good chocolate and the energy drinks on tap.

"I need to sign some charts," Sarree said. "Get me a Monster and see if Vlade's logged in yet."

"Peach?" Bailey asked.

"Course," she told him, nodding.

"I'll be back."

Bailey himself preferred coffee, but there was an espresso machine back there too, which put out extra-large portions on command. Bailey checked the big pocket of his lab coat to make sure his plastic travel mug was there and headed for the crib.

First he checked the computer. Vlade *had* logged in, nearly half an hour ago, which didn't make any sense because why wasn't he on the *floor*, splitting Bailey's cases with him? Next he went to the vending machines, picked up Sarree's Monster drink and four giant chocolate bars (to share with Sarree and the other nurses), and set his cup under the espresso machine after he'd programmed in his favorite afternoon buzz with lots of sugar and cream.

While he waited for the machine to gurgle its way into coffee heaven, he peered into the crib from the window, uncomfortably aware that if he caught another couple doing what he and Dean had been doing three months ago, he'd be torn between being a total hypocrite and reporting them, and a total slacker and not.

He really, really hoped everybody in the crib was fully dressed, but still he checked, because seriously, where the hell was Vlade?

Bailey didn't see anything at first (hooray! Nobody had sex in the crib but Bailey!), but as he shifted his gaze from the darkness of the bunk bed to the oblique angle of the single cot, he could make out... *something*. The pale flash of light as he moved picked up the features of a face held very still.

It looked like Vlade's face, but... but the eyes were open. Not moving.

So *very* still.

With a frown, Bailey opened the door, and the light streaming in from the hallway illuminated a scene Bailey had never assessed, not even in the ER.

His doctor's eyes made the diagnosis immediately, dispassionately.

Adult male, deceased, cause of death most likely exsanguination. Manner of death, stabbing. *Vicious* stabbing, lacerating the flesh of the chest and stomach but probably starting with a long, deadly gash of the throat.

His human eyes were not *nearly* as dispassionate. *Holy fuck, the last time I saw something this bad was on a crime drama.*

And the horror of the *crime*—not of the blood, not of the severity of the attack—was what moved Bailey, of his own volition, toward the bed.

He managed to avoid the pool of blood, a heretofore unnoticed job skill, and after gloving up on reflex, using the box of gloves on the table in the crib, he held two fingers to Vlade's cooling neck and reinforced what he'd already guessed.

Vlade may have clocked in, but he'd never be working a shift again.

Bailey straightened, his foot disturbing something on the floor next to the pool of blood. As he bent to retrieve the small shiny thing, he heard a ruckus outside the crib door and froze.

"Look, it's not my fault I left my lucky coin at the scene" came a thickly accented voice. "It was weird doing it in a hospital. Almost like a murder in a church, right?"

His heart, already doing the merengue in his ears, jumped to triple-time timpani in his throat, and he glanced around frantically for a place to hide. Holy fuck. Holy *fuck*, he was standing in a *murder scene*, and the *murderer was back for his lucky coin*!

Without thinking, Bailey clutched the coin in his hand, approached the cot from the end instead of the side where the blood was, and wriggled underneath it, against the wall, hoping this wasn't where they found his body when Sarree came searching for her Monster.

The door opened, the usual corridor of light blocked by the broadest set of shoulders Bailey had ever seen, or so he guessed from the silhouette thrown by the man's shadow.

"Fuck fuck fuck fuck fuck...."

The man swore gutturally, and Bailey tried to stop breathing.

"Do you see it, Shev?" This voice was sharp and somehow... smaller. Maybe simply higher in register? But it also seemed to fit a man small in station. Without meaning to, Bailey thought about Wallace Shawn, and the way his voice cracked when he yelled at Bob Parr in *The Incredibles*.

"Nyet. Is not here. Damn."

There was an irritated grunt, and the footsteps receded, followed by the slow *thunk* as the pneumatic door shut.

Bailey stared at his Fitbit and tried to control his breathing for another two minutes.

Two seconds in, just as the killers probably rounded the short little hallway into the main corridor, the espresso machine let out the hiss and scream of scalded coffee and steamed milk. Even through the walls, Bailey heard their voices.

"What was that?"

He pulled out his phone and texted Dean.

Killers in the hospital.

Dead doctor in the crib.

Coming back, may see me.

L—

The door burst open, saving him from making a really embarrassing mistake, and at that moment he heard Sarree's voice echoing down the corridor.

"Doctor Dodge!" she called. "Bailey! There is a four-car pileup coming in, and apparently we don't get breaks!"

The door clicked shut, the footsteps receded, and moments later Sarree burst into the crib just as Bailey scrambled out from under the bed.

"Bailey!" she cried, for a moment only focused on her one goal. "What in the name of heaven are you doing in here while—*Jesus Christ Almighty*!"

Bailey gaped at her. "Sarree!"

"It's not using his name in vain when you are calling on him in need," she retorted, staring at Vlade in slack-faced horror. "What happened?"

"There were two men in here," Bailey said, trying to hear his own voice over the roaring in his ears. "Did you see them when you came down the corridor?"

She *forced* her square, lined face to turn toward him and away from the dead man in the crib. "No," she rasped. "I mean… I saw the back of them. A really large man in a boxy suit and a smaller man wearing a little straw fedora, slacks, and a dress shirt. They had slick, shiny shoes, like the oil men."

Bailey nodded, knowing she was talking about the guys who got rich quick by striking oil on their property. They were often the same guys who wrecked pricey cars on the local highways after drinking more than their limit.

"Okay," he said. "Good. I... I texted Dean. Let's get forensics up here, have them wait for Dean, and you and I go do our jobs."

She nodded once, curtly, and then stared. "Bailey," she said faintly, "please tell me you've got spare scrubs in your locker, or a spare lab coat."

Bailey looked down at himself and grimaced. While he'd managed to keep his hands from the bulk of the blood dripping off the cot, his elbow, hip, and thigh were absolutely saturated. "Fuck me," he muttered. "I'll hit the showers, you throw me some scrubs. Give me five minutes to bag and tag this shit, and I'll be out there before the ambulances pull in."

In any other hospital it would make sense that the crib and the showers and the locker room would all be right next to each other, but the crib had been designed for something else—there was speculation that it had been meant as a conference room—and other speculation that the architects had gone "Wait, what do we put in this odd intersection when all the other rooms have a different purpose altogether?"

Whatever the reasoning, Bailey had to stride down the corridor covered in blood before he took another right to the locker rooms and the showers. Like Sarree, he was moving with purpose, his mind on his goal, and later he would marvel that he was so single-minded at being the doctor that met the four-car pileup when his team was shorthanded, that he didn't see the two men striding down the corridor toward him until he took that right.

One of them must have gasped, and he glanced up in a preoccupied way and caught the eyes of the absolutely enormous man, pure brutal muscle and a face like slabs of meat assembled and roughly carved, as they passed each other.

As Bailey turned toward the shower, the man's eyes began to change. From surprise to calculation to realization, and as Bailey kept his no-bullshit stride, he wondered when the killers would put together that Bailey had been there, had accidentally wallowed around in the puddle of blood, and could identify them both by their voices.

And now by their faces.

Oh fuck. Oh fuck, oh fuck, oh fuck.

Falling as Opposed to Jumping

Dean was at the apartment, packing his go bag and giving Bumble one last chuck under the chin before he had to give the lint roller a pass over his clothes, when his phone, set to relay texts over his earbuds, began to tell a three-text horror story with Bailey as the star.

He hit Marcus's number before the final text came through.

"What, you done honeymooning and ready to leave early?"

"Where are you?" Dean asked crisply.

"Leaving the coffee place you love so much. What's up?"

Oh thank God, thank God, thank God, thank God, Marcus was just as big a stickler for being on time as he was. They'd been booked on a flight out, and Marcus had taken a Lyft from his nearby hotel room and grabbed the rental Dean had used for some last-minute errands.

But no errand was as important as the two of them being on time for their plane. That's why they got along so well.

"Complete change of plans," Dean said. "Vlade was hit, Bailey's a witness, and if I'm lucky, I'll get to the hospital and bail him out before our hit men realize it and get him too."

"Well, shit," Marcus muttered. "How in the hell did that happen?"

"Bad fucking luck."

Dean hadn't told Bailey about Vlade. For one thing their little interlude in the hospital cot room had happened about two weeks before Marcus and Dean's carefully cultivated CI had been transferred to Outskirts General, and Marcus and Dean had been *busy*, dammit, trying to make sure he'd be safe.

The sour man with the attenuated build hadn't been Dean's *favorite* person of all time, but he *had* been a font of information about the inner workings of the Russian mob and how they'd been planning to take over the Corazones de Sangre—the Hearts of Blood.

The Karkov branch of the mob had been pretty slick about it, using the muddle at the border and the United States' draconian policies to hide the ladders of bodies they were using to climb to the top of the drug trade. Racism was *such* a good tool to use against the stupid.

A Russian smuggled in undocumented through Cuba and Florida wasn't looked at twice if he had a fake ID that said "Smith," but a Mexican who actually had documentation was still considered good riddance.

Marcus and Dean did a lot of target practice with red hats and ICE windbreakers, and Dean wasn't sure it was even therapy anymore.

Because whether the bad guys were the Russian mob or the Columbian cartels, they were both still winning.

This time around, the mob was smuggling drugs, weapons, and humans with even more brutality than the cartels themselves, and Dean and Marcus weren't going to quibble about how politics could turn things on a dime.

They were going to go after the assholes who had been leaving big shipments of *people* to rot in the Texas heat as a signal to the cartels that nobody was safe.

Fortunately both shipments had been found, but there'd been casualties. One of the survivors of the second shipment had positively identified two men—not "coyotes," which were bad enough, but *buitre* and *diabolico* she had called them. Vultures. Partly because of the flapping black suits, Dean had thought while interviewing the poor woman in the hospital, but also, he was sure, because of their grim delight in death.

She'd heard the men speaking in thickly accented English as they'd crammed the back of the semi to standing room only. They'd talked of "needing to cook the meat extra-long to be juicy," and even knowing she was the meat, she'd rather take her chances inside the truck than try to escape.

There'd been rumors about the big one and his fondness for knives.

When Vlade Karkov had come to them voluntarily, asking for nothing more than a change of venue, Dean and Marcus had jumped at the chance to milk him for information.

They were aware—*very* aware—that he was probably a plant. For every bit of truth he gave them, two-thirds of what he said was lies. If he said the shipment of girls was going over the border at Nogales on Friday, the odds were a shipment of boys was coming up from the border in Nogales on Thursday—but that didn't matter. He'd said Nogales, and Dean and Marcus both had an almost uncanny sense of lie detection with people. Marcus said Dean's came from an inability to manufacture bullshit himself, so he knew when other people were doing it just by the smell. Dean claimed Marcus cooked up so many scenarios in his fertile imagination, he'd already unconsciously run through what was plausible and what wasn't. Either way, both of them knew the sound of truth when they heard it, and so far, their ability to navigate the treacherous waters of Vlade Karkov's attempted false flags had simply added to their stellar records.

And it hadn't hurt that Vlade had kept Dean in Austin after that first encounter with Bailey.

"Fuck bad luck," Marcus said now, breaking into Dean's simultaneous musing and packing. "It's our fault, Dean. We should have let him fool us once or twice."

Dean grunted. Subterfuge wasn't one of his strong points, but he could see where Marcus was heading with this. "What do you mean?" he asked, not because he didn't understand in his gut, but because Marcus was better with words than he was.

"I mean that they probably thought Vlade was passing us the real—not everybody knows about your super brain, Dean—and it's best we keep it that way, but remember? We talked about missing a few of his leads, but…." It was not like Marcus to trail off, but Dean understood.

"Every lead he passed was human trafficking," Dean filled in grimly. It would be one thing if the shipments had been of arms, or of drugs—Dean and Marcus had played the game of "predict the shipment" often enough to be confident that they could track the goods until Vlade was off the hook for the info.

But this month it had been all *people*, and the gathering of the Vultures (as Dean thought of Vlade's branch of the mob) had been particularly bloodless about leaving those shipments to rot just to hurt the cartel's cred.

"Unavoidable," Marcus said now, crisply. "It was unavoidable that Vlade would get popped, one way or another. What is unfortunate is that it happened when your guy could get involved. What's your plan?"

Dean took a glance around the apartment, thinking sadly that he'd been happy here and that Bailey was going to have to go away for a really long time.

And that Bailey's father might need to be picked up as well.

And that Bailey would really miss his cat.

Dean regarded Mr. Bumble (he couldn't keep calling the cat Bumble—it felt disrespectful somehow), and the cat returned a crossed blue-eyed gaze. Mr. Bumble was an unusually chill cat, Dean was beginning to suspect. He didn't mind a trip to the vet's, but that could be because Bailey sedated him whenever he went. Actually, Dean knew where Bailey kept the cat's sedation and medication, and….

"I'll tell you the plan when you get me in ten minutes," Dean said. "You may want to come up. I'll need help."

Marcus didn't ask questions. He never asked questions, not after their first six months together. But then, Marcus had once thrown Dean out of a third-story window, knowing there was a rescue cushion on the ground floor. Dean hadn't known this until he'd been midair and had been able to adjust his body accordingly, and while he'd been briefly terrified he was falling to his doom, he hadn't, not once, questioned that Marcus had done what he'd done because the alternative would have been deadly.

Sure enough, Marcus followed him down right as the room had erupted into flame, taking out their unsubs.

The rest had been sprains and contusions and paperwork, and another story Dean made Marcus swear upon his life he'd never tell Dean's family.

Just like Dean swore to never tell Marcus's parents that Marcus's ratio of bed partners was 60/40 men.

Dean assumed these were the things partners shared, and since he and Marcus never shared with anyone but each other, nobody had disabused him of that notion yet.

And Marcus had not once questioned Dean's attachment to Bailey.

Dean could only be grateful he didn't question it now.

Okay. First things first. Where to deliver the package.

Dean was still moving about the apartment, packing Bailey a go bag. He knew the basics of Bailey's wardrobe and figured jeans, cargo shorts, and T-shirts would about cover the spectrum in June, but he added a hooded sweatshirt just in case, as well as socks, underwear, and a pair of tennis shoes, all of which he rolled into tiny bundles, fitting everything Bailey could possibly wear into a Rollaboard Dean found in his closet.

He packed a satchel with water, power bars, and kibble, and stacked that neatly next to the two small suitcases near the door entrance. He stripped out of his suit and into a pair of jeans and a T-shirt, along with his rubber-soled hiking boots, and then, while the plan was still fresh in his brain and not spoiled by too much thinking, he called his brother.

"Val? Where are you?"

"About an hour from Fort Stockton. Left Vinnie's place near Austin about three hours ago. Just dropped off some breeding cows, why?" Val did a lot of business for Vinnie, who was Val's best friend and sort of a millionaire cattle rancher.

"I need you to do two things for me in quick succession. The first is going to involve talking to a man in Fort Stockton you've never met and convincing him and his dog to go with you. The second is going to be… trickier. Once you have the man and his dog, I need you to head southwest to the Chihuahuan desert."

"The *fuck*—"

"Yes, I know it'll take about five hours. I will have instructions for you by the time you get there."

"Dean, I was slated to do a pickup in an hour—"

"Can somebody else do it?" Dean realized his voice was pitching, and he tried to rein it in. His family was and always had been ride or die, but until this moment, Dean had never really needed them to either ride *or* die. He'd always been self-sufficient, a thing that had hurt his mother and baffled his siblings, and he'd never really understood their need to be in each other's lives to the extent they were.

But now, oh God, now—

"Dean, what is this about?"

Dean swallowed. "Remember that doctor?" he said, his voice at a rasp.

"The one you hit on when I was in the hospital?" Val asked, but his voice was weirdly gentle.

"He… he's in trouble," Dean told him. "It's not his fault. He saw something. I… his father, his father's dog, his cat—they're all he's got. I can get him out of danger, but I need to—"

"You need me to get the guy while you get the bad guys," Val said, and Dean's eyes grew hot. Val was the oldest and the bossiest, and God, he could be an insufferable ass sometimes, but he also had never let any one of them down.

"I can get them," Val said. "And I can get them down to LA. Can you have somebody pick them up when I'm there? I've got Rory in the cabin with me, Dean, and he's got a gig in LA the day after tomorrow, and I'd hate to make him miss it." Val's boyfriend was an old contact of Dean's from the Bureau—and he was a crack shot. Perfect.

"I'll figure it out," Dean said on a breath. "I'll call Chance—he's on summer break anyway. Somebody will come meet you, I promise. But first—"

There was a knock at the door that was unmistakably Marcus's.

"First, you gotta get a move on. No worries, little brother. All you had to do was ask."

"Thanks, Val," Dean said in a rush.

"No worries. Let me know when you've got the rest of your plan doin', okay?"

"Oh yeah. It'll be a doozy."

"Can't wait."

As Val signed off, Dean took a step back and gestured to the go bags and the supplies with a jerk of his chin to the six-foot-plus man with the hard eyes, the square, capable jaw, and the bronze skin. Marcus Cabrillo was an *amazing*-looking man, but even knowing he sometimes swung Dean's way, there'd never been any chemistry between the two of them. Sibling chemistry, yes, but sexual? Not even a little.

"Okay, I've got that. What are you doing?"

"I'm getting the cat into the carrier," Dean said, keeping all the trepidation he could out of his voice.

Marcus stared at him. "Have you ever—and I mean ever—done anything like that before?"

Dean grimaced. "My, uhm, siblings always helped Mom out when it was time to do it at our house. I understand it can be quite… unpleasant."

Marcus nodded. "I, uhm, imagine. Where's the cat?"

"In the bedroom. I closed the door so he's in a limited space."

"Good planning. Here, let me get the first two bags, and hopefully you'll be done by the time I'm back." He gave a baffled smile. "Good luck?"

Dean nodded, thinking of the other calls he was going to have to make. He was definitely going to need it.

IF NOTHING else, the long dripping scratch along the inside of his arm looked like a reason for him to be in the ER.

He strode down the corridors, one of Bailey's washcloths wrapped around the thing, and hoped Bailey and Mr. Bumble could forgive him. He'd been doing so well! He and Mr. Bumble had a rapport! Dean would rub his ears and scratch under his chin until Mr. Bumble flopped over onto his side in perfect bliss. Understanding boundaries himself, Dean had never trespassed to that perfect angel-soft fluff on his tummy—he understood that for the trap it was.

But fueled by desperation and the knowledge that he and Marcus had a limited time to sweep in, grab Bailey, and get out again before Vlade's people started asking questions about the adorable doctor with the tired blue eyes who was so important in his life, Dean had trespassed those boundaries in a big way.

Mr. Bumble had not approved, but the scratch was worth it to get to the hospital in a timely manner.

Dean had to literally vacuum Bailey out of the area and shuttle him someplace outlandish quickly, and while this should have been a job for the US Marshals or even the Rangers, Dean just didn't trust anybody else to do it. Bailey was *his*, and he had to be with people Dean trusted on a molecular level.

Besides, if Dean and Marcus did their jobs right, Bailey would never be a threat to Texas Bratva, and the Corazones de Sangre never needed to know his name.

Thanks to Vlade they'd been close to fingering the key players of Texas Bratva, and the ambassadors to Corazones. Sever the relations between the two groups and they shrink in on themselves like slugs, taking time to rebuild. That time was a tool for Dean and Marcus, and the disorganization caused by breaking off an alliance like that gave them an opportunity to quietly pick up as many key players as possible without triggering a turf war.

Yeah, the war against the cartels was a war of attrition, and Bratva was an awful parasite, sucking the country dry, but while there was no one head of the snake to chop off, whacking off a good three-quarters of the many-headed beast could give them some peace and chill out the drug trade for a good five years. Who knows—maybe there'd be time to fix what was wrong in the world in that time.

Dean and Marcus were ever optimistic, and that kind of dogged determination to fix the world one case at a time was what made them good—if highly feared by their peers—active agents.

"Where do you want me?" Marcus asked, breaking into Dean's thoughts.

Dean had been studying his phone for the hospital schematics. The place wasn't big, but there were always extra entrances and exits, and that's what Dean needed now.

"South side," Dean said. "Maternity entrance. We'll be coming out there."

Marcus grunted. "Because you won't stick out there *at all*."

Dean scowled. "Please give me some credit, why don't you. Besides, I'll be with a doctor. I mean, a *doctor* in a *hospital*. How many times have we actually had a real one of those!"

Marcus gave a low chuckle under his breath, and Dean thought sourly that he was probably thinking about the time Dean had ended up stitching a suspect's lacerations himself, because that particular gang had a habit of offing the doctors they forced to care for them. Marcus had been hiding in a supply closet with the real doctor, which was good because when their slimeball had reached for his gun and found his hand stitched to his chair, somebody had been needed to fix the damage.

That fucker would never use his hand again, because while Dean knew how to stitch up a basic cut, the guy had torn some nerves going for his gun, and those didn't repair.

He'd been about to shoot an innocent woman for doing her job, and Dean didn't have any regrets, but he and Marcus had one more story they managed to carefully screen from their superiors, because, well, they weren't really sure how it would be received.

And nobody could deny it would be easier to get out of the hospital with a real doctor in tow instead of Dean in a lab coat and Marcus cradling a nonexistent gunshot wound.

"Fair," Marcus said. He held up his phone and added, "I'll be tracking you through the building. It'll be fun. It'll look like Pac-Man. Let me know if you need me."

Dean made a sort of ambiguous growl in his throat, and Marcus raised his eyebrows in reply.

"The op I can handle," Dean said with dignity. "I, uhm, don't know how Bailey's going to handle everything else."

Marcus let out a breath. "Well, I've got an idea for how to get him to the middle of the Chihuahuan desert to meet your brother, but let's hold that until we have to push him out of the plane."

Dean blinked slowly, not surprised but very much realizing that if Bailey had been irritated at him that morning, he was absolutely not going to be talking to Dean by the end of the day.

As long as he's alive, Dean thought grimly, that was a chance he was willing to take.

Parachute

ALL THOSE years of being a working student, all those years of taking a hooker bath after forty-eight hours on his feet, and Bailey could still get hypnotized by warm water, even thirty seconds of it, sluicing over his body as he tried to get rid of the blood that had seeped through his scrubs to his skin.

"Sarree says hi."

The masculine voice, spoken casually, made him shriek, and he had to scramble not to drop the soap.

"Dean!" he squeaked. "What are you doing here?"

"Getting you out of here," Dean replied, his voice crisping up. "You about done?"

"Let me wash my hair," Bailey said, although he knew he'd washed his hair at least twice. It wasn't his hair—shaggy as it might be—that was the problem here.

And Dean, damn him, knew that. "Love," he said gently, "you'll never get the blood out of your memory. If it's off your skin, you're done."

Bailey swallowed and realized that for the first time since he'd made eye contact with the two men striding through the hospital as he fled for the shower, his hands had stopped shaking.

"Okay, then," he said, recognizing shock now that it was passing, "hand me a—"

The hand with the towel shot through the curtained cubicle quickly enough to let Bailey know Dean had come prepared.

"Thanks," he mumbled as he turned off the water, grabbed the towel, and began the wipe-down in the same motions.

He'd gotten his hair toweled when the curtain was ripped open and Dean was there, wrapping his arms around Bailey's shoulders and bringing him in so hard, so close, Bailey was forced to shiver out the last of the shock.

"I've gotcha," Dean said softly in his ear. "I've gotcha. We gotta hurry in a minute, but just remember that. I've gotcha."

When was the last time anybody had said that to Bailey? Held him and told him it was all right? Unbidden his thoughts flew to Emmett's death and how nobody was supposed to hold anybody, and he'd had to call his dad and tell him not to even try to make the funeral.

"Thanks," he whispered gruffly. "Thank you."

With a quick kiss to his still-wet hair, Dean stepped back and held Bailey's elbow as Bailey stepped out of the tiny shower cubicle, and then walked him to a small satchel sitting right next to Bailey's other scrubs.

"What's this?" Bailey asked, completely confused.

"You're walking out of here as a civilian," Dean said, digging into the satchel and wincing as a white bandage wound around his wrist and forearm caught.

"I'm what? And what did you do to yourself? Who bandaged that? Where am I going?"

"I did nothing to myself," Dean said, pulling out some of Bailey's casual clothes. "Your cat, knowing I was in a hurry and desperate, gave me the perfect excuse to talk to your charge nurse and explain to her that I was getting you the hell out of here." With that he produced khaki shorts and a T-shirt that featured bigfoot and read National Hide and Seek Champion on the front.

Bailey grimaced, wishing he had something classier in the way of casual wear, and then the full import of what Dean said sunk in.

"Wait a minute—what the hell did you do to my cat?" Forgetting that he was naked for a moment, he held his shirt up to his chest in a delayed attack of maidenly modesty.

"I gave him a sedative and put him in his carrier," Dean said, staring at Bailey like it was a stupid question. "I wasn't going to put you in hiding without letting you have Mr. Bumble."

Dean was the one who called him Mr. Bumble—he apparently didn't get the joke about the Abominable Snowman, and he said he and Mr. Bumble were on much too formal a footing for Dean to forget the honorific.

And Dean, in the middle of an emergency situation, had cared enough about Bailey's feelings to remember his cat.

In the middle of everything else, Bailey was now struck with absolute remorse for his halfhearted attempt to end the relationship that morning, but this was obviously not the time to discuss it.

"That's really nice," Bailey mumbled. He took the briefs Dean held out and slipped them on, and then the shorts, following up with the T-shirt, the short socks, and the basic tennis shoes. When he was all dressed, he was surprised yet again when Dean produced a comb, which was the one item from his toiletry kit in his locker that he always forgot to bring.

He sheepishly combed his hair and took a breath.

"Better?" Dean asked as he disposed of Bailey's towels in the laundry bag where Bailey'd thrown his scrubs and lab coat before he'd jumped in the shower.

"Infinitely," he replied. "Now, are you going to tell me the plan?"

Dean nodded, throwing the satchel over his shoulder. "Before you freak out, I talked to Sarree, your friend, while she was stitching up my arm—"

"*Stitching!*"

Dean sighed and cupped his cheek. "Please, Bailey, you can't afford to freak out about a cat scratch, okay? I'm trying to keep things practical, but, well, I think you stumbled on something dire, so let me finish."

Bailey swallowed and nodded—and recalled that Dean said they hadn't much time.

"Go ahead."

"She's got you on leave—and because she said you never clock in, it's leave that started *yesterday*. She's got plausible deniability that you were ever here, and since she was frightened too, I told her to stick with that story. You were never here, she was never in the crib looking for you. Do you understand?"

"Good," Bailey said through a roughened throat. "I-I would have worried about her."

"Me too," Dean said, his expression—had he known it—tender. "She's your best friend here, Bailey. I'm not stupid. I wouldn't let her twist in the wind."

Bailey gave him a small smile. "Thank you," he said again.

"Don't thank me yet. It's going to be a long hard day, and it's going to start with getting the hell out of here without being spotted. We're going to assume they're still here—"

"They are," Bailey said in a rush. "I saw them as I was coming back to shower. I made eye contact—"

"Did they recognize you?" Dean's voice pitched, and Bailey knew then—*really* knew—how much trouble he must be in, because Dean sounded panicked now, and Dean, to Bailey's recollection, had never even sounded *ruffled*.

"No," Bailey said, shaking his head. "At least I don't think so. I just kept walking and they kept walking, talking together—"

"What did their voices sound like?" Dean asked quickly.

"Very Russian," Bailey told him, frowning. "And they were dressed very… East Coast sharp, if you know what I mean. Texas oilman, but cheaper suits, made out of wool, and shoes that were way too shiny. Wing tips."

"Wow, you *do* have a good memory. Anything else?"

"There was a big guy—like, *gorilla* big—and he must have been the one who stabbed Vlade, because he left his coin."

"His *what*?" Dean asked, grabbing Bailey with almost uncomfortable force.

"His coin—Ouch, Dean, that's some grip!"

Dean released him promptly. "Oh God. I'm sorry, Bailey, but this is really important. Did you *see* the coin?"

"Well, yeah. In fact, here." He grabbed the comb and went to his locker, because matching the comb to the toiletry kit suddenly seemed like the thing he'd been needing to do all his life. That done, he reached into the toiletry kit where he'd put the coin, neatly placed in a specimen bag, now smeared on the inside with dried blood from the coin.

Dean's eyes almost bulged. "Perfect. Oh my God—*perfect*. Okay, I need you to keep that until we can give it to Marcus and have him sign off on it. But first, leave everything here—"

"But *toothbrush*!" Bailey protested.

"I've got your home kit packed," Dean said, and Bailey stared at him.

"I barely had time to take a shower!"

"Your text arrived at a fortuitous time," he said. "Now let's go!"

"Fortuitous time?" Bailey asked, but he was following Dean out the door, thinking if Dean had missed anything—razor, toothbrush, comb— it could probably be picked up at the nearest 7-Eleven or Walgreens. "There was a fortuitous time for me to find a dead body and have to hide under the bed in the crib?"

Dean shuddered. "Good thing you showered," he said, and if Bailey hadn't seen his lips quirking with irony, he would have lost it right there. "God knows what's on the floor in there."

"I hate you," Bailey muttered. "What was so fortuitous about that timing?"

"Easy." Dean—steering Bailey like he'd been born and raised in the damned building—shrugged. "I was already packing. Just had to grab your suitcase."

Bailey made a little squawk of protest, and Dean took him on another left.

"And your cat."

Oh God. "Why my cat?" Bailey asked suspiciously. "I mean, why—"

Dean took him down a corridor that Bailey suddenly recognized. They were heading for the small maternity-ward entrance, which because in Texas irony was never big enough, was also where smokers used to go to indulge in their filthy habits. In a way it made sense. They got six to eight deliveries a day because usually pregnant women went to some of the bigger maternity hospitals in Austin. Given those odds, someone could sneak a five-minute cig and probably not see anybody waddling in to be checked, and if they *did* get busted, as long as they weren't working in L and D, nobody would ever know.

And most women in labor did not really give a rat's ass if their doctors or nurses smelled like nicotine after they scrubbed up as long as the medical professionals were free with the painkillers and didn't make the women stay on their backs.

"How did you even *know* about this corridor?" Bailey asked, his voice rising a bit in panic. This seemed *very* well thought out for an emergency rescue.

"Hello," Dean said, "FBI!"

"Wait, is this how you knew where my apartment was?" Bailey asked, feeling stupid. Hadn't that happened, like, three months ago?

"It was either that or stalking," Dean replied absently. "Bailey, how often *do* people sneak out here for a smoke?"

"A lot less than when I was going through med school," Bailey told him, not wanting to think about those two years he'd been rooming with a bunch of smokers and had needed to feed his own fix.

"I don't want anybody to see—"

Behind them, Bailey heard the clatter of hard-soled shoes and a thickly accented voice saying, "That is him!"

And Dean grabbed his hand and bolted for the door, pressing the Bluetooth earbud he'd been wearing and ordering, "Now, Marcus, now!"

They crashed outside the double doors, scaring a couple of orderlies, who scattered, and then leaped into Dean's rental car, Dean in front, Bailey in back.

"Drive!" Dean barked, and Bailey stared out the window as the two goons who'd come back to Vlade's body slammed outside after them. Marcus peeled away from the curb, pulling an abrupt right, and Bailey was left staring behind him.

"Do you think they caught the plates?" Marcus asked.

"No way of knowing," Dean replied tersely. "Where's your safety?"

"Two hours away, heading east. Yours?"

"Fort Stockton. We'll meet Birdie between here and there in about three hours."

"Birdie?" Marcus replied, a note of whining in his voice at odds with the big man's debonair appearance. "Dean, do we have to?"

"Yes, we have to," Dean muttered. "Did you not hear me make arrangements with Val not twenty minutes ago? It's your own goddamned plan!"

"But I wasn't thinking Birdie. I thought we could call in a favor from the Bureau!" Marcus retorted.

"That's ridiculous," Dean told him. "Val's got an hour's head start on us, coming from a closer direction on a clearer freeway. None of the Bureau airstrips are close enough to where Val's going to be!"

"But Dean," Marcus reasoned, and Bailey felt some satisfaction in the realization that he, Bailey, was not the only man on the planet who felt like Dean could be unreasonable, "that means Birdie has to *fly back*. I don't *want* to jump out of an airplane today!"

"You don't *have* to jump out of an airplane today!" Dean retorted. "I'll get clearance to voucher Birdie as an asset. You and I will *land* in an airplane five miles outside of Sangrino del Corazón, the cartel's compound in Mexico. *Bailey* is going to jump out of the airplane and be transported to safety along with everything he loves."

"We're going to *what*?" Marcus demanded.

"I'm going to *what*?" Bailey snapped, hard on his heels.

"Oh, please," Dean muttered. "I think it should be perfectly obvious. I just told both of you what the plan is, and now I need some peace and quiet while I call Birdie, who needs to be filled in."

AN HOUR later, Dean had spent so much time on his cell, he'd needed to charge it while he spoke into his Bluetooth, and Bailey was overwhelmed at how many *other* people were overwhelmed by the man who'd been sharing Bailey's bed.

Conversations with Dean seemed to go as well for anybody else he steamrolled as they did for Bailey and Marcus, and Bailey had no choice but to sit and listen as Dean gave directions to somebody named Birdie that included a price point that made Marcus wince and Dean promise to double whatever the Bureau paid out of his and Marcus's own pockets.

"Mine?" Marcus snarled as Dean was talking. "My pocket too?"

"Is it your bust?" Dean snapped, hitting the Mute button. "Then, yes, your pocket. Don't cheap out on me now, Cabrillo." Then he unmuted himself and resumed speaking into the phone about destinations and a small airstrip outside a town in Mexico Bailey had never heard of, and then he'd signed off.

Before Bailey could ask a single question or so much as suggest they pull over for him to eat (since he and Dean had never gotten breakfast that morning), Dean had hit another number in his phone.

This next phone call was full of acronyms Bailey didn't get and coordinates Bailey didn't understand, but this time when Dean signed off, Marcus managed a word in edgewise.

"You were a little rough on him."

"He was being slow," Dean replied, sounding deeply in a funk.

"Well, yeah, but Dean, he's our SAC!"

"He shouldn't be in charge if he's that stupid about civilians and necessity," Dean replied and then hit yet another number and was off planning again.

Bailey began to feel a little woozy. He'd really needed that espresso and whatever he'd been planning to get from the vending machine.

"Marcus?" he asked, under Dean's conversation but loud enough to be heard. "Are we going to stop anywhere?"

"Not planning to," Marcus replied shortly. "If you gotta pee, I've got a special bottle."

"I've gotta *eat*," Bailey told him, a little desperation in his voice. "I'm serious. If I don't regulate my blood sugar, I get spacey and weird and nauseous—"

"Diabetic?" Marcus asked, and gratifyingly enough, he aimed for the nearest rest stop that obviously had some fast-food outlets.

"No, just sensitive to fluctuation," he said. It ran in the family, though, so he and his father tried hard not to go too far between meals.

"Fair enough. We do need you firing on all cylinders." Marcus took the next exit and began slowing the car down considerably. "Besides, if you didn't eat, Dean's living on coffee too, and I know that because I bought him the coffee." Loudly into a pause in Dean's conversation, Bailey heard somebody's stomach grumble.

Dean glared at his partner in annoyance.

"Are we getting food?" Dean murmured under his breath. "Thank God. Marcus's gas when he hasn't eaten is *horrific*."

Bailey gave him a long-suffering look, but Dean was glaring into space and chewing out the next person who did not seem to be able to read his mind.

"You're, like, his eighth sibling, aren't you?" Bailey asked Marcus sourly, and Marcus gave him a sheepish smile in the rearview mirror.

"He says sometimes I'm the one he special ordered, but I came with factory defects."

Bailey shook his head. "It's a good thing we met when you were saving my ass," he said frankly, resting his hand on Bumble's pet carrier, where Bumble snoozed happily, obviously deeply sedated. "It's really hard to hate you for being his work wife after that."

"Don't worry about me," Marcus told him kindly. "For one thing, Dean and I just never could hit that way." He let out a sigh. "For another, there's sort of someone else."

"Sort of?" Bailey asked, surprised by the yearning in the big man's voice.

"He's very young," Marcus said. "And I'm waiting for him to grow up a little. It's taking forever."

"He'll be out of college in a year," Dean said, suddenly back in the car with them again. "And I'm dying for a hamburger, no onions. Any objections?"

"Hardee's it is!" Marcus said brightly, and, thank God, they headed for some calories.

Bailey had enough trouble with his own life right now. He didn't need to be sticking his nose into Marcus's.

A DOUBLE cheeseburger with onion rings later—with a stop at a decent restroom and a snooze in the back of the sedan while Dean continued to micromanage the planet—had Bailey feeling a little bit better about things. He was sitting up from his slump over Bumble's cat carrier, padded with a blanket he'd found shoved behind the driver's seat, and blinking rapidly, trying to get his brain to catch up to his body, when Dean spoke clearly from the front.

"Mr. Bumble's still asleep, isn't he?"

"Yes," Bailey said, checking on his cat again. "Jesus, Dean, how much did you give him?"

"He should be out for another four hours," Dean said, sounding apologetic. "I looked up the dosing, but I had to push the envelope. This is going to be a rough trip for him, and I don't want him to wake up until it's over."

Bailey nodded, and then as what Dean said penetrated, he remembered something else Dean had said. For a moment he glanced around wildly at the flat desert vista of southwest Texas and thought, *No.*

And then he remembered that ferocity with which Dean had attacked everybody in his life over the last few hours and thought, *Oh shit. No.*

And then his mouth opened all by itself, and he said, "Please tell me I'm not leaping out of an airplane with my cat."

Dean sucked air through his teeth—Bailey could hear it from the back of the car. "Well, not strictly *with* him. We're sending a supply platform down that Mr. Bumble gets to ride on. Marcus is really good at steering things like that. *You,* on the other hand, are going to have to get a few quick lessons."

Bailey blinked hard and then blinked again. "Why?" he demanded faintly. He was a smart guy. He *knew* he was a smart guy. You didn't work your way through med school bartending without some ability to extrapolate a lot of logical conclusions from a little bit of pertinent information. But he couldn't… couldn't *reason* why Dean was doing this, and therefore couldn't reason a way out of it.

He heard Dean's sigh, and then to his horror, since Marcus was going about 100 mph on a mostly deserted freeway, Dean unbuckled his belt and turned physically around in the seat so he could meet Bailey's eyes.

Bailey thought he was going to die of apoplexy, and he'd never actually seen anybody do that before. "Dean, oh my God, *turn around*! For fuck's sake, put your seat belt on. Have you ever seen what car wrecks can do? Jesus Christ—"

Dean reached out and feathered his thumb across the shaggy hair on Bailey's forehead, pushing it out of his eyes, and Bailey was so arrested by the gesture he actually shut up.

"I'm doing this so the people who killed Vlade can't trace you," Dean said softly. "Vlade was one of our CIs, but we think he was a plant. He kept trying to feed us false information, and we kept figuring out what the real bust should be. He got killed because they thought he'd turned for real."

Bailey crossed his eyes.

"Yeah, it's a mess. There's an unholy Gordian knot being tied right now between Texas Bratva and Corazones de Sangre, and the two men you described sound like the Texas Bratva hit men, right down to the coin, which is Ilya Pardonov's signature. The coin is a replica of the rare Constantine Ruble—there's only about twenty of this particular pressing in the world today, and Ilya stole himself one, and that's what he left at the crime scene. And *you* saw him come back for it. You are a walking, talking conviction—hell you're an entire case—for a gang of violent thugs and the people they've been screwing over who are equally as violent. And given the way they followed us out of the hospital, they're pretty sure they know that. I will do anything, Bailey, *anything*, to keep you and Mr. Bumble—"

"Bumble—"

"Mr. Bumble to me," Dean said, his lean, serious mouth barely twisting at the end. "And I want to keep him safe. So when you land, there will be some people waiting for you—a few you might recognize, which will be nice. You're going to be shuttled around for a bit, but I think I've got a good safe place for you to end up, and hopefully this little jaunt to the desert will help hide even your direction. So if you can deal with jumping out of an airplane—"

Bailey whimpered. He couldn't help it. Sure, skydiving had been on his bucket list, but didn't most people have that on their bucket lists, only to decide in the end they simply wanted to live a few more years and not risk that precious time doing stupid things on their bucket lists?

Again that gentle touch, this time along his cheekbones. "We'll give you instructions," Dean said softly. "And I swear there will be somebody waiting for you. It's going to be fine—"

"Except for that five to seven minutes in the air," Bailey said, trying not to freak out.

Dean's grin surprised him. It was like watching a little kid geek out over dinosaurs. "You've looked it up, right?" he said. "'Cause it's *amazing*. Like the whole world is there in your outstretched arms. You're gonna love it."

And Bailey couldn't help it. That joy in such a hard, determined man—it was *magical*. Transcendent. Glorious. Who didn't want to touch something that amazing? Who wouldn't follow it into hell?

"If you say so," Bailey whispered, already crumbling in the face of that transcendent joy. "I mean, what could it hurt."

Dean chortled like a third grader, and Bailey stared at him hungrily, all thoughts of danger—both to Bailey from the jump and Dean for sitting backward in his seat without a belt—disappearing. The eyes, the cheekbones, the lean lips, the slightly crooked bottom teeth—even the strutting-rooster God complex—all of it seemed unbearably attractive when combined with that goofy laugh, and Bailey was struck with wonder.

Oh man, he was so in trouble. He'd been in trouble when he'd let Dean in his shower that morning. Screw that, he'd been in trouble when he'd let Dean in his front door. Or, hell, before then. When he'd let Dean in his *pants*.

Dean Royal so very obviously had Bailey Dodge's number, and as evidenced by their conversation that morning, Bailey didn't even know he had a phone.

"Yeah," Bailey admitted faintly. "I… I've thought about it. Was thinking maybe the big four-oh—"

Dean snorted. "How about the big three-four?"

"How do you know how old I am?"

He knew the answer before Dean said it.

"Hel*lo*, FBI!" Dean grinned and texted deftly on his phone. "There. I just sent you the basics for the jump you're going to make. You don't get carsick reading, do you?"

Bailey shook his head, feeling dumb from being caught in the hurricane.

"Good. You ponder that for an hour, and then we'll be at the airport. I've got some more prep work to—Oh, wait, how's your phone battery?"

Bailey pulled the thing out of his pocket and shrugged. "Fifty percent. Oh—"

Dean shoved a battery pack at him, complete with charging cord.

"Where did you keep that—"

"Don't ask," Marcus said. "He keeps them stashed around his person and produces them like magic tricks. Just charge your phone, read your briefing, and let him work. He's making *me* nervous too."

Dean sent his partner an evil glare. "Killjoy," he muttered, then turned back to Bailey. "But he's right. Read the briefing. I'm not dropping you out of the sky like a rock out of a boat, Bailey. We're doing all this because we want you to *live*—"

"We?" Bailey asked, suddenly feeling manhandled by the Federal Bureau of Investigation.

"Well—" And Dean's entire fireball demeanor sort of… softened. He gazed down at the seat rest then, the dearest smile Bailey had ever seen crossing his lean mouth. "—*I* definitely want you to live," he said. "You matter an awful lot to me, Bailey. I know we're just beginning, but…." He scowled and cast a sideways glance at Marcus, and Bailey took pity on him.

"I'll see you when all this is over, right?" Bailey asked, reaching forward to brush Dean's fingers with his own.

Dean glanced up, that manic grin back in place. "Oh yeah. You're not getting away from me *that* easy. So study up on the skydiving brief. And remember, when you land somebody will be there to meet you."

"Who—"

But Dean was already on his phone again, turning around and belting up as he went, and Bailey decided that if he didn't want to get caught flat-footed as he jumped out of the plane, he should probably do what he was told.

TWO HOURS later he was in a small plane, wishing he knew enough about planes to know if it was the safe kind or not. He had a semi-eidetic memory, so he had skydiving procedures clicking behind his eyes like a slideshow, and Dean was repeating last-minute instructions in his face as Marcus opened the hatch and wind and engine noise roared around them, filling his senses with a bone-jarring, brain-melting distraction.

Dean paused for breath, and Bailey's gaze went to what looked like a small wagon filled with Mr. Bumble's cat carrier and lots of water and supplies, and boxed in a crate with a hinge and a catch so it would be easy to access once the thing landed.

"My cat—" he whimpered, completely bypassing what Dean was saying. He knew it already. Hit the timer on his eWatch as he jumped. At one minute, pull the chute. Grab the handles, steer gently, try not to land in any cacti, and run in the air before his feet touched the ground. Woohoo! The jump should take about six minutes, plus or minus some wind currents, and Marcus would be steering the other chute via remote control. Once Bailey touched down, he was to release the chute, gather it up, and stuff it back in the bag, then do the same for the chute attached to the box. The bags would fit in the wagon, which was exactly as big as the ubiquitous crap-wagon used by soccer coaches and overwhelmed moms everywhere, and as soon as Bailey had disassembled the crate, he was to grab the wagon handle and walk toward the mountain range in the north. Somebody, Dean promised, would be along shortly—half an hour maximum—to get him. In the meantime, Mr. Bumble had a mini cooling system in his carrier, and Bailey had one in his flight suit. If the cooling systems died before help came, he was to make a canopy with one of the parachutes, find a place to hold down and stay cool, and wait it out.

Help *would* come.

A part of Bailey was skeptical, to say the least. That long, terrible year and a half, part of it without PPE, part of it just… just overwhelmed. He remembered that feeling—the grownups were going to figure this out, right? Somebody would realize that a hospital couldn't function when its personnel kept dropping dead. Right? *Right?*

And help never came. And Emmett had dropped dead, right in the middle of a shift.

And in the end, it had been Bailey and Sarree and the rest of their friends, battling it out because nobody else would. *They* were the grownups. *They* were the last stand between order and chaos. They would die fighting, because that's the only end they could see.

And just when they could all see daylight, the Dobbs decision had come through, and they were fighting a whole other battle.

Bailey had lived so long in a world where *he* was the cavalry, he could not imagine a world where some mysterious force came through and rescued him from the desert.

But he'd spent three months knowing Dean Royal, and he couldn't *conceive* of a world in which Dean didn't do exactly what he promised and keep Bailey out of the fire.

"Bailey!" Dean snapped. "Bailey, did you hear me?"

Bailey gave him a distracted smile. "Yes," he yelled back, over the noise of the wind and the roar of the engine. "I'm going to trust my entire existence to a man I've known for weeks, and a mysterious stranger is going to roar through the desert and pluck me from perdition."

Dean scowled. "He's not that mysterious," he said. "It's my brother, not James Bond!"

Bailey stared at him in absolute surprise, and before he could ask what in the hell Dean's brother was doing roaring through the desert to save Bailey's ass, Dean's mouth was on his, hot and needy and demanding, and Bailey was suddenly very much in the moment, very much in the kiss, very much in that morning when Dean had possessed his body thoroughly and had, it seemed, grabbed hold of his soul as well.

Dean pulled back, leaving Bailey breathless and rattled. Very gently Dean fastened his helmet and double-checked the timer on Bailey's watch.

"You can do this," he said soberly. "And we've got you. Remember the basics?"

"Wait until my wrist unit beeps," Bailey said. "Then pull the cord. Don't oversteer, and don't do anything drastic unless it looks like I'm landing on a cactus."

"We're over a site that used to be a farm," Dean said. "The field below us hasn't grown over yet. You should be safe from cacti, but, you know, just in case."

"Take them seriously," Bailey said. "I'm a doctor in Texas, Dean. I've pulled more spines out of people's asses than you even want to know."

Dean gave him a quick grin. "That's my boy," he said. "You keep being feisty. You'll land fine."

"Dean!" Bailey said in sudden panic. "Dean, I want to say so much, and I don't know where you'll be, and—"

Dean's tap on his helmet was grounding.

"Don't worry. I'll catch you later. Say hi to Val for me!"

And then Bailey was gazing at the open bay door of the airplane, staring at a wide blue horizon, while Dean walked him up to the mark.

A few taps on his watch and….

As easy as falling out of an airplane.

The wind roared through his flight suit, screamed in his ears, battered at his face, and he was in freefall, the ground 8,000 feet and counting.

Bailey shouted in exhilaration and wanted to look at Dean and tell him this was frickin' *awesome*!

But Dean was back on the airplane, and Bailey had to concentrate or he'd never get to tell him anything again.

DESTINATIONS

MARCUS'S FLIGHT suit was attached to the frame by the bay door, which was why he was the one to lean out of the airplane and watch as Bailey—and the crate holding the cat and supplies—landed.

Dean's heart didn't beat normally until Marcus gave him the thumbs-up.

"Val?" he heard himself asking as Marcus slammed the bay door shut.

"About a mile away," Marcus confirmed. "Could spot that purple rig from space!"

Dean's knees went a little wobbly. He wasn't sure why it hadn't occurred to him that kicking his lover out of an airplane at 8,000 feet might be a risky proposition for romance, but until Bailey had regarded him with enormous eyes—and enormous faith behind them—he wasn't sure if he'd ever known fear before.

"Good," he said weakly. "Now for phase two."

"And phase two would be?" As they spoke, both of them were slipping out of their flight suits and donning faded khaki cargo pants, ribbed tanks, and battered madras shirts. They wore socks, because trekking through the desert without them wasn't fun, but the kind that were hidden under the edges of their walking boots. Their casual rucksacks carried two changes of clothes—one of them black microfiber for nightwork—extra batteries for their communication devices, protein bars, water, and, hey, their service weapons and enough C-4 to take out….

Well, Dean's brain kind of skittered around that last one.

It was one thing to talk about "bringing a cartel down" or "bringing the mob members to justice," but it was another to contemplate mass murder in order to assure his boyfriend's survival.

But then after seeing what these two gangs had been doing to *each other* over the last year, Dean wasn't sure he wanted to contemplate what they'd do to his sweet little Bailey for just finding the wrong body.

"I'm on board," Marcus said softly, and in his eyes, Dean could see it. The weariness that had been edging in on both of them. The discomfort that came with knowing they were fighting a losing war in which the only people who were ever brought to justice were the small fish who'd never had a chance to be anything bigger than fry.

"We have to survive getting to the compound first," Dean told him. There was a small airstrip outside of Sangrino del Corazón, the compound that featured a military barracks surrounding a villa that housed the cartel leader's family. Gael Barrera was known for being absolutely ruthless, creatively bloody, and horny as a goat. The villa had grown so large in order to house his wife, two mistresses, and the knot of little Gaels, many of whom were at the preteen age, ready to join their father's ranks to serve as his lieutenants.

"What's the plan?" Marcus asked, and Dean glanced at him, the telepathy of a nearly six-year working relationship in fully functional order.

"Of course," Marcus replied after a moment.

The secret, Dean thought with satisfaction, was that he and Marcus were such sticklers for order on the bureaucratic scale. Dean's genius IQ added to his obsession over details, and Marcus's ability to smooth talk the powers that be gave them the *illusion* that they never walked into a situation without a firm objective to justify what came next.

The secret, the *real* secret, was that Dean and Marcus had survived for six years on luck and quick thinking.

The cold truth was that there wasn't a plan. There was never a plan. There was an *objective*, and there were hard limits. As the plane buzzcut through the arid heavens, Dean and Marcus outlined their objectives and their limits and where they saw the mission beginning and how they saw it ending.

And figured they'd fill in the blanks when they walked into the void.

BIRDIE WAS aiming the plane about a mile from the small village. It had sprung up the way a lot of small towns in Mexico had—people were going *across* the land and needed a fueling place to get them from point A, which was a hundred miles *that* way, and point B, which was two hundred in the other direction. Because it *was* so much the middle of nowhere, other amenities had sprung up: hotels, a few small bodegas, a couple of bars. It would never be a vacation spot, but it was big enough that a couple of gringos riding the all-terrain motorcycles stashed in the tail section of the plane wouldn't really be noticed. It was not unheard of for Americans to get lost in the desert, and Dean and Marcus both had leathers and bandanas to cover up their Bureau-length hair until it grew out, which it had done a couple of times when they'd been undercover down south trying to figure out what was coming up north that they could bust.

Technically speaking—or nontechnically speaking—they were US Feds. They weren't supposed to even *be* south of the border.

Practically speaking, as long as they didn't act on any of their intel unless they were north of the border, nobody in their division asked any questions.

And their division was so grateful for the wins Dean and Marcus had been giving them that they pretended they didn't know the answers anyway.

Vlade had been a *godsend*, because they could legitimately say they got all their info from a CI in Austin, and besides being more worried for Bailey than he knew what to do with, Dean was also irritated that his one excuse for staying in Austin was no longer going to be his excuse, because he was *dead*.

"What are you thinking?" Marcus shouted after Birdie started their descent.

"Fuckin' Vlade," Dean said honestly. "Life was a lot easier when that asshole was still alive."

Marcus grunted. "Think our two hitters know who saw them?"

Dean shrugged, unsettled. "I think Bailey's nurse is going to cover for him, smooth as silk. That woman does not look like she could lie to save her life, but boy did she get some determination in her spine when it came to lying to save Bailey's."

Marcus frowned. "Friends?" he asked uncertainly.

But Dean had done his research on Bailey's life before Dean had powered into it, and he'd pulled up death statistics in Outskirts General, and the unsupervised death statistics as well. Many states had been told to "lie with the truth" during the pandemic by not mentioning COVID on the death statistics if no tests had been run, even when the virus had clearly been responsible for the illness that killed the victim.

The numbers for Outskirts General had been devastating, and the numbers of staff and frontline workers who'd died in the course of those dreadful two years must have felt like severed limbs to the survivors left to fight another day.

"Brothers in arms," Dean told him shortly. "They both lost people during the pandemic, and there was nobody else to come in. You don't rat out your foxhole buddy, you know?"

Marcus's eyes widened. "Ouch," he said softly. "Your boy okay after that?"

Dean shook his head. "His boyfriend died," he said baldly. Because yeah, he'd seen that. People in the Bureau didn't date people who hadn't been vetted. And while Dean and Marcus had both had their share of fly-by-night lovers, when Dean had made the decision to show up on Bailey's doorstep, it hadn't been impulsively or recklessly done.

It had been because he'd been thinking of Bailey nonstop since he'd left the man sleeping, exhaustion written all over his appealing features, and he wanted to know if Bailey would welcome him into his life.

And, yeah, to make sure Bailey wasn't part of the *many* drug pipelines that ventured across the border.

Of course if Dean had thought for a moment he *was* on the take, he wouldn't have even indulged in that rather magical moment in the crib, but once he'd been officially cleared, Dean had been able to barge into the man's life and force him to allow Dean to stay with a completely clear conscience.

"Oh wow," Marcus said, so softly Dean had to read his lips over the engine noise. "Has he recovered yet?"

Dean gnawed his lip, uncharacteristically worried about another person's feelings.

"Not entirely," he said after a moment. "Or he would have told me about the man before now. But enough, I think. He was worried this morning because he felt like I didn't"—Dean wrinkled his nose in distaste—"*share* enough."

Marcus's eyebrows—perfectly plucked to accentuate his liquid brown trust-me eyes—went up to the shaved edge of his corkscrew hair. "Did you… what did you…?" He squeezed his eyes nearly shut and squinted at Dean. "Good God, Dean, I have no idea what kind of sharing you would even do."

Dean shrugged. "It was no big deal. He wanted to know about my family. What's not to tell?"

Marcus shrugged in honest bemusement. "Got me there. Your family is about as transparent as Baja gulf, but was it, you know…." His voice dropped, and Dean knew he had his own demons and secrets. They both did, but not from each other. "Hard?"

Dean thought about it. "It was weird," he said frankly. "It felt like he should have known already. They're, you know, a part of me. How could he know *me* and not know them?"

Saying it out loud made him blink.

"Which is why," he said, filling in the blanks, "he wanted me to meet his father. Oh! I totally get it now."

Marcus slow-blinked at him. "Dean Royal, ladies and gentlemen, super genius."

"Shut up," Dean retorted. Unlike Marcus, who was an only child, he'd had brothers growing up. He knew how these fights were won.

"No, seriously, Dean. How could you not think he'd need you to open up?"

Dean scowled and was about to reply that he had too little experience "opening up" to even know what the signs in a relationship *were* for that sort of thing when the engine noise changed and the plane suddenly went diving for the ground at an angle *not* conducive to good health and a long life.

"Bird!" Dean cried. "Birdie, the fuck?"

"We're taking fire!" Birdie retorted from the cockpit. "Somebody knows my usual spot with the fuel line. Gonna have to go farther south and land, but first…."

Dean could feel the engines screaming and the plane's structure groaning under his feet as Birdie pulled out of the dive and slid left then right in what had to be an attempt to dodge antiaircraft fire.

"First we have to avoid getting shot out of the sky!" Marcus hollered to him and threw him a parachute while Dean scrambled for his flight suit.

Dean slid the chute over his shoulders and then leaned back as far as the pack would allow and buckled in. "C'mon, Birdie!" he shouted in encouragement. Marcus, in the meantime, had managed his flight suit and was double-checking the cargo chutes on their small motorcycles and the supply trailer, both boxed in a large cargo container that dominated the rest of the hold.

Birdie—small, weathered, and as unaware of gender as a cactus— had flown them on more assignments than they could count.

This wasn't the first time they'd thought they were going to die, but as the plane started to climb in a way that defied both gravity and engine strength, he met Marcus's eyes grimly.

Wasn't the first time, but a little prayer that it wouldn't be the last time wouldn't hurt either.

A Horse with No Name

It was a near miss, but in the end Bailey did *not* have that brush with a cactus that Dean had him worrying about. He did everything Dean told him—ran his legs in place like a cartoon animal, pulled left to go left, right to go right, and in the end he landed cleanly in about an acre's worth of cleared space, only coming near the giant cacti toward the end of his run.

He released the chute from his back so he could make a hard turn and skidded to a halt about ten feet in front of a surprised rattlesnake, who after curling up, shaking its little rattle, and watching Bailey back away, went off on its original mission.

Bailey managed to gather his chute after that, but he left his flight suit on when he realized that the cold packs in the suit were doing him a real favor.

God, Dean had thought of *everything*.

Bailey tripled down on that thought when he bundled his parachute and shoved it in the space in the wagon, using a fold to cover Mr. Bumble's crate.

Mr. Bumble was still very out of it, but there was a hamster feeder with water ready to be positioned on the side, and Bailey did that while stroking his cat's fur. There were also, he realized, a few cold packs along the walls and top of the carrier. The outside temperature in the long-shadowed, westering sun was at least 105, but Mr. Bumble sat in relative 80 degree comfort.

Bailey's eyes burned as he finished rubbing the sleeping feline's ears, and then even more as he discovered his old khaki baseball cap wedged between the carrier and the soft side of the wagon, sunglasses tucked inside.

With a determined shove of the hat on his head—and of the sunglasses up the bridge of his nose—he stood and unlatched the plain wooden box so he could grab the wagon handle. He'd seen the road as he'd gotten near the ground and had even spotted what looked like a big rig—all in purple—nearby.

Dean had told him a half hour at the most.

Bailey was very much starting to trust Dean's estimates in things like that. It seemed like a *stellar* bet.

IT TOOK less than fifteen minutes for him to reach the road. Sand had coated it, but the basic pattern of a throughway still held true amid the encroaching cacti, and the rig didn't seem to have much problem powering through the desert.

Bailey stood to the side and watched as the driver found a place to turn around that wouldn't force the local fauna to scratch his paint job, and he was stripping out of his flight suit when the air brakes hissed to a stop about fifteen feet away.

He recognized the rangy cowboy in the passenger seat as Rory McCauley, the man who had offered to keep an eye on Val Royal that day in the hospital, and he gave a tentative smile.

"Fancy meeting you here?" he asked, as McCauley swung the door open.

"Yup. Total fuckin' coincidence," McCauley said dryly. Then he stepped out of the cab and adjusted the seat so somebody sitting in the back of a small sleeper cabin could emerge.

Bailey could not have been more surprised to see McCauley hold out his arms to help his father's dog to the ground.

"Catherine?" he said, remembering suddenly that Dean promised his family would be safe. The big golden retriever gave an even bigger *woof*, galloped toward him, and stood on her back legs to lick his face, because she had no manners, and his father never tried to teach her manners, and right now that big doggy hug was one of the most wonderful things Bailey had ever received.

Then his father clambered out with McCauley's help as well, and with a slightly bemused smile and a squeeze of Bailey's shoulder, he gathered the stuff in the wagon—the water, the food, and then the cat, and one item at a time, he and McCauley made spare, exact work of packing the things away into a sleeper cabin that was feeling more and more like the Tardis and less and less like a real semi.

After only a little fussing, Bailey had his flight suit stripped off and that had been stowed too, and then his father and McCauley hefted the dog back in before they both—to Bailey's surprise—clambered into the back of the cabin and let Bailey pull himself into the passenger seat.

The driver—who had relieved himself on a cactus on the other side of the rig as they'd been stowing gear—was wiping his hands off on a pocket wipe that he pitched in a neat little trash bag hanging from the console between them.

Bailey recognized Val Royal with no trouble at all, but instead of looking pained and fragile and as though the next move might shatter his overtaxed musculature and nervous system, he looked scowly and irritated and ready for bear.

Bailey grinned at him in absolute happiness. God, it was so good to see a relative of Dean's.

"Wow," he said as he belted himself in and Val released the air brakes. Val hit a button and their windows purred up, leaving him in a nicely air-conditioned cab with relatively little engine noise.

"Wow, what?" Val asked. He held his hand between the seats and said, "Mack, could you hand me a—Thanks."

He pulled up two bottles of water and handed one to Bailey, who opened it and guzzled happily. Yeah, he'd had water, but he'd had no idea how long it would last him, and he hadn't really gone far enough for a good break.

Didn't mean he wasn't thirsty.

"Wow, Dean does not fuck around when he's arranging a rescue," Bailey told him when the water was gone. He crumpled the bottle, put it in a bag of recyclables hanging from the console, and enjoyed the sound of Val's gruff chuckle.

"No, I guess not. What surprised you more—to be pushed out of an airplane or to see your dad?"

"To see my dad," Bailey replied, glancing to the rear of the cab to give his father a smile. People told them they were the spitting image of each other a lot, and Bailey always took it as a compliment. Older, with longish gray-blond hair, Connor Dodge was a treatise on how to age gracefully. He had one of those weathered smiles that made Bailey feel like nothing he did was too awful to forgive, even when he'd been a kid and been nothing but mistakes.

Hearing his father's voice on the phone every day after Emmett had died had kept Bailey putting one foot in front of the other, even when he'd felt as though every bit of his will had been sucked out of him with a vacuum and a straw, body and soul.

Connor gave him a sweet smile back and hugged Cathy to his chest.

"You even brought his dog," Bailey said, knowing that talking from the back seat to the front was probably an exercise in frustration and futility. "And my cat." Bumble had still been groggy when he'd been hefted into the back of the truck, but the water supply and a tiny bit of cat treat had placated him. Bailey figured he'd probably snooze a while more before needing to be let out to wander a bit on the lead and halter Dean had included with his crate.

"I understood they come as a matched set," Val said with surprise. "Son, I'm old enough to know you don't separate a man from his dog." He smirked. "Or my brother's boyfriend from his cat."

Bailey laughed a little. "Well, thank you," he said, feeling the gratitude in his heart.

"You want to thank me?" Val asked. "Then, uhm, could you tell me why we all did that? I mean, I trust my little brother and all, and I'll take an awful lot on faith, but I gotta tell you, I was toodling along perfectly happy, heading toward Fort Stockton, when Dean suddenly calls me up and rearranges my life. I would *love* to know why."

Bailey gaped at him, absolutely stunned. "He… he didn't even tell you? Oh my God."

Val hit a switch on his dashboard. "Okay, y'all," he said seriously into what must have been an intercom. "Listen up. Bailey's gonna tell us a story."

Wow. Uhm… *wow.* Well, given what Val Royal had just done for Bailey and his family on faith, Bailey figured he owed the man one.

If all he wanted was Bailey's story, well Bailey would make it a ripsnorter.

He told the story with all its elements and finished with "And then Dean threw me out of an airplane, and you know the rest. Sorry! Sorry for the inconvenience—"

Bailey's father's voice was crystal clear over the intercom. "You literally knelt in a puddle of blood while mobsters came in and pawed a corpse? Jesus, son—you've got balls!"

Bailey snorted. "I didn't think about it that way, Dad," he said. "I mostly didn't want to get gutted like poor Vlade."

"Vlade?" Val asked, his voice suddenly sharp with curiosity. "Vlade… Karcek?"

"Uhm, yeah?" Bailey supplied.

"Wow. Well, that explains what Dean was doing in Austin all this time—besides you, Bailey."

As Bailey stared at him, McCauley guffawed. "Fuckin' *nice*, Val. To your little brother's boyfriend you said that. Don't forget I know your family."

Val grunted. "I mean I know what he was doing there for *work*, asshole."

"What?" Bailey said. "And I don't know if we're boyfriends yet—" About the time he was wondering if he could sound any more like he was in the ninth grade, the other three men in the semi burst into a cacophony of laughter.

"Son, after what these men just did for you, I'm pretty sure you're married in the eyes of their clan."

Bailey could feel his cheeks heat in spite of the semi's stellar air-conditioning.

"I only meant we're new," he said with what dignity he had. "But what was Dean doing there for work?"

"Well," Val said, "from what I understand—and Dean is a closemouthed bastard, which is why I'm the only sibling who knows about *you*, my friend, so don't get your panties in a wad when everybody else gets all in your face. But from what I understand, mind you, Dean and Marcus are sort of… well, the cartel busters of their division."

From the intercom, Bailey heard Rory McCauley snort. "Two most out of control sonovabitches in the Bureau," he said, a note of admiration coloring his voice. "I mean, the shit those two get into—legen*dary*. But yeah, over the last year or so, they've been tracking an unholy alliance between one of the local cartels—Corazones de Sangre—and a branch of Bratva, the Russian mob. I would imagine you stumbled onto a Russian mob hit, Bailey. No wonder Dean wanted to get you out of there before the world even knew Vlade Karcek was dead."

"So…." Bailey swallowed, trying to keep the hurt from his voice. "That's why Dean was in Austin? For this… this Bratva thing?"

"That's why he was there for *work*," Val said gently, as though reading Bailey's mind. "But you should know that he had lots of chances to come home to Sacramento—or to see the family—that he's passed up in the last few months, mostly because he wanted to see you."

"Do you know," Bailey said, unable to keep the bitterness out of his voice, "that until this morning, I thought you and *Marcus* were his only two siblings, and when he said your family was *a lot*, that just meant your parents were really nosy?"

Val's laugh filled the cab of the truck—and so did McCauley's from the back.

"Oh my God," McCauley whooped. "Val, wait until he meets your parents. He'll know why that's so funny."

"Meet your parents?" Bailey said, surprised. "What does he mean by that?"

Val grunted. "Well, for one thing it means I may have been able to put one payload off on one of my employees, but I've got another one waiting for me in LA that is both insured and worth a lot of money to my company. I can't put this one off, so you're catching a ride from Chance and whoever he can con into going with him."

"Reg and Anthony," McCauley said from the back.

"Anthony?" Val sounded puzzled.

"Who's Anthony?" Bailey asked, pleased that he at least knew Chance and Reg were Dean's little brothers.

"Rory's son," Val said, still puzzled. "Great kid, really, but I don't know why he'd be hanging out with Reg and Chance."

"Don't you?" Rory McCauley asked cryptically. "Do you really not know?"

Val frowned. "I didn't realize they'd all gotten tight." He smiled a little. "It must have been at the family reunion."

There was a faint snort, and Bailey wondered if, should he see Rory McCauley's face, he wouldn't be gazing at Val Royal with a hint of pity, but then Val added, "I was hoping Dean would bring you to that, but it must have been too soon. Hopefully you'll be able to make it to the Thanksgiving thing." He raised his voice for the intercom. "You too, Connor. My folks set a big table around Thanksgiving."

"It's been a while since we sat at a big table," Connor began, but Bailey rapidly saw this conversation—and his life and his relationship with Dean—spiraling neatly out of his control.

"Dad, don't get your hopes up. This man just pushed me out of a plane, remember?"

And this time, his *father* snorted. "Son, you just *let* this man push you out of a plane—with your cat, which shows he knows you. I'm saying the cat alone should get you to give him a shot till Thanksgiving."

"He obviously didn't want me around during the family reunion in—When was it?" he asked.

"Early June," Val said. "You two would have been pretty new."

Bailey grunted. "Or he's just a closemouthed bastard who wasn't ready to share his family," he said bitterly.

"So you got some things to say to the man," Val said, nodding. "I totally understand. Me and Dean have been saying shit to each other since he got smarter than me—when he was about eight and I was in high school. Little asshole." He smiled indulgently. "I love him so." He sobered. "And whatever his reasons for not mentioning the family reunion, you're about to be eyeballs deep in family *now*. His *and* Rory's, for whatever reason—"

Rory let out what was almost a giggle, and Bailey fought the totally useless urge to turn around in his seat. Val ignored him and continued.

"—so you need to prepare yourself. Dean likes to keep his secrets to himself, and you, my new friend and hopeful in-law, are apparently his secret keeper. You are going to be grilled like a trout, with lots of spices, until you are delicate, flaky, and tender."

Bailey stared at him. "That's an, uhm, oddly specific analogy," he said, hoping Dean wasn't a member of a closet tribe of serial killers.

"Don't mind him," Rory said. "He's starving. First barbecue place you see when we get back to Texas, call out. They almost all have parking for semis, and we've got to get us some chow."

As if to punctuate this, Bailey's stomach grumbled, and he yawned. "Hey," he said, "does anybody want to switch seats with me? It's getting dark and I'm… I'm feeling a nap coming on, and I've worked at a hospital too long to let a car ride go without catching some sleep."

"Begging your pardon, Mr. McCauley" came Connor Dodge's apologetic voice, "but I would give a lot to look out on the road from the front. Catherine too."

Bailey heard the smile in Rory McCauley's voice when he said, "Not a problem. I could use a nap myself, and the pullout sleeps two. Don't get jealous, Val. I'm pretty sure Bailey's eyeballs are about to roll back in his head."

"Not jealous. Coming to a rest stop soon," Val said. "We can get out, cop a whiz, grab some snacks, and rearrange. Hold on, folks, it'll all be good."

TRUE TO his word, the rest stop came in about half an hour, and everybody used the chance to stretch their legs. Bailey noted that Val and

Rory took turns standing by the truck—like many semis, the thing didn't get turned on and off on a dime. Letting it sit and idle for ten minutes took less diesel than starting it up again, and less time.

When Bailey crawled into the back, a rather tasty homemade chicken wrap in his stomach to hold him until "barbecue time," as Val called it, Rory let him kick off his solid sneaker-boots (as he called the ankle-high cross trainers he wore to the hospital) and wedge himself into the cabin's sleeper. It was surprisingly spacious, so when Rory stretched out next to him, his back to Bailey, Bailey felt no more intimacy than he did bunking with somebody in the crib.

"You all right back there, Doc?" Rory asked, and Bailey grunted.

"Yessir. Thanks for asking."

"Good. Need anything before I cop my own nap? Years in the Bureau—you know how it is."

"Sleep if you can catch it," Bailey agreed.

"Yeah. So need anything?"

"Only one thing," Bailey said with a yawn. "Why was it so funny about Anthony? And who is he anyway?"

Rory chuckled. "Anthony's my son," he said, his voice low. "And it's funny because he's pretty damned in love with Val's little brother, but I don't think Reg knows it yet. And Val certainly doesn't."

Bailey smiled a little. "Why not?" he wondered sleepily. "Why wouldn't Val know?"

"You gotta meet the family," Rory said on his own yawn. "Once you meet them, it'll all become clear. Trust me, Doc. A man throws you out of a plane with your cat and he's pretty sure you're gonna stick, if he has to bungee cord you to his roof."

Bailey chuckled and had an image of being bungee corded to the roof of Dean's rental, the wind through his hair, Marcus—who was clearly insane—at the wheel.

"Whee…." he mumbled, and then the cool dark of the vibrating cabin took over, and he was out.

Out of the Rain

THE PLANE climbed up, up, up and—sort of—leveled out. Birdie came hauling back to the cargo area to grab a parachute and yell at them.

"What are you doing?" the pilot demanded. "Why aren't you prepping the bikes to bail?"

Marcus and Dean stared at each other.

"Are we hit?" Marcus asked, standing up anyway and slipping on his own chute as the plane sputtered.

"No, but I'm not landing here!" Birdie snapped. "Get your transpo ready, and I'll be back in two to push you out of the fucking door!" And with that the pilot whirled around to keep the damned plane aloft.

"Well, this feels like karma," Marcus muttered, but he was on it. The two cross-country bikes had full fuel tanks and landing platforms, because Dean knew how to requisition things months and months ahead of time so nobody shouted about the expense. Together the two of them prepped the bikes, and then Dean opened the bay door again and stared down.

"Jesus!" he shouted. "Bird, I don't even know where we are!"

"About a hundred miles south of where you were gonna be!" Birdie shouted back. "You got supplies, right?"

"I fucking hope so!"

But it didn't matter. Marcus was shoving the first platform out the bay door, having set the chute to deploy in forty-five seconds, and Dean was putting his shoulder behind the second platform, having done the same.

"Christ," he muttered. "If we're lucky they won't collide in midair. What's our terrain looking like?"

"Like a rattlesnake's toilet!" Marcus replied, getting his shoulder in on the action next to Dean's. One of the platforms held a motorcycle cart with the provisions Birdie hoped they had, and this must be that one because it weighed a fucking *ton*. "Let's go swim in coyote shit, shall we?"

They both grunted as the platform dropped out of the plane, and Dean had to pinwheel his arms to stay grounded.

"Don't worry 'bout the transpo, Bird!" Marcus shouted.

"I'm not!" Birdie shouted back. "I'm worried about the fuel I'm dropping! I think they hit the tank!"

"*Fuck*!" Marcus cried, his attention arrested by something right outside the plane. Dean stared where he was staring and realized that flames were roaring down the fuselage, only getting blown out by the change in pressure by the bay door.

"Bird!" Dean shouted, hauling ass for the cockpit, "She's on fire! Get your ass out here and bail with us!"

Birdie had a wrinkled, weathered face, and could have been anywhere between thirty and sixty years old, but Dean had seen enough people give up something dear to them to know the torture in the old pilot's eyes.

"But Dean," the pilot said, the anguish in their voice resonant of countless missions Birdie had helped Dean and Marcus with. Dean had discovered Birdie on a road trip to the Austin field office the first time he'd been posted there, and he'd liked the tough old bird. The pilot's absolute dedication to the craft of flying, the hunger for more and more time in the air—Dean related to it at the time, because that had been how *he'd* felt about his job. He'd just been partnered with Marcus, and he'd discovered that brotherhood didn't have to come with the Royal name, and that Marcus was more excited about participating in his adventures than worried about Dean's person.

And Birdie had been their companion on so many journeys they'd lost count, and now his friend was in pain.

"Bird," Dean said softly, "she's been a good ship. But we'll get you a new one. You're too good a pilot—too good an *asset*—for me and Marcus not to be able to get you a new one."

The engines were whining, and he could feel the heat from here. From the cockpit he could see the burning fuselage, and as he watched, another engine sputtered and died.

"Dean...."

But Dean had no more time for Bird's feelings—Birdie could forgive Dean, he hoped, but only if they all lived.

"Bird, get out now or I will throw you over my shoulder and pitch you out of the plane myself," he said, and something about the flatness of his voice had Birdie giving him a glare of fury.

And of absolute belief.

"Fine, you fucking heartless sadist," Birdie snarled, but Dean could hear the tears in the pilot's voice. With a sad little pat of the plane's console, Birdie set the automatic pilot and followed Dean down the aisle to the cargo bay.

"Go!" Birdie shouted at Dean and Marcus, but Dean and Marcus had dealt with Birdie for too long to fall for that. Birdie had strapped on a parachute when they had, and they'd all made too many jumps to take the time to check gear.

Together they each grabbed an arm and hauled ass out of the plane, ignoring Birdie's scream as they plummeted toward the earth.

They held on until Birdie's cry of *"You bastards!"* died in the wind, and then all three of them checked their watches as they separated and gauged the time to jump that would give them the most control over their chutes.

"YOU THINK Bird'll stop bitching before we find the compound?" Marcus asked after they'd landed. They knew the drill, the same one Bailey had followed: releasing and packing the chute, making sure cooling packs were set with the fuel and water, releasing the latches that held their transpo crates together. All of it, smooth as silk, with the bleak, angry accompaniment of Birdie's bitter harangue about arrogant jackasses who knew fucking everything but how to fly a goddamned plane.

Dean rolled his eyes and then raised his head for the horizon. "I predict the bitching will stop in… wait for it…."

Marcus joined him in staring, and together, they watched as the plane got lower and lower and—

Boom!

The concussion of the plane as it hit more coyote shit and exploded knocked Birdie to the ground and forced Dean and Marcus to brace, reaching out to grab each other's bicep as a stabilizer.

The orange flame that hurled from the wreck was enough to make Dean shudder.

"Hey, Birdie," Marcus snapped as Bir gaped at the destruction. "You see that bigass fireball?"

Bird nodded dumbly.

"That means your fuel tanks were well and truly breached, because that only happens in the movies when your plane's about to *explode*."

They both saw Birdie swallow. "Yes," came the stunned croak.

"So now that we know the damned thing was going to kill you, do you think you can *give Dean a fucking rest for saving your life!*"

Dean regarded Marcus with surprise. One of the things he'd always liked about his partnership with the man was that they were equals, in this together. But that had sounded almost protective.

"That plane meant a lot to Bird," Dean said softly, and Marcus scowled and shook his head.

"So should Bird's life," he said. "It bothers me when people yell at you."

"People yell at me?" Dean asked. He didn't often register that. He assumed part of it was his lack of social awareness that he'd never noticed.

"Sometimes," Marcus said, shaking his head. "Let's say I've grown a sudden tenderness for your feelings and leave it at that."

Dean stared at him. "What? Why?" Then, with horror, "You're not… not *in love* with me, are you?" The absurdity of even asking that question left him gasping.

"No," Marcus said, with such absolute finality that Dean gave a sigh of relief. "But I do *love* you. You may have brothers coming out your ears, but I only have one, and I don't like him disrespected. Is that okay with you?"

Dean gave him a smile. "That's fine," he said happily. "I *do* have brothers coming out my ears, but that doesn't mean people get to be mean to you either." He paused. "Except me. I get to give you shit at any time."

"Oh, of course," Marcus said, nodding. "Goes without saying."

They didn't need any other words as they went back to gathering and organizing, and after another grumpy, pissed-off moment of mourning the plane, Birdie stood to help them.

Twenty minutes later, as Birdie prepared to mount behind Dean on the motorbike, Dean heard a rusty voice proclaiming, "Thanks for not letting me die, you arrogant fuckhead."

"Anytime, Bird," Dean said, meaning it. "Keep an eye on the compass. Seriously, Marcus and I knew where we were *going*, but we have no idea where we are now."

"Yeah, yeah, I get it. Sangrino del Corazón isn't really found on maps."

Dean grunted. "We were *hoping* to find the town before we found the compound. I'd leave you in the town, Bird. You could place a call for exfil, and Marcus and I could go do our thing."

"Wait a minute," Birdie said, forestalling Dean from hitting the kick start. "What's your thing? I don't know your game plan here. What aren't you telling me?"

Dean shot an unhappy glance at Marcus, who against what they both knew about being all alone in the middle of fucking nowhere, glanced around them as though scorpions sporting recording equipment were a common occurrence.

"I'm not gonna say it," Marcus told him. "I mean, *I* know what we're doing, but the less we actually say what we're doing, the more we can pretend we weren't planning to do it."

Birdie stared from Marcus to Dean and back. "Wait. Did I just *crash my plane* in an unsanctioned action? C'mon, guys. The FBI is going to replace my plane, right?"

Dean nodded, no doubt in the world. "Of course they are, Bird. We've got recon near the US-Mexico border totally cleared. You were in perfectly legal airspace when Corazones de Sangre opened fire on you. You're good."

Birdie blinked. "What are you two chuckleheads not telling me?" the pilot asked flatly.

Dean regarded his old partner in adventuring with a level gaze. "Right now, Birdie, you can call our supervisor from town, and they will send a copter to pick you up in exfil. And when they ask you what we're doing, you can say that was never part of our deal."

Birdie's mouth opened a little, lean and lined and a tad vulnerable, and then closed again. "And what if I want payback?" Birdie asked suspiciously. "Those fuckers shot down my baby."

Dean and Marcus met eyes again.

"Either way," Marcus said to Dean alone, "we've got to get going before somebody starts checking to see where our chutes went."

Dean grunted. "My boyfriend's a witness to a Bratva murder," he said. "The same hit men who've been cozying up to Corazones de Sangre. We're gonna head toward town to drop you off, and I want you to think about the one thing that would keep my boy and his family and now *my* family safe, and when you come to a conclusion, then you can let us know if you want to come with us. Until then hold tight, Bird, and keep your helmet and your goggles on."

The diminutive pilot nodded firmly, and Dean and Marcus kickstarted their bikes. The two-stroke engines roared to life, and they hauled ass in the general direction of the town.

"What happens," Birdie yelled at him as they hit their stride, "if we get to the compound before we get to the town?"

"I guess you won't have much of a choice to make then after all!" Dean shouted back, and then kept his mouth shut because he didn't like eating bugs.

THE HANDOFF

THE NAP was surprisingly refreshing, and so was the stop out in the middle of nowhere for a pop-up barbecue pit. They ate on battered picnic tables with vinyl-covered red-checked tablecloths under an ocean of black sky, and cleaned up with about sixty-dozen wipes, and every one of them moaned and made free use of the antacids Val Royal passed around afterward.

And secretly craved more but didn't want to look ridiculous in front of the other travelers.

The place gave ham hocks to big dogs if they were asked, and Catherine got a long, happy gnaw on a rare treat.

Two hours after Val had parked in the hardpacked parking lot—not the only big rig there by far—they all started out again, only now Bailey felt a little less crazed.

Of course he had yet to be grilled by his father, either.

Val's cheerful injunction to make free with the Wi-Fi and watch a movie or something on the screen secured to the back of one of the seats felt—to Bailey anyway—like an invitation to throw up in the impossibly tiny bathroom tucked into a recess near the foot of the sleeper bed, so he and Connor both declined.

But after fifteen minutes of dissecting the barbecue (a habit for some Texans, an obsession for others), an uneasy silence fell, and Bailey felt compelled to break it.

"So, uhm… any questions?"

"Tons," Connor said dryly. "But first, skydiving. Was it everything you ever thought it would be?"

Bailey had to smile. He'd dreamed of flying as a child, and Connor was the one who told him he'd have to try skydiving—but not when the older man knew he was going to do it, because, as he proclaimed, "My ticker can't take it!"

"It was amazing," Bailey confessed to his father. "Just… just *amazing*. Not like falling at all. It really was like flying. And when the chute caught air—it was so peaceful. Dad, I'm telling you, that was worth waiting for."

"Glad to hear it," Connor said, chuckling and settling back on the sleeper so Catherine could join him. Neither Rory nor Val had made any complaints about the dog, and Bailey was grateful. Catherine had gotten both the Dodge men through a really tough time. Now she rested her chin on Connor's lap and gazed at him with adoring eyes while he absently fondled her ears.

"What about you?" Bailey asked slyly. "You always said you wanted to—what was it? 'Greet the open road'?" Next to him, Mr. Bumble made a plaintive meow, so Bailey opened the top of the carrier and smoothed his fur. The cat had enjoyed the walk around the field surrounding the barbecue pit, and Bailey had been grateful he'd chosen to relieve himself off in the tall grass as the lead went taut. But Mr. Bumble wasn't used to *any* of this, and Bailey recognized the need for comfort when it yowled at him.

Connor snorted. "I do like this little compartment back here," he acknowledged. "But I would definitely miss my recliner—and my walks in the morning with Catherine, here." He sighed, and Bailey knew it was because his neighborhood had become more and more developed in the past five years. While Connor Dodge wouldn't have said anything, Bailey woke up from nightmares of the two of them getting run off the road because it felt like the place was all blacktop, no sidewalks, with more cars every day.

"We'll find you a better place after this," Bailey promised him. His father had moved to the burgeoning suburb shortly after Bailey's mother had died, while Bailey had still been in med school. At the time it was closer to Bailey, his only family, and far enough from the city for comfort.

"I'd as soon find a place near *you*, son," Connor said with some asperity, "but I get the feeling you might not come back to roost in Austin when this is done."

And now there they were.

"Dad, Dean and I are very new—"

"Sure, sure."

"And Dean doesn't even live in Austin. I've got the ER—"

"Of course you do."

"And Dean has family. I mean, you can *see* that Dean has family."

"Yes, he does. Good family."

"I mean, I don't even know what we were doing in the first place," he finished bitterly, because all of his father's "sure, sures" were most certainly *not* in any sort of agreement.

There was a taut silence.

"You done now, son?"

"Yes," Bailey said, pouting and unable to stop.

"Let's start with the new."

"We *are* new."

Connor gave a short bark of a laugh. "Bailey, you and Emmett had been together since med school. In that entire time would you have let Emmett throw you out of an airplane?"

Bailey scowled. "Emmett would *never* have thrown me out of an airplane," he said.

"No. Emmett was a thinker and a planner and a good man," Connor Dodge said soberly. "But he was not a seat-of-the-pants thinker, and he wasn't the sort to improvise. And yet you trusted this guy enough to go with him anyway. Why is that?"

Bailey's scowl relaxed, and he thought carefully, Emmett's fading image behind his eyes as he did so. Emmett had been quiet and studious, with pale brown hair that had been thinning a bit in the end. He'd been a planner—much like Dean—but meticulous. The kind of man who did the calculations six to eight times, just to make sure.

Dean did the calculations twice, filed the information away, and moved on.

But then, Dean's intelligence was fiercer, his moods more mercurial—although he appeared just as loyal and dedicated to his own causes.

"They're a lot alike," he said in surprise. "They're both planners, but Dean's... well, Dad, you've got to meet him. When people say 'he's sharp,' they haven't met Dean. He's, like, triple-folded-carbonite-steel kind of sharp, but he never sits still."

"So you trust his plans," Connor said, nodding. "Already. So maybe the new isn't the problem."

Bailey tried to scowl again, but he couldn't. He'd thought of Emmett for the first time in years without that tight knot of tragedy binding up the memory, and he'd found the memory good. A kind, quiet, dedicated man,

Bailey had loved him so very much and would have been happy with him for the rest of their lives. But Emmett wasn't here anymore.

And Dean was.

"No," Bailey said faintly in reply to his father, rocked a little by the revelation. He'd never be "over" Emmett. He'd never not miss him. But he'd lived without him for four years now, and apparently his heart had healed enough to beat some more.

"So about the ER," Connor began, and Bailey glanced at him sharply.

There was something in his father's voice that Bailey didn't like. It was the same tone of voice Connor had used when Bailey had been waiting for his college acceptance letters, when Bailey *hadn't* gotten into his top choice.

"What about it?" Bailey asked, wary.

"Just… you know that nice woman you work with? Sarah… Sarabeth…?"

"Sarree Wilson?"

"That's the one. Do you know she's been calling me up and chatting every so often?"

Bailey stared at his father in the air-conditioned dark of the sleeping cabin until Mr. Bumble bit him to get his attention.

"I had no idea," he said, his voice practically squeaky with surprise.

"Oh yeah, started after Emmett passed. Kept going. She's a nice lady. We exchange Christmas cards. Her husband makes the most amazing fudge."

"I know," Bailey said, still lost. "She brings it to work over the holidays."

"She says you like the Black Forest fudge best," Connor said gravely, showing the same attention to raising his son that he had through Bailey's childhood. "But anyway, she's been looking to retire, you know."

"I know," Bailey replied, remembering their last conversation before Dean had hustled him out of Outskirts. "She's been waiting for me, I think. Until she knew I'd be okay."

"That's right, son, she has," Connor told him. "But I want you to think. Who else you hanging on for, there at Outskirts? I know you and Sarree have been propping each other up pretty steadily, but who are you holding on for when she's gone?"

There was really only one person—they both knew that—and he wasn't around to appreciate the dedication.

"They need good doctors in Texas," Bailey said, but his voice was weak and he knew it.

"They need good doctors everywhere. Wait and see, son."

"You haven't even met this guy!" Bailey finished on a wail, remembering their conversation that morning. Oh God. That morning? Really?

"Whose fault is that?" Connor asked.

Bailey let out a grunt. "Well, sort of both of ours. We… we didn't start out communicating, you know?"

A passing flash of light showed Bailey his father's arched eyebrows. "Oh, *really*."

Bailey let out a mortified burst of laughter. "I… you know, Dad, you don't want to hear this story."

"Oh I do. I *really* do."

Bailey thought about it. And thought. And then his father's chuckle broke into his frantic scrambling for a way to explain that first meeting.

"So, uhm, orgy, was it?"

"No!" Bailey cried in outrage. "No. You know me better than that. Val got hurt in a wreck—he pretty much pulled every muscle in his body and had a roaring concussion. Dean showed up to make sure his brother was taken care of, and McCauley showed up, and Val's best friend showed up too, and after I got everybody calmed down and checked Val out, Dean and I… uhm… had a moment."

"A moment," his father echoed dryly.

"A really *good* moment," Bailey admitted, because it had been. And then, because his father probably guessed this anyway, "My first moment since Emmett."

"Yeah, son. I know. So an important moment."

Bailey shrugged. "I thought so, but I also didn't expect it to go any further, you know? Dean left, I fell asleep, and… and I was, like, 'Wow. That was amazing.' And never expected to see him again."

"What happened?" His father adjusted his seat so he was lying prone on the bed, and Bailey wondered if somebody up front needed a break because he wasn't ready to sleep yet.

"He showed up a week later," Bailey said, that moment so clear in his mind. Dean, head leaned back against the stucco, eyes closed, half smile on his face in spite of the discomfort of his injury. "And I was so glad he was there. And that's how it went. He'd disappear and then show up again, and we forgot to talk about the important things because…."

"Because being together *was* the important thing," his father supplied, and Bailey sighed, because his father, as always, got it. He had since… well, since Bailey was eleven and had a terrible crush on the quarterback of the Dallas Cowboys. He'd been *so* excited about football, but he couldn't remember any of the rules, and when his dad had asked him what about the sport he liked best, he'd blurted, "The guy with the ball is so pretty!"

And that had been it. His father had bought him posters of Drew Bledsoe and told him to maybe tell his friends it was because he was going to "bring it home this year" and not spread the "pretty" part around school. Bailey had taken his advice to heart and hadn't come out to friends until college, when he was pretty sure it wouldn't be a thing. But his father had always known and had always supported him and had always, *always* wanted him to be happy.

"Yeah," Bailey said now. "It was. And this morning I almost… almost made him leave, because I realized I wanted more."

"What did he say?" Connor asked drowsily.

"He said I should have asked him earlier. He had no problems talking, but he needed specific questions or he wouldn't think about telling me things."

His father's laugh sounded slightly more awake. "Uhm… wow."

Bailey snorted. "That's Dean. He"—Bailey's voice grew soft—"said he'd been diagnosed as on the low end of the spectrum when he was in college, because he organized information so specifically and didn't always pick up on emotional cues. I-I don't know if his family knows that, but I get the feeling…."

"They wouldn't have cared?" Connor asked.

"Well, not so much not cared," Bailey said, "but the way Val talks about Dean, about his other family—like the quirk wasn't what mattered. What mattered was communicating with the person. I, uhm, think that's why Dean wouldn't think to tell *me*."

"Mm…," Connor murmured. "Because he's been accepted for his entire life by all his important people."

"Yeah," Bailey said softly. "I hope I didn't let him down."

"You must not have," Connor told him. "You called him with an emergency, and that boy called in the cavalry, didn't he?"

Bailey laughed softly, thinking his father probably *really* needed his sleep now. "Oh yeah he did."

"Someone who would go to the wall for you like this—son, that's special. What's he look like?"

Now Bailey really *did* laugh. "Like Val, but leaner and younger. Just as cocky, though, but you can definitely tell they're brothers."

"Well, Val's a good-looking man," Connor murmured. "His little brother might almost be good enough for my son."

"Dad," Bailey said, figuring it was time.

"'Night, son. Let me know when we come to a rest stop. I don't want to use that tiny portajohn. It's terrifying."

God, Bailey's father was the best.

AFTER ABOUT six hours of sleep, Val was going in the back to rest, and Rory was up, so Bailey asked to sit up front with him. Rory was good company, Bailey realized, but then, Val had been too. Snarky, snappy, the two of them could bitch at each other like an old married couple, and then they'd laugh into song, which only made Bailey laugh more.

And miss all he'd let lapse during the past four years.

Those times leaning on Dean on the couch while they'd been watching TV or listening to music were the closest Bailey had gotten to really appreciating *anything*—movies, TV, music—since Emmett had passed.

Talking to Rory about the beauty of *Grease* was fun, but it made Bailey want to know what Dean's opinion would be.

Four hours later, they switched off, and this time Bailey's dad got to run Catherine around the rest stop for a few minutes. That put Bailey back in the sleeper with Dean's brother and a few questions Bailey had been gnawing on since he'd hopped in the semi at around six thirty in the evening the day before.

"So," he said, as they made themselves comfortable, "do you help Dean out a lot?"

"Nope," Val said, folding his arms and tipping his head back onto the pillows. "You're special."

Bailey snorted and prepared to ask another one, but Val stopped him.

"Look—you may not know this, but we had the intercom on when you were talking to your dad. So here's the thing. Dean's my little brother. No, we didn't have a label for the autism spectrum thing, but yes, the whole family had pretty much agreed that Dean's brain was special. The fact that you figured it out too and basically learned to move around it for him—well, that makes you special too. No, I don't know if you two are destined for each other, but I think he must really care about you to do all the shit he arranged yesterday, so there's that. And"—his voice softened—"he probably knows about Emmett. But he probably doesn't want to talk about him until you bring it up, because it's private. There were seven of us, Bailey, and that means we always had somebody to have our backs, and we always had a best friend or a confidant or somebody to be a part of our lives. But it also meant that if we had something that was private, it had to be locked away in a steel safe and buried under the bodies in the backyard. Private is *important* to a family that has no privacy at all, you understand?"

"Yes," Bailey said, his head swimming.

"So if you're ready to talk to Dean, he'll be ready to listen, but he's not going to open your steel safe." Val puffed out a breath. "Now I need my last two hours or tomorrow's gonna suck. Can I get that?"

"Yessir," Bailey said.

"Good. Nice meeting you, Bailey Dodge. Welcome to the fucking family."

And with that Bailey swore Val Royal fell asleep with the snap of his fingers.

And almost like magic, so did Bailey.

ANOTHER NIGHT at a rest stop, and then they started the last leg of their journey to LA. At around eleven in the morning they stopped at a truck stop diner just outside of the city. Bailey was cramped and frowzled and probably a little bit ripe and wishing for a bed that didn't rumble under him in the worst way when three young men strolled in, looking fresh as daisies and beautiful and clean and not a day over twenty-five, not one of them.

And two of them were the spitting image of Dean and Val, with dark hair, dark eyes, slight builds, and square jaws. One of them had slightly browner hair and the other had big, almost forest-creature eyes, but yeah, Bailey was starting to see the family stamp like a glow-in-the-dark pass to a members-only club.

Royal family blood was apparently very exclusive.

The young man next to them was taller and rangy, with an impressive chest and an almost familiar strut, including a chin with a divot down the center and fine lines already branching out from light hazel eyes.

Impressed, Bailey looked to Rory, who grinned. "That's my boy," he said, preening. Then he stood and walked over to hug the young man with absolutely zero self-consciousness, saying, "Anthony! I didn't know you were coming!" and Bailey liked this whole family even more.

"Heya," said the young Royal with the forest-creature eyes. "It's good to meet you." He grew his hair long over his brow and sort of floppy, and he punctuated his words with a little toss of his head that threw the hair back and revealed his sly smile. Oh wow. This kid—innocence, beauty, that beguiling summer-child smile.

Dynamite. Undiluted TNT. And Dean's youngest—had to be the youngest—brother had it all.

"You must be Chance," Bailey said, feeling a little befuddled by that beauty. He held out his hand and then turned to the other boy, who was *not* "plainer," but he was *quieter*. He kept his brown hair cut shorter and hid his hazel eyes behind glasses and his smile muted, and when Bailey turned to him for a handshake with "And you must be Reg," he startled to even be noticed.

Bailey remembered Dean's voice when he'd talked about his younger brothers—indulgent, protective, gentle—and he got it. It wasn't just that they were the youngest of seven, it was that they'd been *allowed* to be young. Had Bailey been any less innocent when he'd been a premed, absolutely sure that being a doctor meant helping people and not playing politics? Had Dean ever felt forgotten and anonymous in his big family, with every child vying for a spot with a distinct personality?

These young men were still children to their big brother, like Anthony was still a child to his father, Rory.

"Oooh," said Chance, after the introductions were finished. "You just sat down? Can we eat too? I'm *starving*, and I bet they have ham and hash browns, right?" He smiled winningly at Val, who rolled his eyes.

"Yes, I'm buying, you freeloading little shit. Reg, you up for breakfast?"

"Sausage, fruit, hash browns, and—" Reg paused to yawn. "—coffee. I drove down while Tony and Chance slept."

"You let him call you Tony?" Rory asked in surprise as they all settled down into the large booth Val had procured. "You told your mother and me absolutely not."

Anthony gave his father a mild gaze and said, "Pop, do we need to have a talk?"

Rory gave a quiet, bemused shake of his head, and while Bailey recognized some sort of family code, he couldn't say exactly what had been communicated. It didn't matter because Chance was obviously used to being the center of attention, and he took over from there.

"Reg drives like two grandmas," he said blithely, taking the menu lying under Reg's hand. "Both of them arguing over who's going too fast."

Reg pinned his little brother with a bored look. "Chance thinks because he drives the Grapevine in a Ford Fiesta twice a month, he can push a minivan to ninety and do the Muhammed Ali bob-and-weave among the semis without ending up a grease spot on the freeway."

Bailey's eyes widened, and Anthony nodded. "True story. Twenty miles out of Bakersfield I *begged* Reg to take over." He glared at Chance. "I am *absolutely* driving the whole way back."

"It's my folks' minivan!" Chance complained, and Anthony rolled his eyes.

"And they *love* me and want *you* to live." He yawned then, one of those monster yawns that seemed to take over your entire body, and then added rather pathetically, "but I'm all on board for the coffee thing, though."

"Dad or I can drive," Bailey said. "We both got plenty of sleep in the cabin."

Chance, who had been a little deflated at the criticism of his driving, was suddenly all perked up again.

"I love that thing! Val used to haul me around on my summer breaks—we'd go to Oregon or Seattle or Vancouver. I could sleep for *hours* back there, and then I'd run around the city while Val was doing business or catching up on his own sleep." Chance gave his older brother a look of pure hero worship. "Most of the time we'd have a couple hours to tour together. It was *great*."

Val smiled gently back at Chance. "You were an ideal passenger," he said. "Half the time I'd forget you were there."

"I know you did," Chance said affably. "Because you'd start singing along with Mom's musical theater stuff." He turned to Bailey and Connor. "He's not bad, you know."

"*I* know," Rory said. "And I heard him do an *amazing* version of 'The End of the Day' from *Les Mis* that I'll tell you about one day."

Val sent Rory a killing look that had overtones *not* sex that Bailey didn't understand.

"When was this?" he asked suspiciously.

"Oh, this was the day we first met," Val said grimly, eyes set as though trying to bore a hole through Bailey to make him understand.

No holes necessary. Bailey realized that whatever misadventure had thrown Val into his ER had happened to the tune of *Les Mis* and thought now that he *really* wanted to ask Dean about that day.

"You met before yesterday?" Anthony asked sharply. The waitress arrived to take their order, which was good because it gave Bailey a chance to organize his thoughts into something that children could hear. Well, not exactly *children*, but Dean's family, which, he realized, was starting to feel like his own.

The waitress left, and Bailey gave an abbreviated version of the events of that day. "Dean and I… uhm, connected when Val was getting checked over for a concussion," he said smoothly, "so when Dean was in town the next week, he looked me up."

Reg and Chance exchanged glances, and then Val and Rory exchanged glances, and then Connor gave an inelegant snort.

Bailey could only glare at his father. "Don't," he warned.

"Boy…," Connor said, shaking his head.

"Dad, can we just leave it at that?"

"You are fooling *nobody*," his father said. He was sitting at the end of the booth, one hand on Catherine's noble head as he fondled her silky ears.

"Maybe one person," Val said, winking at Bailey. "But my family won't let you live in denial that long." Something flickered over his face, though, and Bailey gazed at him curiously.

Then he glanced at his phone and suddenly, like a slug to the gut, Bailey knew what was bothering Dean's brother.

He never told us when we'd hear from him, he realized. It had already been thirty hours.

He met Val's eyes and said, "Soon," hopefully, and Val nodded once, grimly, as though Bailey had said a prayer.

Chance burst into their thoughts then with a question about Marcus, and something about the plaintive note in his voice seemed to echo in Bailey's own heart.

"How'd he look?" Chance asked, glancing anxiously from Val to Bailey and back. "I mean, we saw him at the family reunion, and he didn't seem to be, uhm, you know, tied down. Did he seem… settled? Has he gained any weight? Said anything about a soulmate? Those kinds of things?"

Bailey stared at the boy, the nonconversation Dean and Marcus had engaged in about somebody younger that Marcus was waiting on to grow up suddenly making sense. "No," Bailey said flatly. "Marcus looked just as insane as any other single man on the planet. In fact, he drives like a freaking maniac, if that makes you feel better."

Chance's adorable smile surfaced again, and Bailey wondered if Marcus had *ever* stood a chance. "So much better," he said earnestly. "You have no idea how much better I feel about that."

Next to him, Reg had taken off his glasses and was massaging the bridge of his nose. "Wow," he mouthed to Val, who rolled his eyes.

Bailey turned his attention to Chance, who was oblivious of the byplay. "He and Dean were a pretty impressive team," he said, not sure if he should feed Chance's apparent crush. "I mean, Marcus drove, and Dean planned and bossed everybody around, and Marcus read his mind. I, uhm, don't think they'll be working with anybody else soon."

That smile again—gah! Bailey had a thought that if Dean ever smiled at *Bailey* like that, he was a goner. Lights out. That's all she wrote. Here lies the ghost of Bailey Dodge's resistance to falling drastically in love with a man crazy enough to toss him out of an airplane with his cat.

Then he remembered the way Dean had climbed into the shower that last morning and gentled Bailey's skittishness with warm hands and matter-of-fact chatter, like he was calming a rogue horse.

Apparently Bailey Dodge's resistance was already dead and buried, and Bailey had simply not acknowledged the gravestone.

He glanced at Val again, who—arrested in the middle of checking his phone—caught Bailey's gaze and nodded.

Yeah. They hadn't heard from Dean in nearly thirty hours. It was a hell of a time for Bailey to admit to himself that he was in love.

WISHES, PLANS, AND HALLUCINATIONS

TURNED OUT they actually *were* closer to the compound than the town, but Birdie insisted it didn't matter. The diminutive pilot had one thought on the brain during the entire three-hour trip through the blistering heat.

Revenge. Payback. Utter destruction and chaos.

Fuck all the fuckers that fucked Birdie's beautiful bird.

At one of their hourly pauses for water—necessary in the heat, particularly after the cold packs in the flight suits failed—Dean finally said, "For Christ's sake, Bird, we hear you. Man, if you'll shut up long enough for Marcus and me to come up with a plan, we'll even let you set the C-4. Is that good enough for you?"

Birdie gave him a rather watery gaze. "You're good people," Birdie said. "Thanks, Dean. I might fly you again someday."

Dean stopped and cocked his head. "Marcus, did you hear that?"

Marcus—who was in the middle of gulping his own water ration—cocked his head and listened.

"No, not out in the desert," Dean snapped, thinking about what Birdie had said. Although he didn't blame Marcus for trying to listen over the engine noise that had rattled their bones for the past couple of hours. Marcus was like he was, his skin and his hearing and his sense of balance were fuzzed out for being out in the heat on the motorcycles for such a long period of time. They had sunblock—hell, they had solid zinc oxide, because just plain sunblock wouldn't do it—and they were riding the bikes at a moderate speed to not overheat the engines. But that didn't change the fact that they would both hear the rumble of the bikes and the plane and even the car they'd abandoned back in El Paso long into the next week after an adventure like this. A pool helped—Dean swam as often as possible, and so did Marcus—but until then their travels would rumble under their skin.

"Then what?" Marcus asked irritably. "I thought we were paying attention for signs of the compound. Or town. Or whatever."

Dean swallowed, sort of wishing he wasn't always the first person to see the scary shit.

"Compound is thirty miles northeast," he said, nodding to a smudge on the horizon. "Town is fifteen miles north past that."

Marcus stared at him. "Do I even want to know?"

Dean held out his phone—it was set on compass. "I've been doing some calculations," he admitted. "Airspeed, wind, where we were over the desert when the shots hit, where we were when we jumped, how fast we've been going since." About twenty miles an hour, as the crow flew. The road they were traveling on wasn't a maintained highway—there were lots of detours for clusters of cacti and, in one instance, a small rock canyon that literally *echoed* with rattlesnakes. Dean would be waking up screaming about that one for a couple of years, he was absolutely sure of it.

"Are you positive?" Marcus asked.

Dean grimaced. He had sunshades in his pocket, but his and Marcus's helmets had vision enhancement in the goggles, and since they'd gone from skydiving to motorcycling, they'd kept the helmets on.

"Look that way," he said, nodding to the northeast, "but put your helmet back on."

Marcus did, and for a moment everything went still, with only the whisper of a thin, hot wind in their ears to penetrate the silence.

"I can see the antiaircraft guns," Marcus said in surprise. "That's why you've been tugging us east."

Dean grunted. "We should stop five miles out," he said. "At least until nightfall. Set the chutes for shelter, catch a nap—"

"Forge a plan," Marcus said grimly. "I'm hearing you."

He glanced around them, the flatness of the plain making them both feel naked and exposed. "Is five miles far enough out? These things make a hell of a clatter with no ambient noise to drown them out."

"Under normal conditions a small motorcycle runs at about eighty decibels," Dean told him. "Which carries about half a football field on a quiet night. But they've got watchers, and while we can see the antiaircraft guns from thirty miles out on a plain, I think five miles is plenty safe." The chutes were desert camouflage, so they wouldn't draw attention, and pulled taut over a boulder—or even over the bikes—they'd provide shade to rest under and cover them from sight.

"And if we draw close enough to the road," Marcus reasoned, "the main road from town, we can get an idea of who's coming and going."

Dean nodded thoughtfully. "Let's swing wide, then." They had extra fuel in Marcus's trailer, insulated by the cold packs and shaded by the chutes. "It may take us an extra hour, but we can set ourselves far enough from the road to stay hidden and close enough to establish a lookout. And if Bird can aim the infrared distance imaging—"

"We can get a sense for who's where," Marcus finished for him. "I like it. Now see, *this* is a plan."

Dean pulled out the infrared gadget and showed Birdie how to use it. Then they turned it off and set it to charge through an outlet in Marcus's bike's electrical system, where it fit neatly in a saddlebag while powering up.

"FBI," Birdie murmured. "Nice. And since we're coming up with a plan, fellas, I feel compelled to bring us back to what Dean was saying in the beginning."

Both of them focused solely on the little pilot, all ears.

"First of all," Birdie said, "since I'm not working on not steering us into a rattlesnake pit or a cactus cluster, I've been counting planes overhead—there's not many. But while I don't have your far-distance gadgets, I *have* seen two on a trajectory to land in that direction, which makes me think that place has an airstrip."

Marcus and Dean exchanged glances. "Promising," Dean said tentatively. It was, in fact, what he'd been hoping for when he'd broached the subject in the first place. A good plan relied on intel like that. "Anything else?"

Birdie gave an evil smile. "There's not a thing out there I can't fly." There was a pause while that sunk in. "If you two can think of any way to disable those antiaircraft guns, I think I've got our exfil."

Marcus regarded Birdie skeptically. "And you have your new plane?"

Birdie shrugged philosophically. "A little paint, a few screen doors—"

"Some new call numbers," Dean supplied dryly.

"And a bucketload of revenge," Birdie finished, happy as a, well, *bird*. "Let's see if we can make it so."

Dean and Marcus both grunted. Make it so? Possibly. But it wouldn't be easy *or* quiet.

But then, they sort of owed Birdie, and neither of them liked to leave debts hanging.

"We'll try to work it into our schedule," Dean promised. "But if it's a choice between flying out dead or biking out alive...."

"Oh, alive is definitely preferable," Birdie agreed, nodding emphatically.

"That's a priority, then," Marcus said, and they all took one more swig of water, replaced their helmets and their goggles, and got their asses in gear.

TWO HOURS later, as it was getting too dark to ride, they found their spot. As they swung wide around the compound, they realized that the desert had a slight rise and steep drop toward the east. They headed that way and found themselves in the shade of a small promontory that rose maybe ten feet above the gentle decline of the desert floor. After shooing out some rattlesnakes and a *plethora* of scorpions by focusing the exhaust against the wall and revving the engines, they killed the power and used small shovels to scoop out a shallow trench at the base before using the chutes to cover everything, including themselves, leaving the chute vents as lookout points.

"You sure we got all the scorpions?" Marcus asked as he and Dean lay on their stomachs and peered out of their shelter. They'd left the sides open to ventilate the space, and now that the sun wasn't beating down on their heads, they did experience some relief from the heat.

"No," Dean said shortly. "You know the drill. Don't take off your boots, and sleep with your mouth closed."

"Sleep, he says," Marcus muttered, and Dean figured they'd have to take turns keeping a lookout… and guarding the other from vermin.

Birdie, on the other hand, had set the fuel canisters and provision platforms on the ground and curled up in the trailer like a puppy. If Dean or Marcus could have even fit in a space that small, the pilot might have had some competition, but as it was, they let Birdie get all the sleep possible.

It was going to be a *long* night.

Neither of them thought about checking in, using their cell phones, contacting HQ or their families. Something out there had shot them down. Some*one* out there suspected they were out here. A compound militarized enough to have antiaircraft guns would have a communications center, and it would really suck to give away their location because they couldn't go twenty-four hours without tugging on their family's apron strings.

But that didn't mean Dean didn't *think* about Bailey, as Marcus settled down to sleep (with a scarf wrapped around his face and his hands tucked into his sleeves) and Dean took the first watch.

It just meant he didn't reach for his phone or attempt to call Val or his and Marcus's AIC back in Austin.

Their AIC was used to not hearing from them anyway, and as Dean settled down to a long night, he knew he couldn't think of any better place for Bailey to be than with his family.

AT ROUGHLY 4:00 a.m., twenty-eight interminable hours of rotating between sleeping and stakeout after they'd arrived, Marcus flicked at the scarf around Dean's face and then shook him awake.

"Are the scorpions gone?" Dean asked from behind the scarf. Yes, he'd known they were there, but he'd made the scarf tight and kept himself in that half somnolence that had stood him and Marcus so well on previous operations.

"God yes. I have no idea how you just sit there and let them…."

Dean tore the scarf off and shook it hard before batting at the back of his neck, shaking out his sleeves, and checking the folds of where his khakis were tucked into his boots obsessively. And finally indulged in a good minute of shaking out a collective nap of the heebie-jeebies.

"Never mind," Marcus said dryly, when Dean's little performance was over. "I forget you can do that."

"Do what?" Dean asked grumpily.

"Compartmentalize so completely," Marcus said. "Put your discomfort in a box labeled 'after my nap' and then get all the oogies out at once."

Dean grunted. "They're like flies. They just keep coming back. As long as I don't move suddenly or violently they don't sting me. The scorpions are just doing their thing. It's the stinging that's the problem."

And most people didn't react badly enough to the venom to do more than suffer some swelling and discomfort. The ones that had been grouping and regrouping along the edges of their parachute tent were less venomous than bees.

But that could still creep a guy out.

"Sure, sure," Marcus agreed. "Anyway, if you're all clear—"

Dean gave his neckline one last pat down to make sure nothing had snuck into his shirt. "We are."

"Then you need to see this. You told me you saw these trucks on the way in after I went down around ten, right?"

"Right," Dean said, checking his pocket for scorpions before pulling out a tiny, deadly accurate pair of binoculars. "Are they leaving now?"

"All three," Marcus told him. "They're heading back toward town. I'm wondering, do they need all that food, water, gas, etc. for a day, or are those coming back in the next two to three days?"

"Why?" Dean asked. "Whatcha thinkin'?"

"I'm thinking Trojan Horse," Marcus said. "One of us needs to take a bike to town and find the supply trucks—"

"Easy enough," Birdie said, surprising them both. "They've got that creepy bleeding-heart insignia on the back." Birdie waved a larger pair of binocs in the air, probably personal and wedged in Birdie's parachute pack. "I'll do it."

"But Bird—" Dean objected, only Bird was already pushing Marcus's motorcycle out of the shelter, the empty trailer weaving a little without the weight to pin it down.

"Don't 'But Bird' me, young man," Birdie snapped. "I can fill the bike's tanks and the spare and have it ready in town, and I can let you in when that thing returns in the next few days."

"Bird, we can't—"

"You've got enough supplies to last the two of you a week," Birdie said, looking at them over a hunched shoulder. "You did *not* count on feeding me, which is not your fault. Let me set the bike up as exfil and fill it with supplies. If I don't come back in two more moonrises, or you don't see my signal in the next truck delivery before that, assume I'm cheesed and do your thing, guys, but for now, trust me."

Birdie gave a wizened smile, complete with a wink, and then asked, "Wait—do you idiots have any C-4?"

"Yes," they both said, a little alarmed at the question.

"Awesome. Back in two days."

And then Birdie was gone.

"Oh my God," Marcus muttered. "That small irritating human had better not screw us over."

"Oh no," Dean said, certain of this at least. "You and me are Bird's best bet at payback for the downed plane. I'm pretty sure Bird's not going to let *anything* get in the way of revenge." He gave a grunt, and from far away, they heard Birdie start the engine. "Bird's right anyway—the bikes have enough fuel to get us into town *or* get us to the compound. Not both. If Bird sets up the bike and supplies for exfil, we've got some options."

Marcus grunted back. "But in the meantime, it's us, in this pit, with the motherfucking scorpions."

Dean nodded. "Hey, think we could rig sort of a platform with the other chute and some rocks? It would keep the little bastards off us?"

"Mmm…." Marcus cocked his head. "No, Dean. I think they've got nests in the rock face, and while we might be able to cover the rock face with the other chute, that would mean they were wriggling around underneath it. I think we should refold the chute and save it for anything else and settle in for a long July nap in the asshole of the Chihuahuan Desert."

"Could be worse," Dean said. "Could be Fresno."

Marcus chewed on that for a moment. Fresno was a central California valley town known for its homeless population and its poor air quality—and its lack of access to any of the neat places that California was known for.

"Fresno's not bad if you've got air-conditioning," he said after a moment. "They've got a nice little state university there."

"So you're saying you'd rather be in Fresno?" Dean asked, making sure.

Marcus shrugged. "Hey, in two days we've got the possibility of getting shot at here, so that's a plus for the Chihuahuan Desert."

"I'm saying," Dean told him. "It could definitely be worse."

"I'll let you know if we don't kill each other in two days," Marcus told him direly, but they'd killed time before without killing each other. "Anyway, go back to sleep. You were only an hour into your nap, and now that I've seen you do the heebie-jeebie dance, I'm wide-awake."

Dean rolled his eyes. "You just want a chance to see me do it again," he accused, but he was busy wrapping his scarf around his head and sealing off the neck areas, as well as tucking his hands in his sleeves and reupping the snugness between his boots and his khakis.

"Two days, Dean. We've got to get our entertainment somewhere."

Dean grunted and settled in for his nap, making doubly sure his baseball hat was tight to his head and covered by his scarf. "I feel you. Did we bring cards?"

"Damned straight. Tomorrow's gonna be one long game of cribbage."

"We can keep points using dead scorpions," Dean promised, and then he put his various fears, paranoias, and phobias into the other box and closed his eyes.

Royal Welcomes

BAILEY WAS actually relieved to drive the family minivan, although he was surprised to find that after his father and Catherine noped out in the back row, he ended up next to Reg while Anthony and Chance napped in the middle seats.

He was pleased for a chance to talk to the quietest Royal without any interruptions from the rather boisterous crowd he found himself with.

"So," he said as he started out, following Reg's directions to the 5, which would take him straight toward Bakersfield—a place that Dean assured him was *not* particularly glamorous but which held all the comforts of home. "You're a cautious driver?"

Reg made a sound of disgust. "Only compared to my little brother," he muttered. "My God, he's terrifying."

Bailey couldn't argue there—although for entirely different reasons. "How long have he and Marcus been dancing?" he asked, figuring that would give Reg something to chew over.

"That feels awfully personal," Reg said, surprising him.

Bailey *hmm*ed. "You'll have to forgive me. I was an only child. Having an entire family to gossip about is such a luxury. And Dean really only started opening up about you guys recently."

Next to him he could feel Reg relax. "I guess that's understandable," he said. "It's just… my baby brother has carried such a torch. I hate to encourage him when Marcus is older and way more worldly, you know?"

Bailey remembered the odd note in Marcus's voice when he and Dean had been discussing somebody Marcus was waiting on to grow up. "I get the feeling Marcus is just as worried about making a move on one of Dean's younger siblings," he said carefully.

Reg made a subtle "*hmm*" in the back of his throat.

"What?" Bailey asked, amused that it should be as hard to get information from Reg as it was from Dean.

"I think if Marcus was to make a move on Chance," Reg said carefully, "he needs to be very, very prepared. Chance has been planning their wedding for four years, since Dean first brought Marcus home.

Yes, he was just about to graduate from high school, and Marcus was so terrified, he hit on *everybody* else in the family, including our straight brother, Prock. Chance was warned off since then, but… you know. Whatever happens between them….”

“We’d all better put on our flak jackets and our helmets and duck,” Bailey said, getting a full picture of the potential disaster.

“And be prepared to pick up the pieces after the explosion,” Reg told him grimly, and then he cast a half-guilty glance behind him, probably to make sure Chance couldn’t hear.

Bailey felt him stiffen again, and in response to a quiet voice from the back, he said, “Good. Did *you* hear what we were saying?”

Anthony’s voice was a little louder and clearer this time. “No, Reg, because you’re not broadcasting. Don’t stress so much!”

“Sorry,” Reg said, a thing that sounded automatic.

“What’s the rule,” Anthony said.

“Oh God, really—”

“Reg?”

Reg huffed out a little breath. “Unless I back a car over your foot *unintentionally*, then I never have to be sorry. And if it’s intentional, you probably deserved it.”

Anthony’s response was cut off by a yawn, and Reg turned back toward the front. “Just as well,” he grumbled. “I’d get carsick if I had to spend too much time turned around like that.”

Bailey grunted. They were still in the city, and traffic sort of crawled along at forty miles an hour in what seemed to be an urban knot of overpasses and entrances.

“Does it get any faster than this?” he asked.

“Once it opens up around Burbank,” Reg promised. “And then you need to put your foot on it and just accelerate steadily because you’ll be making a steep climb into the mountains. It’s really twisty up there. There’s a reason it’s called the Grapevine.”

“Oh!” Bailey cheered up. “I’ve heard of the Grapevine. Never driven it, but nice!”

Reg grunted. “If you’re this excited about the Grapevine, you should take the next exit and go back the way we came. Disneyland is back there, you know.”

Bailey let out a dry chuckle. “I’ve never been. Is it everything they say?”

"Yes," Reg said, with no apology in his voice whatsoever. "My parents pretty much mortgaged their retirement to take us. It really is the happiest place on earth."

From the back seat, Bailey heard Anthony say, "I'll take you someday."

Reg didn't answer him, and Bailey risked a quick glance to see his cheeks had heated.

"So," he asked, voice quiet, "tell me about Dean."

Reg gave a quick glance over his shoulder, and then practically broke his neck whipping around to face front.

"What about him?" he squeaked.

"What's he like as a brother?"

Reg let out a sigh. "Protective," he said after a moment. "He was always smarter than we were, stronger than we were, and he always knew the bad stuff we didn't. He made it his job to protect everybody from the bad stuff. My folks were always bringing people into the house, letting them sleep in the basement if they were having trouble with their parents, that sort of thing. Dean would walk into their room armed with statistics on domestic disputes, and Dad would say, 'And that, son, is why you are not expected to answer the door should anybody's parent come knocking.' And Dean would be left sputtering that he was *trying* to protect the family while Mom escorted him back to bed and said that the family welcomed anybody under the roof who needed sanctuary. And on the one hand, I think it was funny, and it was great to see him taken down a peg or two, because he *always*—and I mean *always*—knew what was best, and that was fucking irritating."

"But on the other hand?" Bailey asked, feeling for Dean. He could see this so clearly. Dean's pragmatism in the face of what was, apparently, his family's absolute generosity. Dean must have been *so* very baffled to see his logic twisted back on itself.

"On the other hand," Reg said softly, "I think he must have been so lonely. He understood, knew, remembered *so much*, and the simple stuff that the rest of us got in our bones eluded him. He and Val used to get *so mad* at each other, but I remember once somebody was giving Dean a hard time—he was in high school at eleven, you know?—and Val literally left junior college to drive to high school and help Prock and Sal stuff kids in lockers. How *dare* anybody hurt his little brother. And Dean... he was so tough, but they got home, and he started to sob, and then he started to *yell*, because dammit, just once couldn't *he* be the one who took care of himself? And Val was hurt at first, and then he squared his jaw—just like Dad—and said, 'Stanford Dean Royal, you will *always* be my baby brother, and I will *always* stand up for you. Get over it. You may be this family's biggest pain in the ass, but you are also our pride and joy, and we won't let *anything* happen to you.'"

Bailey's heart ached suddenly, because he could see that happening, the two of them so stubborn, so proud, and so wanting to take care of everybody else in the family.

"What happened then?" he asked.

"Hugging and crying," Reg said, a little bit of kind laughter in his voice. "Dean and Val could piss each other off so bad, but it always ended up in hugging and crying. It's why we bugged Val when we knew Dean was seeing somebody. We figured he'd know."

This was a surprise.

"Did he?" Bailey asked.

"Oh yeah," Reg said. "But Val's as good as Dean at ducking family texts. We didn't hear from him for three days, and then it was to come get you."

Bailey laughed outright then. "So you all knew about me—but not the particulars."

"Yeah." He could feel Reg's regard. "Did you know about us?"

"Not until yesterday morning," Bailey said with half a laugh. "Because I almost broke up with him, because I thought he was withholding information."

"Was he?" Reg sounded riveted.

"Nope. Turned out I only had to ask."

Reg grunted. "And that, as you have probably figured out, is typical Dean."

"I'm starting to get that picture," Bailey told him, and at that moment traffic opened up. Bailey gave a happy "Whee!" as he stepped on the accelerator and headed for the hills.

Two and a half hours later—after one rest stop in Kettleman City for coffees, sodas, and a chance for Catherine and Mr. Bumble to be walked on a little green outside a strip mall—Anthony directed Bailey down a long roller coaster of a straight road where fifties-style ranch houses sat back on absurdly large property packets while Reg took his turn napping in the back. Much of the scenery was brownish, with tiny little lawns, many of those with white picket fences inside a larger chicken-wire or chain link property fence. There were even, to Bailey's surprise, a couple of pools, barely glimpsed in what amounted to the backyard.

"I thought you people were always in a drought?" he said.

"Sometimes," Anthony conceded. "But sometimes not, and then the pool comes in handy when it's hot."

"I imagine so," Bailey said. It was barely twelve o'clock, and he could already feel the unrelenting dry July heat starting through the windshield. "I have no idea if Dean packed my trunks."

"If he didn't, I'm sure there's a zillion pairs you can borrow," Anthony said blithely. "Reg's parents are uber prepared—and sort of the king and queen of 'there's always room at the table,' you know?"

"How long have you known them?" Bailey asked.

"Only a couple of months," Anthony said. "But my parents had both lost *their* parents before I came along, and my stepdad's folks are—" He grimaced. "—not kind about the LGBTQA crowd." He pronounced it all together, like "elejebetequa," and it took Bailey a moment to realize that the young man had just told him that his step-grandparents were bigots. "I was *so* excited," Anthony told him, "when my dad told me his new boyfriend had parents who liked the whole family to *be* the whole family. They invited me to their big reunion picnic at the beginning of June, and it was one of the best days of my life." His voice dropped. "And Reg was there, so that was nice too."

"Best friends?" Bailey asked, although he suspected it was more than that.

Anthony's sidelong glance confirmed it. "You don't *seem* stupid, Doc," he said softly.

"Well you don't *seem*… coupled," Bailey retorted, thinking he might be getting the hang of this brother thing.

"Mm…." Anthony gave one of those glances behind him that indicated he needed everybody to be asleep. "Reg is used to being the quietest Royal. The one everybody overlooks. He needs to get used to being the most important person, at least to me. Baby steps, Doc. Baby steps."

Bailey blinked at the young man who had just shown far more self-awareness than Bailey had in the last four years, but before he could think of anything to say, Anthony spoke hurriedly.

"A left up there—you see the cattleguard and the gate? That blue house with the mother-in-law cottage and the pool gate and the big backyard—"

That self-awareness vanished, and Bailey was suddenly in the presence of an excited little kid who got to visit grandma and grandpa, and as the other occupants behind him started to shift groggily awake, he slowed the minivan down and made ready to turn left.

TWENTY MINUTES later, after being shown to a guest bedroom in the big house, where Mr. Bumble was left to roam with a sandbox and some food and water handy—and after seeing his father shown to the mother-in-law cottage, the better to accommodate Catherine until she and the multitudes of indoor cats had a chance to get to know each other—Bailey, his father, *and* Catherine, sat in the shade by the surprisingly roomy pool while the three younger men swam and played like teenagers.

Their hosts were Ed and Julie Royal, who had greeted them with a plate full of sandwiches—from peanut butter and jelly to lunch meat to chicken salad—and the off-brand sodas of their choice in big plastic cups of ice, as well as a cold pitcher of water.

Julie Royal was a sixtyish wiry dynamo of a woman, who had been weeding one of the many vegetable boxes in a garden that took up about a quarter of the big backyard as they'd driven up. She was dressed in an oversized T-shirt with the sleeves and neck ripped off and a pair of what had once probably been her husband's basketball shorts, as well as a big floppy garden hat, and she smiled up at them as her husband wiped some of the sweat off her forehead.

He'd been the one to greet them while she'd hurriedly washed up and prepared their lunch, and Bailey had gotten the feeling that meeting someone—anyone—in their son's life was a big deal for them.

He could suddenly see why Anthony had been so delighted to be here.

"Relax!" Julie said, smiling at the both of them. "We're so happy to meet you. I've got to say, Dean has *never* invited us into his super-scary job life before, so you're, like, a triple treat." Her voice dropped conspiratorially. "Did he really push you out of an airplane?"

Bailey had to laugh. "He briefed me first," he clarified. "And it was Marcus who did the pushing. Dean wasn't secured to the frame and didn't have his chute on yet, so he stayed back from the bay door."

He was startled by Julie's cackle. "Oh, Ed, it's so cute. He's exactly like Dean! Did you see how he tried to make it a smaller thing with that 'just the facts, ma'am' schtick? It's adorable!"

Ed, who was a scant few inches taller than his tiny wife, with largeish ears and a grin that stretched between them—gave a happy grimace. "Julie, honey, they're new. Give them a chance to get their feet on the ground before you call them adorable."

She shook her head and patted Bailey's knee. "Oh, he doesn't know. I mean, he *does* because he *can* be the most romantic man in the world, but you know, don't you? That the two of you are something special?"

Bailey's ears heated, and his father chuckled. "They're not in the admitting stage yet, Miss Julie. It's fine. He's just happy to meet you all."

Julie grinned at him, and Ed spoke up.

"You two are welcome to stay here as long as you like," he said. "Connor, we had to hustle to make the cottage habitable—it's been a while since it's been used as more than storage. Let me know if there's any repairs to be made. Leaky faucets, cold water, anything." He gave a whimsical little smile. "I'll try to be a good landlord."

"Well, you should let me help with that," Connor said, perking up. "I was a contractor in my younger days. That's a neat little place—good bones. But I'd love to fix up the wiring and the plumbing for you. It would be the least I could do, given you've put us up here on no notice."

Ed practically bounced on his toes. "Now I wasn't a contractor," he said, "but I can hold a hammer and a wrench. I would *love* a good project." He gave the pool a dark look. "And my youngest appears to have some time on his hands. Now it gets too hot to work out here much past one, but if we make a list of projects today, you and I could meet in the kitchen early tomorrow and do some damage."

"Absolutely!" Connor stood and patted his thigh absently so Cathy would follow him, and together they ambled past the swimming pool and toward the small structure in the corner of the backyard, beyond the garden.

"Well, bless him," Julie said, smiling at them in bemusement. "Ed has been *dying* for a new project." She turned her beaming face toward Bailey. "Your father has just made my Christmas card list."

Bailey gave her a quiet smile. "He'll love staying out here for a bit," he confessed. "His neighborhood is getting a bit… suburbanated is how he puts it. Too many houses, not enough sidewalks. He used to be able to walk Cathy by keeping her by his heels, but now he's got to put a lead on her, and while *she's* a good girl, you can see it pains him."

"Well, as long as he doesn't take up partying or playing loud classical music at midnight, he's welcome to stay as long as he likes."

Bailey hated to bring this up, but staring at the chain link fence around the property, the Victory garden, the battered picnic table, the cottage with the peeling paint, he felt like he had to. "Are you sure you wouldn't like us to pay rent of some sort, ma'am?" he asked uncertainly. "We hate to be a burden—"

She waved her hand in dismissal. "Of course not," she said. "Now if either one of you cares to make dinner or spring for groceries, Ed and I wouldn't say no. But if all you're doing is drinking my soda and eating PB&J, well, that's no more or less than the kids and their friends have been doing since Val got old enough to bring Vinnie home for Friday night scramble."

Bailey remembered Vinnie, but he hadn't realized the friendship had been thick enough to harken back to middle-school days. "I've met Vinnie," he said, "but what's Friday night scramble?"

She cackled. "Well, I worked at the local IGA—it's a chain store now, but for thirty years, we'd comb the shelves on Thursday nights for the expired food. Some of it we gave to the local seniors clubs, and some of it went to the food shelters, but the owner knew me and knew I had, in his words, *dozens* of kids floating around the house. My kids were always good at bringing home their friends, mind you, and then word got out, and they'd bring home the kids who maybe didn't get fed all the time at home. So the kids would come over on Friday night—usually we'd have at least twenty, counting mine—and I'd have frozen pizza after frozen pizza cooking in the oven, and everything from Pop-Tarts to chips to canned fruit or applesauce or Little Debbie and cookies on the kitchen table, and bags full of canned goods, soup, and such. And the kids would eat and play games down in the basement—or later in the little cottage—and when it was over, they were invited to bring home a bag of food for their folks." She gave a happy little sigh then. "It's been a while since we've had a houseful, but even grown, my kids still invite their friends over on Friday nights. There's always a combination here. Even Prock, who brings his little girls, or Laure, who brings the boys."

"Wow, that's a lot of work, ma'am," he said respectfully, and again, that casual wave of the hand.

"Nonsense. Do you think I've had to do dishes or clean up on a Friday night even once in the last thirty years?" She laughed heartily. "No. It… it's a good sound when people are enjoying your hospitality. It's a good feeling when your kids think of your home as a safe space." Her expression grew sober. "We… I mean, I have no idea how so many of our children ended up on the rainbow side of things, but so many of their friends didn't have homes like ours."

"Where everybody was loved?" Bailey asked, not wanting to get into politics.

"Not just the queer kids, either," Julie said baldly. "So many kids who… I don't know. I always assumed that I was simple. I couldn't see a thing wrong with them. They seemed like perfectly nice young people to *me*, but folks get strange when their kids get older. Let's just say we had a number of kids staying in our basement or in the cottage until Ed and I felt okay about letting that kid go home."

Bailey felt his eyes burn, and he swallowed. "My charge nurse," he said gruffly. "At the hospital. She… she brings fudge and homemade teddy bears and kid's sweaters into the ER. It's like the one night a week she doesn't spend at home, she spends with friends who make these things, and she says the same thing. That she's simple and can't think of a thing to do on her off hours besides make things for the people who end up coming into the hospital on their worst days. I don't think it's being simple at all," he said after a moment. "I think it's knowing that *kindness* is simple. Putting rules on it, caveats, conditions—that's when things get complicated."

"I'm not smart enough for complicated," she said with a laugh. "Neither is Ed. Not destined for greatness, either one of us. But our children…." She glanced over at the young men at the pool. "That's why the names, you know."

Bailey blinked. "What about the names?" He tried to remember if Dean had mentioned anything about his name during that quiet revelation the day before.

Julie's gurgle of laughter should have been a warning, but it wasn't, not even a little bit. By the time the two dads (as he now thought of them) returned from the cottage, all flushed and excited with a list of supplies they'd need to get that afternoon to start work in the morning, Bailey knew so much more about Dean and the close network of siblings who'd been blessed—and cursed—with names from lives few of them had been destined to lead.

Except for Dean and Chance, Bailey thought, casting an aching glance at the pool, where Reg had peaced out and was stretched in the shade with a paperback book while Anthony continued to do laps and Chance napped in the sun, golden and unimpeachable.

So many sacrifices, so much dreaming and hope, so many "simple" choices to create a generation of children who would continue to put good into the world, continue to be each other's ride or die, continue to hope and dream and *learn* and aspire and try.

Bailey wanted so badly to talk to Dean then, to tell him that he *loved* his name, and his siblings' names, and that he wanted in—in on a family that would provide hope and food and kindness to an entire town full of children, in on two parents who couldn't afford their own education, or even a lot of money for their children, but who wanted their kids to feel like they could aspire to be anything they wanted, in on the entire Royal family.

Bailey's father was right—he and Dean weren't at the accepting place yet, but they couldn't get there until Bailey saw him again and told him… *everything*. From loving Emmett to grieving him, from meeting Dean to the scary L-word that Bailey had been thinking in his head, in his heart, for *weeks* about Stanford Dean Royal, but hadn't had a chance to talk to Dean himself about.

It was now more than forty hours since Dean had pushed Bailey out of an airplane, and Bailey was half crazy with the inclination to go flying back over the desert and jump out again, all so he could talk to the man he loved, so the two of them could go about forging their own place together in the world, so Bailey could be part of this family too.

GIN

"You do not have gin," Dean told Marcus, his eyes half closed, his cards resting on his chest.

"I do too," Marcus said.

"You do not. You would have needed a book of kings and one of threes, and since I have the last king and the last three in my hand, you either didn't count right, or you pulled them from another deck." He scowled at Marcus grumpily from under his lashes. "I could have been sleeping if you were going to cheat."

Marcus grunted. "I was *bored*," he confessed. "And losing. I wanted to see how alert you were."

"How alert was I?" Dean asked, wondering if he should wrap his scarf around his face again and just give it up and sleep. The heat was making him somnolent—but the boredom was making them both itchy.

"You can still keep track of a deck with your eyes closed," Marcus said in disgust, throwing down his cards. Casually, he leaned back and took a gander through their vent to the outside world and saw the usual stand of nothing. Birdie had been gone for about sixteen hours, and if the compound got supplies *every* day, those trucks should be back soon, although that didn't mean *Birdie* would be. Either way it was late, late afternoon, and the heat was unbearable under the shade of the parachute and unlivable outside of it. They'd been on uncomfortable stakeouts before, but the tension of knowing what they had planned at the end of *this* one was making them both fratricidal.

Dean didn't deign to answer, and the ensuing silence sat thickly on the two of them. So thickly, in fact, it was almost like a noise.

In fact….

Dean's eyes shot open, and he and Marcus both scrambled to a squat. There was no "Did you hear that?" because if they hadn't both heard that, they wouldn't both be staring at the opaque sides of their little shelter, wondering if they weren't both about to be taken out by an armed drone.

"It's small," Dean breathed, and Marcus gave a short nod. By now the buzzing was close enough that they had an idea of how big the thing was, as they hunkered down behind a flimsy piece of cloth, and the idea that the drone was too small to carry a weapon might be the most comforting last thought either of them ever had.

At that moment there was a zoom and a rustle at the side vent of the tent, and a dinner-plate sized object hurtled in and fell at their feet. The giant bumblebee sound stopped abruptly, and Dean went to their lookout portal while Marcus bent closer to check out the drone for explosives.

As he pulled his helmet goggles on for an enhanced view, he caught his breath. Way out—*way* out on the road connecting the compound and the town—was a supply caravan, heading toward Sangrino del Corazón.

Rising up from the corner of the last truck, barely discernible at this distance even with the goggles, was a wire-thin antenna where most antennae wouldn't be. As Dean watched, the antenna retracted, disappeared, and the last truck in the caravan was the same sand-covered canvas as the rest of the caravan, with the exception of the stowaway in a hastily soldered hidden compartment underneath.

Or so Dean surmised as he adjusted the goggles to their maximum and studied the last truck with increasing desperation.

There it was. The antenna that had steered the drone made one last retraction into the undercarriage and the betraying shadow of Birdie's hastily improvised compartment.

"Holy moly," Marcus swore by their tent's entrance, pulling Dean's attention.

"What?"

"There's a message attached to this drone—paper."

"Holy moly?" Dean sniped, pulling the goggles off before his head threatened to split open. "What are we, six?"

"Okay, then. Holy *fuck*, Dean," Marcus retorted. "If that would help, then holy *fuck*." He held up a strip of electrical tape that had obviously been peeled from their new drone. Underneath was some basic note paper, scribbled on with what was probably a ballpoint pen.

"I had no idea Bird was so hi-tech," Dean said with no inflection whatsoever, and Marcus let out a strangled yelp of a laugh before handing the packet over. Dean pulled out the Leatherman tool that no op would be complete without and released the blade so he could work diligently on extricating the notebook paper from the tape without tearing it. When he was done, he spread out the pieces so Marcus could see too.

There were two pieces of paper—the first one had a series of bullet points.

- Bike's at Gonzalez Wreckers. 3 days before it gets wrecked.
- Family SW corner
- AAG NE—Win!
- Door by N entrance 3 a.m.
- FUCKING QUIET

Dean raised his eyebrows as he stared at the combination of intel and instructions. Next to him he heard Marcus let out a low whistle.

"What?"

"Just glad Bird doesn't want our jobs is all," Marcus said. "How in the hell did Bird learn all that?"

"Probably hid in a corner and listened," Dean said. Birdie's age and gender weren't the only thing obscured by clothes, haircut, and a ballcap. After time out in the sun and the desert, Birdie's ethnicity was anybody's guess. A hunch of the shoulders, a hitch in the walk, and Birdie could be anybody's wizened abuela, limping in obscurity from store to store.

But that didn't mean this wasn't a stunning piece of intel.

"The family and the antiaircraft guns are in the exact opposite ends of the compound," Marcus said, to make sure they were both on the same page.

"Yes, they are."

"Bird can let us in by the antiaircraft guns," Marcus extrapolated.

"Yes, Bird can."

"You and me have the explosives."

"We do."

"What else do we need?"

Dean looked at Marcus with a measured glance. "We need to know the Russians are going to blow up too."

Marcus grunted. "God, must you ask the impossible?"

Dean shook his head. "Not impossible. In fact, logical. Our assassins just knocked off their double agent. If they're in bed with Corazones—"

"And they are," Marcus supplied.

"And they are," Dean agreed. "So they executed a major action, and they're trying to suck up to Gael Barrera. Bird saw planes landing after ours got shot down—it's probably why our plane was targeted in the first place. They were expecting important people, and we weren't them. The problem is making sure our bloodthirsty Bratvas are in the place we want to make boom."

Marcus grunted. "God, Dean. It's got to be a hornet's nest in there. They shot down our plane. Bratva fucked up and is looking for a witness. Are you sure Bird's going to be able to let us in?"

"Bird letting us in? Yes," Dean said thoughtfully. "But being able to gather enough intel to blow the place up in good conscience? That's gonna be rough."

Marcus grunted. "So that's our plan? Run around and gather intel, then meet when we know what to do with it?"

Dean nodded slowly. "Yeah. But don't get too discouraged. That's only one of the pages Bird sent us."

Marcus perked up. "And the other one is…."

"The layout of the compound." Dean flattened the other piece of paper, holding the first one with the list behind it. "And now we know something about Bird that we didn't before."

"Scary smart?" Marcus breathed.

"Yes, but also probably an engineer before a pilot," Dean surmised, glancing at the exacting block printing that matched that of the first page of the missive. The sketch was rough but precise, with every building labeled and every potential need outlined.

"So that's more like it." Marcus set the drone down carefully and, after checking for vermin, sat down next to it. "Pull up a seat, partner. Let's make a *real* plan."

Dean nodded, and Marcus produced a very clever little pen from his pocket, and together they started to outline in earnest.

AT MIDNIGHT, they gathered their supplies and bungee corded them to the trailer, covering the neat bundles with their friend the parachute/tent. They walked the bike a good 200 yards from their modest little cliff face so the sound didn't echo before Marcus got on in front and Dean grabbed his waist and they took off for the compound.

Dean closed his eyes for some of it, not sleeping, of course, but relaxing, because if Marcus was driving, he'd be on the alert. He let Bailey fill his thoughts: That shy, adorable smile, the freckled and peeling nose, the surprising insights into people, whether they were movie or TV people, the way he seemed to yearn for the things in the pictures in his apartment—hiking, exploring, going to museums and such—but had allowed his life to become his cat and his job with not much else in between.

Dean wanted to be spooning *Bailey* right now. Dean wanted to tell him about hiking in the foothills in the spring, or having a picnic at his parents' in early summer. Wanted to take him to Grass Valley to show him Dean's brother's antique store, and let Laure fix him a home-cooked meal.

Dean wanted to see his shy doctor *live*.

But first he had to make sure he wasn't assassinated for seeing too much.

Soon enough the compound loomed up in front of them, although it was facing the northeast road to town. Marcus shut off the engine a mile before the gates, and after strapping on their service weapons and filling their collapsible water bottles—and making sure their enhanced-vision goggles were firmly attached to their heads for when they were needed—they set off toward the northbound door.

It was a small service door, set between massive cooling towers, and Dean could see that Birdie's plan wasn't so featherbrained after all.

If this part of the compound was the service/ventilation part of the place, it would be damned hot in and around it. Nobody who didn't have to would willingly stand in 100 degree heat at two in the morning, even to cop a smoke or see the stars.

They were sweating by the time they made their way through the thundering hum of the towers toward Birdie's ushering hands.

Once inside, Birdie locked the door behind them and, finger to lips, pulled them deep into a labyrinth of air-cooled serving towers, just as the plans had indicated.

Antiaircraft guns and radar and running a complex this big required computer power—this was where the servers were held. And while nobody was needed in the corridors, which was a blessing, two hot and sweaty soldiers—and one diminutive Birdie—stuck out like a sore thumb.

Marcus and Dean followed Birdie until the little pilot guided them to a tiny staff room perhaps twice the size of a linen closet and distinguished from such by a microwave, a mini fridge, a love seat, and a small couch—and a lavatory around the corner.

"All the comforts of home, I see," Marcus said, collapsing on the couch in a cloud of dust.

"Cartel guys are like any other employer," Birdie said, coughing behind a grimy hand. "Except his employees carry guns and it's hard to dispose of bodies out here. Barrera wants his guys to not think about rebelling, he's got to not treat them like chickens waiting for the axe."

"But he's not going to let them get too fat and happy either," Marcus concluded, and Birdie nodded.

"I heard a *lot* hiding out under that fucking supply truck. Dean, you were spot on about the two Russian guys on the heater for fucking up. They came back with us—I could hear their hard-soled shoes ringing on the floor of the canvas-covered truck, for fucks sake. The truck pulled in, the guys got out, and they had a fucking *escort* to go see Gael Barrera. I wouldn't put odds on those guys making it through another night, you know what I mean?"

"But they're alive now?" Dean asked.

"Yeah. There's a sort of… well, it's not quite a jail. It's more like a controlled barracks. Our guys were put in there, under guard, and the bitching was loud and in Russian. The whole compound could hear it down the hall."

"Too bad they made you, me, and Bailey at the hospital," Marcus said with an unhappy glance at Dean. "It would be great if Barrera took them out himself and thought he was done with it."

Dean nodded. Their plan, such as it was, was contingent upon the family—*all* of the family—being separated from the military part of the compound.

"Bird," Dean said, feeling the pain of this in his gut. He and Marcus had hard lines—and he was pretty sure Birdie did too. "Is there any way to take the whole compound out without putting the family in danger?"

Birdie grimaced. "I can give you about eighty percent," Bird said frankly. "But for us to really cripple them, all it would take would be to use the C-4 on the antiaircraft gun and the computer station. Once we take out their surveillance, their computing power, their infrastructure— I'm saying. It took ten years to build this shit up."

But the Russians. And their information....

Dean started to pace. "Marcus," he said slowly, reaching out absently to touch the file cabinet, "what would be the one thing that would make Gael Barrera focus on somebody besides the witness to the Bratva hit?"

"I don't know. A carpet bombing by the US military? A turf war with one of the other cartels?"

Dean felt it then, the tingling sensation that came with *it*. The idea that was going to solve all their problems. *The* it.

"Maybe Bratva breaking out their two hit men and blowing up the antiaircraft array?"

Marcus and Birdie stared at him.

"Why in the fuck would they do that?" Marcus asked in disbelief. The hit men had fucked up—Bratva would as soon cut them loose, particularly since their partnership with Sangrino de Corazón was going so swimmingly.

"I don't know, comrade," Dean replied in Russian. "Why would they?"

Marcus's face went blank, which meant he was rapidly assimilating everything Dean had just said. In Russian he replied, "I haven't the faintest idea. But I think it should happen."

"Da," Dean said, his mind darting around like a million fish. In English he said, "Bird, we're going to need some cartel uniforms and some AK-47's. You're in charge of the C-4. Marcus has the bags. Blow up the computers, the antiaircraft array, hell, even the weapons. Everything in the northeast quadrant of the compound, go for it. But if you so much as see a doll or smell a diaper—"

"Abort, abort, abort," Birdie said, nodding like this was a crapton of relief. "What's our exfil?"

"Well, I assume you're going to leave the hangars alone?" Marcus asked.

Birdie grimaced. "I'd love to fly out of here, but we'd have to get to the planes, and taking one of the fucking Jeeps would be really goddamned dangerous."

"Suggestions?" Dean asked.

Marcus closed his eyes, and Dean knew he was running Birdie's map through his head. He opened his eyes and said, "Two things. One is a Jeep *would* be dangerous—it would leave our heads and faces exposed."

"We know this...." Dean made go-on motions with his hands.

"It would be *perfect* if our two Bratva boys escaped in a Jeep, you think?"

"Oh my God," Dean said, and just like the tingle meant he had *it*, the shudder meant Marcus had put the cherry on top of *it* and turned it into the sundae of his dreams. "They'll be so busy chasing the damned Jeep—"

"They won't even realize we're the ones in the plane," Birdie finished on a cackle, and they all took a collective breath.

"So," Dean said. "Where does everybody eat or gather?"

"There's a mess hall toward the center of the compound," Birdie said. "From what I heard, Barrera eats there at night, talking among the troops, that sort of thing, and then he retires to the civilian villa, where he plays daddy dearest with what is probably an entire fucking romper room of kids."

"Okay, then," Dean said. "We should have a complete division. No civilians in this part of the compound. Marcus and I break the Russians out, making a hell of a ruckus *in Russian*, and then we get those boys to a Jeep. Then, while they're standing on it and distracting the rest of the compound, Bird, you'll have our exfil prepped and the C-4 ready to blow. We'll spend the night shift out and about getting the lay of the land—maybe dropping some C-4 nodules if we've got time—and then catch eight hours here. It's not used a lot, is it, Bird?"

Birdie indicated no with a jerk of the chin. "Did you spot the dust on the file cabinet?"

"Yes, and the drawers are empty. I could tell. No, this place doesn't get many visitors." Dean let out a puff of breath. "Which is good news. Between the club chair and the couch and one person sitting on guard at the table, we might get some sleep. It's *glacial* in here."

"Glorious," Marcus mumbled. Dean smiled at him wearily as Marcus's chin touched his chest.

"Well, maybe you and Marcus can rest here for an hour or two," he said to Birdie. "I'm going to take a cruise around the compound and see if I can't get some uniforms while nobody's at the commissary."

Birdie's plans had indicated barracks and a commissary—much like any military organization anywhere. Well, why not? So much of South America had been destabilized by American CIA interests in the eighties and nineties that building up a dependable government had taken sweat, blood, and lives. The cartels had filled in the vacuum—and often offered a stability that the governments at the time hadn't. Unfortunately their brutal origins bred brutality, and the now-thriving government of Mexico was having a hell of a time fighting what amounted to small fascist regimes in the middle of their country.

It was a mess. Dean, for all the numbers that fell behind his IQ, couldn't untangle it. All he knew was that he didn't like it when people got hurt. Trafficked people. People who fell susceptible to drugs. People hurt in violent crimes. He and Marcus had long since started to work on the least violent options to help people not involved in the cartels just live their damned lives—and that included Bailey.

The fact that he wanted to see Bailey again, longed to spend some time with Bailey in peace—or making love, which was *not* peaceful—made this the most important mission Dean and Marcus had ever attempted.

It was absolutely imperative that Bailey be allowed to live his life in peace after this, whether or not that peace included Dean.

With this in mind, he scouted the complex and found the laundry and the closed commissary. Quietly, he let himself into the commissary and stole three of the requisite uniforms—green khaki, ribbed tanks, red kerchiefs, and hats. It was a simple getup, without stars and bars, and Dean thought part of the reason a uniform was required was to delineate people in the military part of the compound from people in the civilian part.

He was pretty sure that when cartel personnel were sent off campus to do business, they dressed in civilian clothes, the better to sneak into people's lives and homes and perpetrate mayhem.

He changed into one set of the uniforms and grabbed two AK's from the armory, also located in the commissary. He thought about giving one to Birdie but thought Birdie would be better off with a service revolver. The AK's had a massive pushback that the revolver didn't. Birdie was probably strong enough to wield one, but Birdie's real strength relied on stealth.

Besides—carrying one buddy's extra weapon over his shoulder while strapped with a personal revolver was one thing, but carrying two was ridiculous.

He returned to the staff room well and truly exhausted and more than ready to catch his nap, slipping in a mere breath before a claxon blared over speakers placed all over the compound, probably to indicate changing of the shift.

"Jesus," Marcus blurted, sitting bolt upright from the couch. "Bird, you couldn't have warned us?"

"Didn't know!" Birdie snapped, scrambling to stand by the comfy chair that had served as a sleeper. "Holy shit! How long were you gone?"

"Couple hours," Dean said, yawning. "Brought you guys presents. Next person who sneaks out needs to bring food."

"I slept all day under the fucking truck," Birdie muttered. "Had cold packs most of the time. Comfy as a kitten."

"I'll do it," Marcus volunteered, standing and starting to strip. He used the small sink and the faucet to dampen his tank and wipe his pits down as he did so, because he'd always been meticulous. "I'm starving."

Dean yawned and nodded as he stripped off his overshirt and used it to cover himself when he took Marcus's place on the couch. "Same," he said.

"Yeah, you get some sleep." Marcus chuckled. "Knowing where to find the dining hall will be essential for what we're doing tonight."

Dean grunted and closed his eyes, as safe here as he'd been under the parachute in the desert but admittedly more comfortable. "Plan later," he muttered. "Bird, water's in the plane."

"Will do, boss," Birdie told him, and that's all he had to remember for a few.

Restless Hearts Sleep Alone

"Bailey, son," his father said in a pained voice. "Do you really think you want to spend your time helping?"

To his credit, Connor Dodge didn't put any emphasis on *helping*, although yesterday's repeated accidents in the mother-in-law cottage had proved that Bailey was anything *but* help.

"Fine," Bailey muttered, gazing at the two spilled buckets of nails and screws in dismay. He could *swear* he was a competent adult when he was in the hospital, but something about working side by side with his own father….

"Son," Connor said, his voice set on *extra* kind, "why don't you go relax? Spend some time reading by the pool? I know you don't get a lot of chances for vacation, but why not make this one?"

Bailey stared at his father like he'd sprouted another head. A burst of sheer frustration drove him to his feet, and he stalked out of the mother-in-law cottage snarling, "Fine! I'll sit and be useless, and you can go ahead and rebuild the Taj Mahal!"

Behind him he heard his father sounding dismayed and Dean's father soothing him. Yeah, well, Bailey got the feeling Ed Royal was used to calming volatile tempers.

With a harumph, Bailey strode directly to the pool, let himself in through the chain link gate, stripped to his cargo shorts, kicked off his boots, and dove in.

The water was surprisingly cool, and he surfaced, trying not to sputter, before setting off on a blistering freestyle, hampered by the baggy shorts and soggy underwear. He ignored that and continued for a good five laps, until the bright sunshine, the coolness of the water, the thrill of physical activity—all of it—settled into his muscles and he relaxed enough to start having fun. When he finally pulled to a halt, out of breath but a little less pissed off, he found Reg squatting at the end of the pool, waiting patiently for him to be done.

"Hello," he said brightly. He liked the quietest Royal. In the past three days he'd met them all but Sal, who lived several hours away. Prock and his wife and children had been a delight, and Laure and her two teenaged boys had been a wisecracking family in the best of ways. Reg had, in his understated way, floated among them all, holding the baby for Prock, lending a phone charger to Russell, Laure's oldest, fixing Prock's wife's phone in a matter of moments. Whereas Chance was bright and shining, distracting everybody's attention with a smile or a joke—or often a very naïve statement that *seemed* like it was too innocent to be true but that Bailey was starting to suspect Chance really was—Reg was the family angel, quietly helpful in all ways, embarrassed by any notice whatsoever.

"Hi," Reg said, pushing his glasses up his nose. "I, uh, are you done with your laps?"

Bailey thought uncomfortably of his sodden cargo shorts. "Yeah. I should get out and start to drip dry, at least, before it gets so hot my skin starts to peel off my shoulders."

Reg nodded. "Come on, let's sit under the umbrella. I got lemonade and big plastic cups with *ice*."

Bailey grinned at him. "Your mom sure does know how to do summer right."

The Royal family wasn't fancy. The soda was bargain brand, and the lemonade was the kind from frozen concentrate. There were no fluted glasses or expensive tumblers—Julie had alluded to their "fine gas-station china" on the first day, but a giant plastic cup full of ice was still pretty blissful in the middle of Bakersfield in July.

"There's also curried chicken salad," Reg said, looking quite pleased. "It's my favorite."

Bailey had an idea that Julie had done that on purpose. Anthony had gone back home the day before—apparently he lived about forty-five minutes away, and he and his father owned and operated a shooting range, both of them giving lessons along with a recently hired manager. Reg and Anthony weren't an item—*yet*—but Bailey could see by the way Reg's shoulders drooped that he missed Anthony, even for the work week when he went to keep up his livelihood.

"Why don't you go with Anthony and work from his house?" Bailey asked, sitting on the patio chair in a plop of clammy cloth.

Reg scowled at him. "That's forty-five minutes away," he said. "Most of my siblings are here."

Bailey raised his eyebrows. "You'd still see them," he said tentatively.

Reg shrugged. "Anthony's busy. He doesn't need me hanging on his coattails."

Privately Bailey thought Anthony would *love* to come home and have Reg in his house, finishing up the IT work he did through telecommuting. But Anthony had pretty much told Bailey he was biding his time until Reg felt like he was important enough to be somebody's number one priority.

Bailey wished them both luck.

"So what's doing today?" Bailey asked, picking one of the curried-chicken-on-wheat sandwiches and taking a happy bite. Simple, yes, but still superlative.

"Well, I finished my commission this morning," Reg said, matter-of-factly. "And I thought we could address what's making you so edgy."

Bailey almost choked on his sandwich. "I beg your pardon?"

Reg took off his glasses and rubbed his eyes with his thumbs. "Was it a secret?" he asked. "I mean, you've been super polite to Mom and Dad, but so's everybody. But you spent two hours last night *pacing* around the property. I know what a walk looks like, and I know when somebody's stress walking, and that was definitely pacing. And you just managed to piss off your dad, and he's got 'laconic cowboy' in his DNA."

Bailey grunted. "I was just *trying* to help," he muttered.

"You were just *trying* to get out of your own way and into somebody else's," Reg said dryly, and Bailey wondered if the rest of the family had caught on to that dry sense of humor.

"Well, that too," Bailey admitted.

"You're worried," Reg said bluntly, and hearing the words from someone in Dean's family—when he'd been trying so hard *not* to be worried in front of them—was enough to make Bailey's shoulders sag in relief.

"Oh my God, am I," he admitted, feeling pitiful. "I am *so* worried. It's dumb—I know it's dumb—because Dean has left me a dozen times since we got together, and I never knew what he was doing or how dangerous it was, but this time…." He rubbed his stomach, and Reg made a mirror gesture with an expression that was pure sympathy.

"Me too," he said softly. "Want to do something about it?"

Bailey cocked his head, surprised. "Like what?"

"Well, for starters we could figure out what he's doing. And, well, for finishers, I might be able to track his location."

Bailey gaped at him. "You can *what*?"

"Shh!" Reg flailed and glanced around. "Do *not* let this get out, okay? I just… well, I worry. I mean, I worry about *everybody*, so I've pretty much done this for *everybody*, but I worry most for Dean because he's… he's not really *conscious* of risk to himself, you know what I mean?"

Bailey frowned a little, thinking of the *intense* amounts of micromanaging that had gone into his jump from the airplane. "No," he said bluntly. "He… he seemed to plan for every contingency when he was getting ready to drop me, uhm, off in the desert."

Reg nodded as though this information didn't contradict what he'd said at all. "Yes. He'd planned for *you*, but I'm betting that his plan with Marcus consisted of…." He trailed off, and the next few moments consisted of him mimicking a conversation between Dean and Marcus— and boy, was he spot on. Mannerisms, gestures, even Dean's trademark scowl. Bailey had no doubts as to who was who in this scenario and how scarily accurate Reg's rendition was.

"So, we fly somewhere dangerous." This was definitely Dean.

"Yeah, yeah." And right there he'd nailed Marcus.

"And then we get out of the plane somehow."

"Sure, sure."

"And then we disable the bad guys."

"Oh, of course."

"And then we obtain our objectives."

"I'm with you, bro."

"And then we exfil to safety."

"Brilliant! It's a plan!"

Bailey stared at him, torn between laughter and panic. Reg had done the conversation *pitch perfectly*, mimicking Dean's flat, no-nonsense tones and Marcus's more eager, excited chorus, and changing his body posture to echo each person he mimicked. And when he hit, "Brilliant! It's a plan!" Bailey realized that it was *all true*, and that Dean and Marcus's plan was to *have no plan*.

"That's terrifying," he said, as the reality sank in. "It's like you were there in the plane with them."

"Oh, I've heard them talk," Reg said grimly. "Which was why I snuck into Dean's room three Christmases ago and stole his SIM card, planted a bug in it, and replaced it. Someday, Dean's going to find out, and either he'll be super pissed and never speak to me again, or I'll be bailing him out of the shit and he'll be fine with it. Either way, let's see where he is, figure out what he and Marcus are doing there, and maybe plan to go get them in case they need us."

"Wow," Bailey said, feeling a little like he did in Dean's presence, but even more so because gentle, quiet Reg seemed like the last place he'd find that much potential for evil. "You're as scary as he is."

Reg shrugged. "We're sort of tightly knit. Even Sal, who likes to pretend he's above us all. I'm pretty sure he and Laure have weekly conferences where they map out our love lives to see if we need any help."

Bailey thought about Dean's only sister, outstanding cook, mother of two teenagers, CEO of her own home-office based headhunting business.

"If I knew your sister was planning my love life, I'd be *very* afraid," he said bluntly, and Reg shrugged.

"I think Sal introduced her to her husband, and yeah, I know he died young, but it was true love. It's like he wants to give her that moment back, and she wants him not to mourn his friend, and they've been doing that for a good fifteen years."

Bailey's eyes widened. "Wow. I… you know, for some reason I assumed she was divorced." He took a breath. "I should talk to her," he said after a moment.

Reg cocked his head over his plastic gas-station cup of lemonade. "Why?"

And Bailey heard himself saying it. "Because I lost somebody too. I-I guess I want to ask somebody, you know. About moving on."

Reg's eyes widened. "Oh. Wow. Ouch. Are you? Ready to move on?"

Bailey laughed a little, and it wasn't entirely a happy sound. "I must be. I'm about to concoct a plan that might send me back into the desert after your brother because I don't want to live without him. I'm pretty sure that's a big thumbs-up!"

Reg nodded, completely equanimous, as though Bailey hadn't just ripped open a big fat painful revelation. "Good," he said, no irony whatsoever. "Because we can't let on to my parents or siblings that we're doing this. They'll worry, and that's no good. You and me need total commitment."

Bailey didn't even want to think of what they'd find if they jumped down the "track Dean's phone" rabbit hole. But he didn't want to think of what could happen if they didn't.

"Or we need to be committed," he said dryly.

"I understand those places are very peaceful," Reg said, his lips not even *twitching* as he did so. "I brought my Tor-networked laptop. It's in the house, where we can use the secure Wi-Fi in my parents' office."

"Secure like…."

"So encrypted I haven't seen spam in years," Reg said, matter-of-fact like. "My parents have no idea how many protections they've got on their laptops."

Bailey ran his fingers through his drying, tangled hair. "Does your family have *any* idea how much you know or how terrifying you are?"

Reg gave one of those now-frightening "quiet" smiles. "Nope. Please don't tell them. It will only freak them out."

"Sure," Bailey said. And part of him knew *he* should be more freaked out. But part of him was thinking *finally* they could check in to see how Dean was doing.

He *really* needed to see how Dean was doing.

"After lunch," Reg repeated. He grabbed another curried chicken sandwich. "My mom made these for me special. I really don't want to waste them."

"GOING TO use the office, Mom!" Reg called casually as he and Bailey entered the house. Bailey had excused himself to put on his other pair of cargo shorts and to hang up the pair he'd worn in the pool, and the result was his skin was pleasantly cool and more susceptible to the eightyish air-conditioning in the house. Over dinner the night before, Prock, the "dead center" sibling, had assured him that the AC was perfectly capable of offering subarctic temperatures, even in the overwhelmingly dry heat of a central California summer, but that his parents didn't like to tax the unit too much, because once in a while 105 degree temperatures gave way to 115 degree temperatures, and they didn't want to burn out the unit.

It felt exactly like his own father's house, Bailey had told him, and he and Prock had bonded over parents and their foibles.

But now, following Reg into the small den, the *first* thing Bailey noticed was the temp was a cool and glorious 72 degrees. Glancing around, he realized that the out-of-date paneling and wallpaper that marked the rest of the house was missing in the small, plain room. The walls were thickly plastered and not just dry-walled, Bailey saw, and painted a peaceful pale yellow with pale green accents on the doorframe and the electrical outlets. The desk was modern, spacious, and comfortable, and the chair ergonomically superior to pretty much any other piece of furniture in the home.

And the place where the window should have been had been plastered and sealed over—if Bailey could recall, the stucco on the other side had been patched and painted as well.

And the small game closet had the door removed, and all of the shelves were full of advanced electronic equipment that would rival the NSA.

Bailey glanced around the room again and realized that the place was probably as hack-proof and surveillance-proof as a SCIF—a sensitive compartmented information facility—in the Pentagon, and he found himself staring at the quietest Royal.

"Do your parents know what this room is?" he asked, wondering at how much damage somebody with an unwholesome intention could do from a room like this.

"Oh hell no," Reg said absently. "I asked Dad if I could redo the den, and then I rewired the Wi-Fi, and then I thickened the walls and specially funneled all the power to a different transformer. I had a friend from high school help, and we put the AC unit on the same transformer so we wouldn't tax my parents' electric bill, but since they're *insane* and apparently *like* sweat in their armpits I also gave it its own separate thermostat so the server towers wouldn't overheat the place." He paused. "And there's special foil insulation under the plaster to make it fireproof. And there's a trapdoor under the desk that leads to a crawlspace under the house that comes out in the mother-in-law cottage. Which reminds me, I need to make sure my dad doesn't plaster or paint that over, so thank you, I'll go out there tonight."

Bailey couldn't help staring. "You… you did all this without your parents' knowledge?"

Reg gave him a mild look. "I'll tell them if they need to know."

"But why the secret tunnel? Who are you working for that you need a secret tunnel?"

Reg laughed. "No, no. Nothing like that. See, my folks went on a trip right after Chance graduated from school, and I asked if I could redo the den since my job needed more computing power and memory space—particularly when I'm doing design and coding and stuff. They said yeah, I could do it then, as long as I didn't let any of the cats escape, and I got some of my friends and some of Dad's friends to help me. And because of all the computer specs—and the fact that I wanted it subarctic in here when I was working—everybody started to joke that it was like a secret spy room. The tunnel to the mother-in-law cottage was a joke, really, but we realized that if the place was ever on fire, there was enough fresh air blowing up from there to make it a safe place to get out if the other ways were blocked. And since I'd blocked up the window...."

Bailey nodded helplessly. "Wow," he said. "Just... damn, son. Does Anthony have any idea about this?"

Reg frowned a little. "Why would Anthony know about the secret passage to the mother-in-law cottage?"

Bailey shook his head. "So I could tell him?" he asked.

"Oh, well, sure," Reg said. "It was mostly a lark, you know?"

"Sure," Bailey said. He was going to tell Dean about it too. But all that depended on whether or not they could get Dean the hell out of Mexico with his skin intact. "But about Dean...."

"Okay, then," Reg said, and with that he opened his laptop and did shit that Bailey didn't even recognize. He assumed he was logging into a special server, but given the setup he saw in the erstwhile closet, he could have arranged his *own* server, one completely clear of any pesky entanglements like, say, the websites belonging to the DOJ, who were apparently blissfully unaware of this unassuming kid who'd been tracking one of their own for nigh on three years because he'd been worried about his sibling.

"So," Reg was murmuring, obviously oblivious to the boggling Bailey was doing in his own head, "here's where Dean was three days ago, about an hour after he left you. He's about a hundred miles away from where Val picked you up. I'm going to assume the plane landed about forty-five minutes after you got pushed out of it, because the distance tracks. Mostly." Reg frowned, and Bailey was afraid to ask him what he suspected. "Okay, either way the phone needed to be charged between then and now, so we're going to assume Dean's alive to have done that."

"He's got sixty-zillion phone batteries on and around his person and stuff," Bailey said, remembering Marcus remarking on it. "It's sort of a glitch for him."

Reg made a happy little wiggle with his shoulders. "I taught him that," he said proudly.

Bailey wanted to ask this kid what happened to him to make him so damned careful, but now was not the time.

"So how long did he stay there?" he asked, and Reg tapped a menu by the little red dot Bailey assumed was Dean, and got a readout of movement by hour.

"Well, they landed and then took off again," Reg said carefully. "They're going around thirty, forty miles per hour, and they're riding on old roads—the sort that aren't nice to vehicle suspensions or chassis— I'm going to assume they're on motorcycles or in a Jeep, but probably motorcycles. They're going faster than a Jeep." Reg frowned. "Maybe a bike with a trailer? Their speed isn't... usual. It should be twenty to twenty-five in a Jeep or forty to fifty on a motorcycle, but it's thirty to forty—"

"Does it matter?" Bailey asked, not wanting to talk over him but needing the big picture before he could triage the situation.

"Probably to Dean," Reg said. "We need to keep it in mind. Okay, then. They travel for about six hours after they drop you off, and as it's getting dark, they make camp. Now, according to my sources, they are out in the middle of Snakeshit Acres, but what do I know."

"What," Bailey joked grimly. "No satellite access?"

Reg gave him a baleful look. "I try not to do anything that can get me convicted or exiled to another country," he said, with so much sincerity Bailey was suddenly very afraid.

"Understood. So they camp in the middle of Snakeshit Acres, and then...."

"And then...," Reg murmured, almost to himself, "they camp some more. Why are we camping in Snakeshit Acres, Dean? What's out there that keeps you and Marcus camping for two nights? Hmm...." Reg grunted and continued to scroll the timeline. "Okay. So, last night they... well, they traveled a little. Didn't so much *leave* Snakeshit Acres as tour the grounds. And then...."

Bailey frowned at the map with the little red dot blinking. The dot didn't *go out*, which was good because Bailey might have dropped dead right there from heart failure, but it did… fuzz?

"What's causing that?" he asked.

"Interference," Reg said bluntly. "Okay, so *my* map says Snakeshit Acres, but given Dean and Marcus stayed still like mice for two days and now their signals are getting fuzzy, I'm thinking there might be a big building or complex that's not really Snakeshit in Snakeshit Acres."

Bailey grunted with relief as he saw the other dot that was Marcus. "It looks like Marcus maybe charged his phone too," Bailey said.

"He probably kept his off," Reg told him. "Which makes me think they were *really* camped out. Dean kept his on and charged for emergencies, Marcus shut his off to save battery. And last night, as we slept, they snuck? I mean, it *is* sneaking if it's late night/early morning, right?"

"Especially if you're in Snakeshit Acres that's not really Snakeshit Acres," Bailey confirmed, both of them staring at the dots and the scroll of activity beside them.

"So they're in a complex or camp or something," Reg murmured. "Something with enough of a computer tower or enough electronic equipment to make it harder to track their phones. Given that they camped out next to it for so long, I'm going to assume they want to be there, but what are they doing there?"

And with that, he turned his hazel-eyed gaze to Bailey, who rubbed his stomach.

Oh God.

"This whole thing started when I saw a murder," he said softly. "And then I saw the two hit men—Russian mobsters, Dean told me. Easily identifiable. And—" He swallowed. "—well known for their ties to the local drug cartel."

"Oh wow," Reg said, taking a deep breath. "Okay, so that's why you got pushed out of the plane. They took you far away from where anybody could see you land, pushed you out, and arranged for pickup. Boom! Suddenly you're *here*, and my family is taking care of you so you don't have an electronic footprint or a paper trail. Have you told anybody where you are? Even texted somebody?"

Bailey shook his head. "No. Dean told me not to, and my dad too. In fact I turned off my phone once I got picked up." Dean had told him to do that somewhere in all that rush on the way to the airstrip. To turn off his phone as soon as the plane revved. If his father hadn't been on the ground to greet him, he might have rethought it, but no, Dean had planned for everything. "I had Val text my friend Sarree when he got back to Texas, so she'd know I was okay, but that's it."

"Good," Reg said, staring at the screen. "Because I think my brother and Marcus are doing something *huge* and dangerous out in Snakeshit Acres to make sure *you* don't get hunted down because you saw a couple of Russian mobsters in the middle of cartel country."

Bailey rubbed his stomach again and thought of Dean, plastering himself along Bailey's back, holding him so tight Bailey forgot all about holding on to hurt, holding on to escape.

"Oh God," he muttered. "Reg, he's got to be okay."

"I'm putting an alarm on this little dot," Reg murmured. "The minute it goes on the move again, you and I are taking the family minivan to go greet it. How's that sound?"

Dangerous. Reckless. The exact opposite of what Dean and Marcus had wanted them to do.

"I'm totally in," Bailey said, because fuck Dean if he thought Bailey was going to leave him out there in Snakeshit Acres without Bailey as backup.

Meanwhile, Back in Snakeshit Acres

Morning dawned and they took turns—one of them would scout, one of them would nap, one of them would stand guard. Birdie's presence made this a lot easier, and Dean thought muzzily when he woke up from his sleep that it was too bad Birdie would never make it in the Bureau. Dean and Marcus could pass for good old American boys—Agent Johnson and Special Agent Johnson—but Birdie would never be anything but Birdie. Besides, an absence of a criminal record was absolutely necessary, and given Birdie's stories on previous adventures, there was a lot of getting bailed out of the clink for good old Bird.

But that didn't mean Marcus and Dean didn't trust the pilot with their lives now.

"Okay, then," Dean said as the six o'clock meal drew near. "Are we ready for this?"

"No," Marcus said. "But if we plan too much more, we'll never do it."

Dean nodded, because that only made sense. They were speaking Spanish—lightly accented with Russian—which they'd been practicing all day. It was the *lightly* accented that was the hard part—otherwise, they sounded like Boris and Natasha in a Telenovela.

Although their little room was protected from much of the outside noise by the low hum of the computer servers and the machinery that kept them cool, they could all feel it—the awareness that people were going to move as one, a hive responding to its lead mind.

With a nod to Birdie, who nodded back, they exited the room and took two hallways to their left, blending in seamlessly with the majority of the soldiers in the compound to head for the group meal.

Dean'd had time over the past twenty hours to marvel at how well run Corazones de Sangre was—there were schedules, obviously, traditions, and probably even rank, although it wasn't emblazoned on the simple uniforms. The cartel had been born in a time of political unrest and had established a power base and a way of caring for its citizens.

Violent? Absolutely. Civilized? No. But there had been a vacuum and chaos, and this had taken its place. As the last three days in the desert had proven, there weren't that many options, and there were very few places to go.

Which left Dean wondering why the seeming merge with Bratva—particularly the two assholes who had botched the hit on Vlade. Whereas Gael Barrera was at least striving for some sort of stability for his people, no matter the detriment to everyone else, he was at least providing for *his* people. The Bratva branch seemed bent on a sort of gluttony of vices. Leaving the trafficked immigrants to rot had never been Barrera's style until Bratva got involved.

Dean and Marcus were hoping Barrera was regretting letting them in on the action.

In fact, they were counting on it.

The sound of shuffling feet and the happy hum of soldiers—both male and female—on their way to chow time was easy to get lost inside. There appeared to be about 2000 people in the military part of the compound, and given that supply trucks came and went and the personnel on the place were probably in a low-grade state of flux, nobody even gave Dean and Marcus a second glance. They carried themselves like the others—unconscious mimicry was one of the first things they'd learned going undercover—with good posture but not *too* good, and a sort of loose-limbed readiness that came with training and a regimen of PT and a nutritious diet.

They hung back for a little so that by the time they were in the food line, being served from caterers tables in the back of the room, far from the dais filled with the higher-ups on the food chain, they could have a good view of who sat where. It was then they made the discovery that—as it so often did—fortune in this case favored the batshit insane.

Their guys—and it was easy to spot the two hit men Bailey had tagged for Vlade Karkov's death, because they were both wearing expensive and overheated wool suits in the desert, as well as completely unsuitable hard-soled shoes—weren't sitting on the dais. They were sitting at the first table off the raised platform, their backs toward the door, two guards behind them, hands on their sidearms.

Their lucky-coin guy was making helpless twitching movements with his fingers, as though searching for his lucky coin to fidget with, and Dean could admit it—the gesture was one of the most pathetic things he'd ever seen.

Both men were sweating and regarding their food, which Dean, Marcus, and Birdie had pronounced first rate—home-cooked carnitas with stone-ground corn tortillas and tomato salsa—with all the excitement they'd regard chopped scorpions as an appetizer.

There was no doubt in Dean and Marcus's mind that those two men were reasonably certain they were sitting down to their last meal.

"We could leave them," Marcus murmured in Russian.

Which was a reasonable suggestion. Whatever had gone down, killing Vlade—and leaving a witness—was obviously a big enough mistake that Barrera couldn't leave these two Karkov assclowns alive.

But getting rid of them might mean they'd have to get rid of the witness, and that was why Birdie was currently planting C-4 all over the compound, because hopefully after the two Russian liabilities were no longer on the ledger, rebuilding the compound would keep this particular cartel busy until Bailey's name—or at least his *existence*—had long been forgotten.

"Should we relieve the guards?" Dean asked.

Marcus gave the situation another look-see and said, "Most of the tables near them are sparsely occupied. Let's get some food, sit down, listen to the nightly address, see if we can grab them during the first exodus."

Dean made a sound, although he did take a step forward in line.

"Or we edge out before the end of the nightly address and miss the rush," Marcus said.

"I'm thinking," Dean said, and they continued their advance in the buffet line.

They weren't the last to sit down with their plates, which worked well because nobody paid attention when they took advantage of the sparsely populated tables. They ate, studying the dais under their brows as they did so.

"Shit," Dean murmured. "Two of his sons are with him."

Gael Barrera was the center of the dais, surrounded by his colonels and staff. Thin, proud, earnest, and handsome, he looked more like a college professor than the leader of a criminal enterprise, and at his right hand were two boys—far too young to be soldiers, even in the face of the fourteen- and fifteen-year-olds Dean had seen on base. The boys were both excited to be there, dressed in the uniform, faces clean, hair combed back under their khaki caps. A mother had prepped them both to be there by their father this night.

"With any luck, they'll never see us coming." They ate happily, because the food *was* superior, and then, as expected, they felt a shifting. People went to the bathroom and returned, people disposed of their trays, got one more water—it was sort of a human rite of settling in, and that's when they made their move.

First they set their trays in their washing station because they may have been enemy combatants but they weren't animals, and then they edged behind the guards looking over the two party boys and bumped their shoulders.

"We can take over," Marcus said with one of his personable smiles. "There is custard for dessert." There was too. Dean rather regretted not getting any.

The way the two guards lightened up was rather sad. Dean hoped they didn't get in trouble. They disappeared, nodding in gratitude, and Dean and Marcus waited for them to get their custard in the dessert line and sit down before Dean bent down and prodded the lucky-coin hit man with the muzzle of his service revolver.

"Time to get up," he said in Russian, and he watched as both men straightened in both fear and hope.

"Come with us," Marcus added, also in Russian. Quietly, without so much as bobbing a head or walking out of step, the four of them started to make their way, Marcus and Dean in the rear with guns drawn, taking the two hit men toward the exit.

Three steps. Two steps. One step.

"Papa, didn't you say they were bad men?"

The Spanish, spoken in a clear, bright child's voice, acted like a spur in Dean's ass, and he and Marcus jammed their guns in the backs of their targets, and they began to run.

As MANY times as Dean and Marcus had walked this hallway in the course of the day, as many times as they'd studied the plans with Birdie, this part still remained the weakest part of the plan. The hallway sat adjacent to locked doors of what looked like classrooms—because it figured that this cartel would be training their people on computer, weapons, and emergency medical procedures—all of which were locked after use in the day. So instead of a warren of convenient hiding places, the corridor stretched long and deadly, like that one hall in a high school with all the lockers lined up on either side. A death trap, waiting for the unwary AP honor student to be walking in the late afternoon, about to be cornered by all the jocks.

There was nowhere to go but all the way through, and they had maybe ten feet to go when Dean heard that small voice, belonging to the boy—maybe ten—who shouted, "Stop! I have a gun!" Right as a frantic adult shouted, "No, mijo, don't!"

Dean growled, "*Go!*" to Marcus and turned around, his revolver pointed at the source of the voices, only to be brought up short.

It *was* the little boy, yes, and he *did* have a gun. A toy gun, wooden, that he was wielding as though he'd been trained how to use it in place of the real thing.

His father was caught between grabbing for the gun and pulling his own, and in that moment, Dean was face-to-face, drawn Glock to drawn Beretta, with Gael Barrera, the leader of the Corazones de Sangre cartel.

And next to him, looking frightened but resolute, Barrera's young son.

Dean stayed, gun still raised, staring directly into Barrera's tense face. And then, mindful that he and Marcus had drawn lines, he said, "You needn't worry. I don't kill children."

Barrera nodded and held his gun steady. "You could have shot him. I saw you had your gun aimed before you knew."

But Dean had hesitated, and here they were, with Barrera's men piling up behind him, obviously chomping at the bit to draw their guns and obliterate Stanford Dean Royal from the roster of all living things.

"I don't kill children," Dean said again. And then, for honesty's sake, "I'm not really excited about killing anybody, really."

Barrera raised his eyebrows. "And yet you invaded my compound to release a couple of hit men?" He scowled. "*Incompetent* hit men, who have managed to foul up my business for *months*, which is what I get for trusting these—"

The word he used then wasn't in any book of street Spanish provided by the Bureau, but Dean got the idea.

His two hit men weren't Gael Barrera's favorite people.

"So," he said, thinking quickly, "you can either have me killed here and let your son see it—" To his relief, a look of revulsion crossed Barrera's face. Good. Not a great human, no, but a decent father. "Which would be a terrible way to pay me back," Dean felt compelled to remind him.

Barrera raised a sardonic eyebrow. "You are right," he agreed smoothly. "I do owe you for showing mercy to my child. But I can't simply let these men go. They were to be… dealt with for incompetence. What do you suggest I do?"

Dean smiled and thought about their plan for putting the two men in a gas Jeep and pointing them in the direction of the open desert. "Maybe send your kids back to the villa. It's going to be busy here for a bit," he said, and he watched Barrera's eyebrows—both of them this time—go up.

"You do not kill children?" he said carefully.

"No," Dean said, and this he meant. He was impressed by the fact that Gael Barrera didn't use his sons as human shields, even though Dean had displayed this weakness for all to see.

"Anything else?" Barrera asked.

And this was where Dean's inflection *really* got tricky. "Could you... I don't know. Stay away from the northwest quadrant outside the gate," he said blithely. "No reason to go there at all."

"Northwest gate," Barrera said, nodding sagely. "Okay, then. Is that all?"

And this was where Dean had to pray. "One more thing," he said.

"Yes?"

"Give me three steps," he said, and then he started singing the Lynyrd Skynyrd song as he turned and bolted for the cross in the corridor and the open maintenance tunnel door Marcus had ready for him.

He slid through the door, and Marcus swung it shut and bolted it from the inside mere heartbeats before the shouting mass of men scuffled past the outside, searching for him at top volume. The men weren't stupid; more than one man tried the handle of the maintenance corridor, but the door was locked. What could they do?

Or course they *could* have chosen to shoot the thing down, which was why Marcus and Dean were running top speed, heading north, Marcus counting doors as they went.

"Five," he murmured. "Six, seven—here!"

And with a sudden wrench he skidded to a halt, hauled the door open, and dragged Dean in after him.

They were in the thick of it now, surrounded by fuse boxes and electrical panels, as they followed the almost secret passageway indicated by the plans toward the more militarized buildings in the north of the compound.

"God," Marcus muttered, hammering one of the electrical panel covers with the flat of his hand. "One good hand grenade and—"

"And everybody will know where to find us," Dean reminded him. "Where are our two 'rescuees'?"

Marcus gave a crusty laugh. "I'm guessing they're heading toward the Jeeps at the northeast entrance, why?"

"Because half of Barrera's forces should be traveling that way too." Yes, Dean had told Barrera the north*west* entrance, but he figured Barrera would assume he was lying.

"Excellent," Marcus said. "I gave them weapons."

Dean wanted to cackle, although a bloodbath was hardly grounds for celebration.

But then, chaos and misdirection would certainly help their cause. As they rounded another corner—this one leading to a slightly larger room, absolutely crammed with electronic servers controlling things like heating and lights and airflow—Dean pulled out a small incendiary device.

"You know what I said about telling them where we are?" he asked as Marcus carefully peered around the corner of the door leading toward the outside buildings.

"Yeah?" Marcus said. "We've got five seconds before we'll be all clear."

"Good. Because I think one of these will tell them where we *were*."

Marcus grinned over his shoulder at Dean in appreciation. "I like the way you think," he growled, and keeping one hand on the pressure handle, Dean pulled the pin.

"Okay, then," Marcus said. "Three, two, one—"

He opened the door, and they both ran through, and Dean turned and tossed the grenade into the electronics and electrical hub on his way out. The door swung shut behind them, and they started running toward the north*east* side of the compound, where the planes took off. They were long gone, and looking very purposeful and as though they belonged there, when they heard the muffled explosion, and the lights in the compound flickered and went off.

"That's what I'm talking about," Marcus said with satisfaction, but he said it for Dean's ears only, and they continued through the compound.

IT TOOK them less than ten minutes to find where a small cargo plane stood gassed on the runway, with a cagey-looking Birdie doing a last-minute systems check underneath it.

"Where's our comrades?" Marcus asked, hitting the release that would lower the back hatch.

"I sent them out the northwest gate," Birdie said. "Didn't want them bringing anyone this way while I prepped the plane."

Marcus grimaced. This was the problem with thinking on the fly. "Bird, we ran into Barrera, and Dean sent him off the scent so he'd assume the Russians were leaving by the north*east* gate. *We* have to go northwest when we leave, remember?"

Birdie screwed up a visage that was mostly lines around the eyes and grooves around the mouth. "We can circle around."

"What about the antiaircraft guns?" Dean asked. "Are those out of commission?"

"It's gonna be close," Birdie said. "We want to give them time to shoot the fucking Russians, and we don't want to be around when the C-4 fulfills its destiny, if you know what I mean."

Marcus glanced around and saw a few members of the ground crew staring at them as though trying to figure out *why* they would be leaving on a mission *right now* and said what Dean was thinking.

"Either way, I think we need to get out of here before they reset all their electronics or start shooting at us on general principle."

"Roger that," Birdie said. "Dean, stop double-checking my checks and get your ass on the plane."

Dean hated to do that—he *always* double-checked the checks, and Birdie usually let him get away with it because they'd flown some hairy shit together, but more of the passing soldiers were stopping to stare at the one plane in the compound ready for flight, and they were flat out of time.

He clambered aboard, and Birdie had started the engines and was telling them to belt their asses down before they even pulled the ramp up.

The taxi down the miniscule runway was met with panic fire and a burst of static over the radio as the control tower—or what was left of it after Dean's grenade to the electrical grid—protested that they had no clearance.

Well, no shit, they had no clearance—they weren't supposed to be there!

Two bullets *thunk*ed into the rear tail section as the plane lifted, but they didn't penetrate the hull, and Dean and Marcus—who hadn't had time to belt yet—quickly latched themselves in as the bumps under the wheels leveled out and Birdie hauled up on the throttle to get the plane to clear the compound walls.

Dean started calculating vectors in his head, about how fast they had to go, how much lift they had to have for the plane to get X number of feet off the ground with Y being the distance of the runway and—

"Stop that!" Marcus shouted. "I don't want the last words I hear to be 'The math doesn't math!'"

Dean nodded and kept his mouth shut after that, but inside he was doing a little happy dance, because the math *did* math, and barring any giant gusts of wind, they might just… might just….

He craned his neck and shifted his shoulders so he could look out the tiny portal, and his blood froze in his veins.

"Bird!" he croaked. "Do you see what I see?"

"*Fucking Russians!*" Birdie snarled. "*Right underneath us!*"

Oh God. Oh God. Could they overtake the Russians before the—

Behind them, he saw a flash of light and two projectiles… up, up… out of his vision… but he could see their arcs… up, up, up, up….

Birdie hit epic airspeed and sliced the plane to the right so only one of the rounds from the antiaircraft guns pierced their tail gear.

The whole plane shuddered, the airspeed radically decreasing as Birdie tried for control. Dean was twisted fully around now, and in the distance he could see the explosion that took out the antiaircraft gun, while below them the smoldering hull of the Jeep was cartwheeling freely through the desert.

And Birdie fought valiantly to keep their plane from joining it.

"Dean?" Marcus called a little desperately.

"Marcus?"

"I meant it."

"Meant what?" But Dean knew.

"I'd follow you into hell."

"Same. But don't pack for the trip yet."

"Doing math?" Marcus asked as the plane began to descend rapidly.

"Nope," Dean said frankly. "Praying."

"Same."

They gave each other a tight grin. There were no parachutes on this plane—Dean had seen that when they'd loaded on. There were no towns. There were two hundred miles of desert between where this plane would land and where they could find water… or food… or medical aid.

Bailey, I really love you.

Dean and Marcus bent double, laced their hands over the backs of their necks, and prepared for a crash landing.

And prayed.

When Things Fail

BAILEY HAD spent five years trying to remember the last time he and Emmett had so much as kissed.

It wasn't that they hadn't loved each other. They'd loved each other very much; he knew that was true. But they'd been exhausted, physically and mentally, and both of them had been coming off of their own bouts with COVID. A brush of hands, a rub of two cheeks together, a lingering glance or, hell, so much as a wink was practically porn for them by the time Emmett had gone to work, collapsed, and died.

But Emmett had known Bailey loved him. Of that, Bailey had zero doubts.

But Dean had kissed him, then given him to Marcus, who had shoved him out of the airplane, and that had been that.

Bailey kept reliving that moment for the rest of the day after he left Reg's frighteningly up-to-date computer room and retreated to his own bedroom, where Mr. Bumble waited for him to lavish attention upon his soft, white-furred body. He'd been told the room had once been Laure's, and she'd told him over dinner that the best part of being the only girl was getting her own bedroom, even if it was small. Once she'd moved out, it had been furnished with a queen-sized bed and a dresser and—her mother had been happy to point out—a new area rug in wild shades of purple and green. The comforter on top was worn, with purple flowers, and the walls were cream with some faded, framed prints. It was a comfortable place, much like the house itself, and because it was one of the few places in which everything matched, Bailey wondered if it was for special company.

The thought sent a wave of affection for Dean's family roaring through his heart. They weren't rich or educated—but by God the Royal family was *fine*. And noble. And all of the things a family was supposed to be.

He sat on that bedspread—soft, cotton, practical, and pretty—and wiped his burning eyes on his shoulder as he petted his cat and fell painfully in love with Dean's family.

He wanted to share this revelation with Dean himself, and the fear—the reality—that he might never get a chance to almost leveled him.

Which was when something in him snapped.

He took out his phone and pulled up Val Royal's number.

He got Rory McCauley instead, which was fine, because that's who he wanted to talk to.

"Heya, Doc," Rory said. "Val's driving. What's on your mind?"

"It's been five days," Bailey told him.

"I know it."

"Is this normal? I don't think this is normal."

"For two agents to be out of contact? No, it is not normal," Rory replied, and he sounded cagey, but he was probably trying to not freak Val out. Bailey could appreciate that, but he was so far beyond freaked out, he thought he'd rather like Val to join him.

"Where are you?" he asked bluntly.

"About to drop off a load to El Paso," Rory said. "Why?"

"Because Dean and Marcus have been stuck about a hundred miles south of Juarez for the last four days," Bailey said bluntly. "And I want to go find them."

"And you would know that *how*?" For the first time Rory McCauley sounded surprised, and Bailey was so far beyond terrified that he didn't care what secrets he spilled.

"Because Reg tracked his phone, on his computer with all this special unregistered stuff I'm not supposed to know about. But we can see a little blinking dot that is Dean. And it has been more or less still for the last four days."

"So…," Rory said slowly, "what is it you propose to do?"

"I propose to charter a small plane to Juarez, rent a car, and *find that motherfucking dot*!" Bailey almost shouted. "But if you guys are closer, you might be able to beat us there."

Rory grunted. "Son, I've got a number you can call for an outfit in Napa. Tell Glen Echo it's me and that he owes me, and I can pay whatever he wants. Tag us with your ETA—we'll meet you in Juarez."

Bailey managed to breathe for the first time in three days, and he almost cried when the text came through with the contact. "Thank you," he all but whimpered.

"Dean's family," Rory said simply. "Which reminds me—have Reg call Anthony. You're not doing this alone. The two of them should come with you, but, uhm, you know. Don't tell Ed and Julie, okay? Just tell them you're meeting us in LA."

"Course," Bailey said. After spending four nights under their roof, he got it. Protect the parents, protect the peace. Maybe, if he'd been in the family for a little longer he might have protested—but right now, his entire heart was beating in time to that pulsating little dot in Reg's illegal computer.

THE AIRSTRIP was midway between the Royal family house in Bakersfield and Anthony and Rory's gun range about forty-five minutes away. Bailey packed a small bag, apologized to his father for his blowup that morning, and left explicit instructions for how to care for the white cat he was leaving in these nice people's spare room.

And then he and Reg got the hell out of dodge—but not entirely unscathed.

"Chance," Reg was saying as he floored the poor family-mobile, "there is no guarantee there are enough seats on the plane."

"Then I'll drive the minivan home," Chance said stubbornly.

"You will not," Reg snapped. "You'll leave my body in the back and take my spot on the plane. I *know* you, you little shit!"

Bailey had never had a little brother—he'd had no idea they had supersonic hearing and some sort of sixth sense for any trouble going down that did not involve them. He'd been throwing his and Reg's bags in the back of the minivan and suddenly Chance had booty-bumped Bailey's ass to the back and was buckling into the front seat and giving his brother hell.

Bailey was thirty-four years old—he'd *thought* he knew how to handle himself with adults, but he'd never come face-to-face with true love before.

"I would not leave your body in the back of the car," Chance was saying now, sounding hurt. "I *love* you, Reg. It's hot outside—you'd *die*. But I would totally leave you on the tarmac after convincing you it should be me who goes to rescue Marcus and not you."

"We're not rescuing Marcus—"

"Oh, the hell you're not!"

"Okay, so we *may* rescue Marcus, but don't forget, the person paying for the plane, you blockhead, is *Dean's boyfriend*. So you need to give him some deference because he's *actually in a relationship* with our brother, and he gets to call the shots."

"Well, was it his idea to call Anthony?" Chance shot back, sounding as childish as Bailey had heard him.

"Rory told him to. What does Anthony have to do with this?" Reg asked—and Bailey wanted to cry, because in this area only, Reg was literally the dumbest Royal, and he wasn't sure if Chance had the maturity to—

"Nothing," Chance muttered, crossing his arms. "Never mind. It's fine. I'll take the minivan home. Just…." His voice cracked. "If I can't go, tell Marcus I… you know. Thought about him."

Bailey's heart cracked a little. This family—*this* was why you had brothers. So they could give up their heart's desire to cushion their brother's heart for a breath longer.

For a moment, he loved Dean so hard he couldn't breathe. Dean hadn't just pushed him out of an airplane. He'd pushed him into *this*. Into this mess of love and kindness and fun and entanglements and *life*. Dean had pushed him into the arms of his family, and not Bailey alone— Bailey's father, Bailey's cat, and Bailey's father's *dog*.

Dean wanted them to be safe. He wanted them to be *loved*. And Bailey wanted nothing more than to be safe and loved with Dean by his side.

But first they had to find that pulsing dot on the screen.

THEY WERE met on the tarmac by a couple of male models, or at least that was Bailey's first surprised take. Glen Echo—six-foot, slender, blond, and blue-eyed, with one hell of a rakish swagger—took one glance at the three of them, and then at Anthony who had beaten them to the small, private airstrip by about four minutes, and shook his head.

"You're looking for how many people?" he asked.

"Two, maybe three," Bailey said, wondering if he was the only one who knew about Birdie.

"Mm… I can take two people there, with three possibly injured in the cargo part of the plane," he told Bailey. "However, I understand you're meeting McCauley in Juarez, amirite?"

"Yes," Anthony said, drawing up near them, "but he'll probably be in the semi—they left their trailer in El Paso and were heading that way."

Glen gnawed his lip and glanced at his flight partner, another specimen of rakish swagger, with dark hair, golden skin, and deep-set, liquid brown eyes. "Damie?"

"Take 'em all to Juarez," his copilot said. "Leave one or two to watch the plane and make plans depending on what we find."

"Damien Ward, for the King Solomon solution," Echo said, giving Damien a high five. He turned his game face toward them when he spoke next. "Okay, Damie'll show you where to park. You two—" He gestured to Bailey and Reg with his chin. "—bring the bags. Damie and I have a fairly extensive first aid kit—"

"I'm a doctor—I brought my black bag with pain killers and antibiotics," Bailey said quickly.

"Good," Glen said with a solid nod. "We'll take stock and stow the gear." He paused in the middle of turning around and pinned his gaze on Anthony. "Wait a minute," he said. "Do I know you?"

Anthony shot Glen a grin and extended his hand. "Little McCauley," he said. "I'm Rory's son. We met about ten years ago when Dad was still in the Bureau."

"D'oh!" Glen said. "Damie! You remember him? God, he was a precocious little shit!"

Anthony held his hand to his heart. "I carried a torch," he said. "My mom drove us out to see Dad take off, and I was, like, 'I'm gonna *marry* that man someday!'"

Glen laughed delightedly. "Well, that's a shame, 'cause I'm already married." He managed to look a smidge embarrassed. "And he's about your age, too, which seems to me like some sort of punishment for something I didn't know I did."

"I know," Damien teased darkly. "Believe me, I know."

The three of them laughed, and Damien went with Anthony and Chance to make sure the vehicles were stowed close to the hangar, leaving Bailey to walk with Reg and Glen to the plane.

"So," Glen Echo said soberly as they walked, "I know you're flying to get your friend—"

"Our brother," Reg said. "Mine and Chance's. And his partner in the Bureau—"

"And their pilot," Bailey put in. "They wouldn't leave Bird behind."

"Bird?" Echo said, arching a brow. "Bird flew them? Oh hell, son—why didn't you say so? We'd fly through a hurricane to make sure

Bird's all right. Best pilot I've ever known. Okay, then. How long have they been missing?"

"Well, they pushed me out of an airplane over the desert about a hundred miles south of Juarez five days ago," Bailey said. "This one," he nodded to Reg, "has ways of tracking his brother's phone. They were holed up about a hundred fifty miles south of Juarez for two nights, and on the third, they moved about two miles north, and have been there since."

Glen grunted. "A hundred fifty miles south of Juarez," he muttered, and then he stopped his swaggering pilot's stride and turned toward Bailey. "What were they doing there?"

Bailey grimaced. "They were trying to track down a couple of, uhm, Bratva hit men who had links to a, uhm, local cartel—"

"Corazones de Sangre?" Glen asked, eyebrows raised. "Why would the Bureau send them to do that?"

Bailey felt so very small. "I, uhm, was a witness to a hit," he said. "Dean said he was going to, uhm, bring the hit men in so they wouldn't try to, uhm, silence me."

Glen Echo dragged his hands through his hair. "So, Dean and his partner—"

"Marcus," Reg supplied.

"Yeah. They were going to go off a couple of hit men in the middle of a cartel compound."

Bailey and Reg glanced at each other. "They never said that in so many words," Bailey said after a moment. "They…. Dean just said they were going to keep me safe."

"Oh, baby," Glen muttered. "I know what *that* means. Okay, then. Do you still have Dean on your illegal tracking software?"

"How do you know it's illegal?" Reg squawked.

Glen stared at him. "Because he's with the FBI, junior. Don't shit yourself—I'm not getting anybody in trouble. If what you've got helps us get our people out, that's fine. But you keep an eye on your equipment so we know if our folks are on the move, yeah?"

"Yeah," Reg said, nodding his head. Bailey had seen the younger, more timid man swallow nervously, but he didn't hesitate.

"Good man," Glen said, with a hearty slap to his shoulder. He caught Bailey's eyes. "And you, sir, have the appearance of a man who's been through battle."

"Only in the ER," Bailey said, but Glen shook his head.

"That's battle," he said, without equivocation. "I don't see you backing down." He paused for a minute, and his eyes softened. "So what's your personal stake here?"

Bailey couldn't even smile. "Dean Royal," he said, the name coming from his lips before he could stop it. "I'm not going back to his parents without him."

Glen nodded like Bailey hadn't just laid his heart out for the world to see. "Well, then, let's get this show on the road."

Fifteen minutes later found them up in the air, strapped in tight to the comfortable passenger seats in the front of the plane, their gear stashed in a corner of the cavernous space in the back. Bailey had noted the four field gurneys, with sturdy vinyl padding and foldable all-terrain wheels, strapped to the side, as well as two ice chests that Glen had shown him were full of saline and plasma, which could be held up by eyebolts on the sides of the plane.

Glen had explained that his vehicles were made to be versatile. He could take rich folks into the mountains with their hunting/fishing/kayaking gear, or he could go searching for those same folks when they didn't report back.

Underlying everything, Bailey noted, was the smell of wet dog.

Glen had chuckled. "Yeah, my brother runs a dog-training business for search and rescue hounds. We work together a lot, which is good because he and Damie live together, and Preston has certain rules about how long Damie is allowed to go without them hooking up."

"Rules?" Bailey said, curious in spite of himself.

Glen glanced at him shrewdly. "Something along the lines of 'Don't make me hare into the wild yonder searching for you because I love you, you idiot.' I'm thinking you could identify."

Bailey thought about Dean pushing him out of that plane, with no promise of when he'd be back in touch. "A little," he said darkly.

Glen nodded. "Thought so."

And now here they were. They were not so far south that the sun had set already, but it was getting close to seven as the plane took off. Bailey had fidgeted in his seat, trying to put that jumpy, fretful feeling in his stomach to rest. They were *doing* something, weren't they? He'd gotten help?

But Glen had been very frank about the twin-engine turbo-prop's capabilities. Twelve hundred miles in six hours was probably the max, and it would be a buzzy dragonfly ride to Juarez, which was nearly a thousand miles away. Still, Glen had a fuel stop planned at El Paso, and Anthony'd had the good sense to stop at a burger place for food, and the seats were relatively comfortable.

Bailey needed to chill out and pace himself—he knew this from med school, from the ER, from his entire life. A man learned patience when he was waiting for an emergency he knew for sure was going to come.

Still, after Reg was done eating, Bailey touched his elbow from the seat behind him. The sky had smudged with purple night over the desert, and stars threatened to peek out overhead. The droning of the twin engines was finally working its magic, and Chance had finished his food and curled up and gone to sleep with the dedication of somebody who probably still had two inches to grow.

Reg turned to him, pulling an earbud out as he did. "'Sup?" he asked, reinforcing how young he was compared to Dean.

"Has there been any movement?" Bailey asked, rubbing his stomach nervously for the umpteenth time in an hour.

Reg took his phone from his pocket—he'd been listening to music—and pulled up a screen, frowning. "Mm… hold up." He touched the screen on Dean's pulsating dot and grunted.

"What?" Bailey asked.

"It's… well, he's moved about a half mile in the last five minutes, but not linearly."

Bailey squinted. "So he's been running around?"

"Yeah. A lot, actually. And quickly. And hold on a sec…." A different pulsating dot joined Dean's. "He and Marcus are still together—like, running in lockstep. But… oh wow."

"Oh wow?" Bailey asked, and his voice pitched enough for Chance to mumble in the seat next to him. "Oh wow?" he said again, this time in a stage whisper. "The hell does that mean, Reg?"

"It means they're on the move," Reg said. "Fairly quickly—about a hundred twenty knots, actually, which is *our* airspeed, which means—"

"They're on a plane?" Bailey actually found this was reason to hope. "Which way are they heading?"

"Northwest from their position—so exactly toward Juarez." Reg glanced up from his phone and smiled hopefully. "They might meet us there. That would be… well, a little like we made a mountain out of a molehill, but….” He shrugged.

Bailey swallowed, trying to contain his relief. It wasn't for certain; it wasn't seeing Dean *right there*, but God, it was hope, right?

“Can I see your phone for a second?” he begged. “I promise not to touch the screen.”

Reg handed it over without question, and Bailey thought for the hundredth time that this family was sort of magical, and then he concentrated on the two dots. Sure enough, much like one of those diagrams you saw in a commercial airliner, the dots were coursing a stately path along the very simple map presented on the phone's face. There was nothing much underneath it, but the dots continued to course, continued to—

“Oh shit!” Bailey squeaked, but it was loud enough to turn both Reg and Anthony toward him in their swiveling chairs. “Look!”

As the three of them peered at the little screen, the two dots slowed their course, slower, slower….

“If that's a plane,” Anthony said gruffly, “it's about to crash.”

“Oh God,” Bailey said. “How far away are they? How long will it take us to get to them?”

“Hold on,” Reg muttered. “Anthony, give me your phone so I can do some calculate—”

“Oh shit!” They all said at the same time. The two dots had stopped. And then they'd gone out, leaving nothing but the blankness of desert on Reg's phone.

Bailey felt himself vibrating with fear, and Anthony took the phone from Reg's shaking hand. “Cell phones break in airplane crashes,” he said softly. “And everybody, including my dad, says Bird is the best pilot he's ever met. Now I'm going to show their last known to our two pilots, and you two are going to take twenty deep breaths, do you understand me?”

“Dean!” squeaked Reg.

Anthony cupped his cheek with undisguised tenderness. “Baby,” he said softly, “we're going to get there. Did you do your calculations?”

“Four hours,” Reg whispered. “That doesn't count getting gas in El Paso.”

“Then five hours,” Anthony said, stroking Reg's cheek with a tender, work-roughened thumb. “You and Bailey here are going to have to put all your fears on hold for five hours. Can you do that?”

Bailey wanted to sob. He wanted to *howl*. He'd done this before—oh God, he'd done this before. He'd seen proof that all his heart's plans had come to nothing but ashes, and he'd grieved. He couldn't… he couldn't… he couldn't….

And he remembered Dean, getting in the shower behind him, holding him, talking him out of his mood. Talking about his family. *Giving* Bailey to his family. It was the best, most perfect gift a man had ever given him, and Bailey couldn't pay that gift back now by giving up.

"Yes," he whispered, wrapping his arms around himself so he wouldn't fly apart. "I have to."

"When you're done telling the pilots," Reg said, in a still, stony voice, "I'll text Rory and Val. We've got a place to start. It could be so much worse."

So much worse, Bailey whispered to himself. He knew what looks much worse looked like. But this wasn't that, he reminded himself.

Not. Yet.

Surprises in All Sizes

DEAN'S HEAD hurt.

His head hurt, and his body hurt, and his phone felt like an ichthyosaur with a broken spine in his back pocket.

He could hear Marcus moaning.

And nothing.

Every soft groan coming from Marcus's mouth sounded like a bullhorn in a refrigerator, because their surroundings were so quiet.

They'd been all loud and tumbly just moments before.

"Dean?" Marcus all but sobbed.

"Buddy?" Dean asked.

"You alive?"

"No," Dean decided. "Everything's dark, and my head was blown up by a hand grenade."

"That's weird. Mine too."

The odds against both of them sitting, headless, and having a conversation were what finally forced Dean to open his eyes.

The darkness was almost as complete with his eyes open as it had been when they'd been closed. Slowly—because even moving his eyeballs hurt—he searched the space in the unfamiliar plane and found Marcus, wedged against the passenger's side of the plane. He had blood trickling from his temple, and his leg—which had been on a part of the fuselage that had buckled—was a horror show.

"Oh God," Dean whispered, staring at not one but two ends of bone sticking through the skin. "Marcus, don't look at—"

"Seen it," Marcus said, his eyes locked determinedly on Dean's. "It's bleeding a lot, Dean. I know we don't have shit in here, but even a cargo plane's got to have a first aid kit."

Dean nodded and ignored his head and its imminent threat of dropping off his shoulders. Marcus needed him.

"I'll find it," he choked. "Let me check on Bird. Then I'll come here and work on you."

As he stood, the broken pieces of his cell phone clattered in his back pocket, and he tried not to remember they were in the middle of the fucking desert and nobody in the Bureau—hell, nobody but *them*—knew where the fuck they were.

There'd been one case of water—*one*—rattling around the back of the plane when they'd gotten in. Dean remembered thinking what the hell? They'd get to Juarez in a couple of hours. How bad was it to only have a few bottles of water for two hours?

He'd better never tell that to Birdie, who was superstitious like most good pilots and would never let him live it down.

"Bird?" he rasped, taking a creaky step toward the front of the plane and feeling the hull of the thing shift beneath him. In a quick glance—but one that felt like it ripped his eyeballs out of his aching head—he saw that the rear of the fuselage had broken off, and the back end of the plane was mostly sand.

Well, shit, there went their one case of water.

He got to the front of the plane and crouched down next to Birdie, who was moaning against the dashboard, bleeding on the gauges and the steering column.

"Bird," Dean muttered, shaking the narrow shoulder. "How you doing?"

"Feels like my head exploded and my brains ran out my ears," Birdie muttered.

Dean grunted, because, well, *same*, and started to gently prod at the collapsed dashboard to see if Birdie was pinned.

"Relax," Birdie muttered. "I can move my legs." There was a grunt that was almost a laugh. "Too small. Whole life, been too small for sports, too small for dances—today, I'm too small to die."

"When we tell this story," Dean said, reaching down to pull Birdie's legs sideways gently, the better to help Birdie out of the seat, "we'll be sure to say you were too mean to die. Can you stand?"

"Too mean to die…." Birdie let out a rusty chuckle and accepted Dean's help out of the seat and into the aisle, the better to go sit down and be grossed out by Marcus's leg.

Dean scrounged around the plane, found a first aid kit from where he'd been sitting, and rummaged through it. Antibiotic wash, tons of gauze, a stitching kit, which would do them no good right now, and some syringes of morphine.

Dean glanced at the mess of Marcus's leg and contemplated the morphine.

"Marcus?" he asked, his voice a little shaky, "how's your math right now?"

"I can count to three," Marcus panted. "Like, my leg's busted in three places."

"Can you do morphine math? Like how much to give you to put you out of pain while I splint it without killing you?"

Marcus moaned a little. "I'd rather you kill me with it," he admitted, tears in his voice. "I'd take passing out as a kindness."

Dean grabbed one of the syringes and some alcohol swabs and wandered over to sit next to Marcus, his energy and ability to move almost exhausted. "Anything for a buddy," he muttered.

Marcus let out a half sob, and Dean pulled out his knife and used it to shred Marcus's khakis far enough up from the bloody mess of his leg to find a bare patch of skin to prep for the shot. He and Marcus had lots of first aid training, but a compound fracture was a rough thing for a trained doctor—hell, for a trained orthopedist. If Dean was going to dump antiseptic on his hands and try to straighten the leg enough to stop Marcus's bleeding, he wanted Marcus to be as unconscious as possible.

With a deep breath—and a hope that he wasn't going to OD his friend—he plunged the syringe in and prayed.

Next to him, Marcus's breathing started to relax, the steady moans that he'd tried to repress easing.

"Better?" Dean asked after a couple of minutes.

"Much," Marcus mumbled.

"Good. Bird, can you walk?"

"Sort of," Birdie said.

"I need you to find that case of water. We've got some work to do."

AN HOUR. It took him and Birdie an hour to get the leg to the point where they felt comfortable wrapping a pressure bandage around it. Everything Dean had ever learned in emergency first aid classes came into play, and as glad as he was that Marcus was unconscious for what he was doing, he missed Marcus's contribution to his little adventure in doctoring. Birdie was good for following directions, but Marcus was one of the few people who could follow Dean's wayward brain.

But finally, after using three-quarters of the water and all of the antibacterial rinse on washing the leg off and setting it, Marcus was as stable as they could get him. Everybody had sipped some water, and Birdie had set up the plane's emergency beacon.

There'd been a short, hot discussion on whether the beacon would bring friendly or unfriendly rescuers, and then Dean had pointed out that if there were no rescuers at all, they'd die slowly, as opposed to quickly if the next folks they saw proved to be unfriendly.

Birdie shut up after that. They were both concussed and woozy and ready to consign their fates to the night-closing desert outside their fragile little eggshell of safety.

At least, Dean hoped, the scorpions would leave them alone, but he couldn't vouch for the rattlesnakes. He'd have to check in the morning to see if any of them had crept in through the broken edges of the plane's tail.

HIS HEAD ached so fiercely that even sleep wasn't a refuge, but that didn't mean he could emerge from it easily. He whimpered and tried to open his eyes as voices approached from outside the plane, but nothing could penetrate the foggy veil of pain and darkness in his eyes.

Until he felt a smoothly gloved hand on his forehead and heard a dearly familiar voice murmuring, "Concussion, some soft-tissue damage in the neck, lots of bruising in the shoulders, chest, and abdomen. We'll need to test to make sure there's no internal bleeding, but mostly I think he needs some painkillers and some sleep."

Dean had heard Bailey's doctor voice before, but never aimed at himself.

"Bailey?" he mumbled. "Am I hallucinating?"

"No," Bailey said softly back. "But you'll wish you were. When you get better, I'm going to yell so hard and so long, you'll say to yourself, 'God, I wish I was still in that wrecked plane, dying in the desert.'"

"As long as you're here with me," he mumbled. "But I'd rather not die." His biggest fear bubbled to the surface. "How's Marcus? He can't die either."

Bailey's restrained chuff of breath told him that was a trickier proposition.

"Our two rescue pilots are getting the gurney in here for him," he said. "How much morphine did you give him?"

Dean called up the number, which had been lasered into his brain as he'd tried to do calculations on grains of the drug versus Marcus's body weight. When he said it, Bailey let out a breath.

"Close," he said. "That was as close to an OD as I'd ever want to give."

"His leg's a mess," Dean said, keeping his eyes shut. He didn't want to see the blood on his own hands. "Had to... feel for arteries. Couldn't penetrate arteries with bone shards."

Bailey grunted. "And you didn't want your friend to suffer," he said softly.

"Tell me he'll be all right." Dean wasn't too proud to beg.

"We'll get him to the hospital in Juarez, and you and Bird too," Bailey said, and the brief, dry touch of his lips on Dean's forehead was more reassuring than anything he could recall. Dean felt consciousness slipping away again, and he tried to fight it. Bailey was here. He had something important to tell Bailey, and he couldn't let it wait. Not after the last five days....

"Bailey...." he whispered.

"Shh, Dean. Not going anywhere."

"Love you." He sighed, and then he fell off the ledge into the blissful dark.

Maybe it was the five days out of the ER. Maybe it was the time with Dean's family. But Bailey could actually *feel* his doctor cloak settling on his shoulders once he knew Dean was alive.

Before that, he was a mess.

It didn't help that in circling the area where the cell phones had last pinged they'd seen the burnt-out husk of a Jeep with two still-smoking bodies in the front seat. Bailey wasn't sure what noise he'd made, but it probably hadn't been human, because Reg had grabbed his hand, and Anthony had set about coldly cataloging all the reasons the two bodies in the Jeep couldn't be Dean and Marcus.

"One of those guys is enormous, and the other is much, much smaller. We're looking for two five foot nine or ten guys who *don't* wear wool in the desert, and these guys are probably six five and five three."

Reg squinted at him as he aimed his field glasses through the plane's portal. "Those are *really good* field glasses."

"Yeah, well, my dad got them when he was in the Bureau," Anthony said, still peering through them.

Bailey was more interested in how he knew the identity of his would-be assassins. "How do you know—"

"Purple," Anthony said promptly. "One of those guys is wearing a purple wool suit in July in the desert—wool doesn't combust like cotton, and I can see a wool fedora still smoldering from here."

"So, uhm, what do you think happened?" he asked, although he had a pretty good idea.

"Oh, they were hit by an IED of some sort," Anthony said, with the surety of somebody who made munitions and ordinance his livelihood. "In fact," he murmured, about a minute later, "I'd bet they were hit by antiaircraft fire that went through the tail section of that plane *right there*."

"Oh my God," Bailey said. "Oh my God. Oh my God. *Dean!*"

He didn't remember much, not of the desert landing, nor of their two pilots disembarking. In fact, everything was a sweaty, panicky blur until Glen Echo clambered *back* into the landed twin-engine and shook him and Reg by the shoulder.

"They're alive, Doc—but they need you."

ONCE BAILEY had confirmed Dean was alive but unconscious, he turned his attention to Marcus's nightmare of a leg.

"Oh God," said Damien, their other pilot, taking a look over Bailey's shoulder. "Those are the fucking worst."

Bailey glanced at him. "You have experience with these?"

"Both as the recipient and as someone who's nursed a fellow sufferer," Damien said grimly. "The good news is, we can get this man to a hospital in less than five hours, and that was *not* the case for me *or* our friend."

"Spencer's was grosser," Glen said clinically. "I'll go get the gurney."

Bailey barely suppressed a snort of laughter. He guessed the company billing wasn't bullshit—these guys *were* search and rescue, which meant as first responders, not much shook them, not even the giant knot on Dean's temple or the fact that the pilot probably had a cracked skull and had bruised every organ known to medical science.

Bailey helped Damien and Anthony position Marcus for an easier transport to the gurney. "How was your friend's injury grosser?" he asked, genuinely curious.

"He got his falling out of a helicopter into a flood," Damien said. "By the time we got to him, it had been festering in a flood for twelve hours. It was like, one dump of antibiotics away from gangrene."

Bailey grimaced. "Yup. I think Glen's right."

"Which means you can tell the kid waiting in Juarez that it's gonna be okay, right?" Damien said soberly. "He was in bad shape about this guy."

"I'll tell him," Bailey promised, thinking of Chance's quiet sacrifice to stay behind. "And Reg too. They *need* Dean and Marcus to be okay."

"Will they be?" Damien asked, and to his credit, he was earnest about it, and not cavalier like he could have been.

"I hope so," Bailey said, and his voice came close enough to cracking that he didn't use it much after that.

IT WASN'T until they got back in the air that Anthony thought to contact his father, who told Val and Chance and organized the hospital crew, and after a tension-wrought five hours of Bailey and Damien keeping up a steady stream of IV fluids, antibiotics, and painkillers for all three of the injured, Glen brought the plane in for an effortless landing, so smooth Bailey almost fell asleep between the time the wheels hit the ground and the time the back hatch was opened by the ambulance drivers, ready to take their patients away.

An eternity later, he found himself—rumpled, dirty, and exhausted—asleep next to Dean Royal's prone figure. He was sharing a room with Marcus and Birdie, because Mexico apparently didn't fuss about patients who knew each other sharing rooms. Marcus would be asleep for many, many hours following a good five hours in surgery, and while visitors were allowed, *everybody* was cautioned to keep things quiet and the lights dim in deference to a concussion trifecta.

Bailey dimly hoped that more brains had been knocked *into* heads than knocked out of them.

He would dearly love to help with the knocking.

My *God*, he was angry.

He hadn't allowed the anger to build until he'd known they would all be all right, but he was *furious*. It wasn't until this blissfully peaceful moment, staring hungrily at Dean's face, that he reckoned with what had almost happened.

He'd closed his eyes tightly, hoping for some equilibrium, when he felt Dean's rough hand cupping his cheek. "You're going to kill me, aren't you?"

Bailey felt that permission in his bones.

"You're goddamned right I am," he growled, keeping his voice down but infusing it with every moment of worry, every moment of fury, every moment of painful self-revelation that had peeled the skin off his nerves in the last five days. "Do you have any idea what you've done to me?"

"Pushed you out of an airplane?" Dean asked, like he really wasn't sure.

"Oh, that is the least of your sins," Bailey snapped. "You *went away*. There I am, thinking, 'Oh my God—we might have a future!' and you *went away*!" He fought to keep his voice even. "I need you to not go away," he tried to snarl, but it came out more like a whimper. "I've had a lover go away and it… it *ruined* me. It destroyed me. I thought I was *dead*, and then you ravished me in the goddamned ER crib, and suddenly I had a pulse. And then you *came back* to me, and I was *stunned*, because living didn't suck like I'd been afraid it would, and right when I thought, 'Wow, we might be able to live *together*,' you *went away*!"

"Oh, baby," Dean murmured, rubbing the moisture under Bailey's eyes away with a cracked thumb. "I won't go away if I can help it. Emmett couldn't help it—you know that, right? He was just doing what you do. Being a hero. He was just being a good guy. He wouldn't have left you if he could have helped it. Who in their right mind would want to leave you?" He smiled slightly, and his eyes—half-open and hazy—closed with obvious reluctance. "I'd do a lot to come home to a man like you."

He fell back under then, and there was nothing left for Bailey to do but cling to his hand and cry. He didn't even ask how Dean knew about Emmett—he figured the answer would be, as it always was, "FBI." Of course Dean knew about Emmett; Dean knew everything about Bailey, from how he liked to be touched to how he liked his eggs done. He knew Bailey wouldn't jump out of an airplane unless his cat was next to him and his father was waiting for him on the ground.

And he knew Bailey had been hurt before he'd shown up on Bailey's porch with a sprained elbow and then ravished Bailey into next week.

But he'd kept showing up. And when Bailey needed shelter—hell, when Bailey's father needed shelter—Dean had provided. And when he'd been off slaying Bailey's dragons, his family had stepped in, like Dean had known they would.

Bailey had no choice. He'd figured that out five days ago, and he knew it even more keenly in his blood now. He had no choice. Whether Dean went off on an adventure and never came back, or went off and came back until they were both too old for adventures, Bailey had no choice but to be with this man, the man who held his hand when he was hurt and made a home when he wasn't.

It hit him then, like a slug to his stomach, that he might not ever be going back to Outskirts General Hospital ER again. Sarree could retire. Austin would function without him. But Bailey wasn't going to live anywhere Dean couldn't come home to.

Simplest decision of his life.

"Dean?" he asked plaintively, wondering if he was still awake.

"Yeah?" Not entirely awake, Bailey thought, but he wasn't ready to give up the conversation yet.

"Why do you work in Sacramento when your family lives in Bakersfield?"

"Dunno," Dean muttered. "Ask Marcus. His idea."

"If Marcus was willing to transfer to Bakersfield, could we live there too?"

He watched the smile overtake Dean's face even as he slipped under.

"Sure, Doc. Sure."

REG, ANTHONY, and Val came in after a bit and relieved Bailey and Chance, who had been there to make sure none of the patients awoke without a familiar face. Val apparently knew Birdie, so that was nice. Both Birdie and Marcus had declined to alert family that they were injured, which made Bailey curious, but not so curious that he refused Rory's lift to one of two hotel rooms they'd rented. Their pilots had taken off, with a promise to return in three days when the patients might be mobile, and all Bailey had to do was eat from the takeout order that Rory had brought with him, shower, change into the clothes from his knapsack, and sleep for a solid eight hours.

When he returned to the hospital with Chance, they were both surprised to see two men—in their fifties, wearing suits and Fed haircuts—in the room with Marcus and Dean, both of them shouting at the top of their lungs while the injured miscreants winced greenly and tried not to throw up.

Bailey was striding into the room to aid the two nurses, who were begging the men to quiet down, when the more senior looking of the men shouted, "And if you two want to move to fucking Bakersfield, you go the fuck ahead. Take it as the demotion it is, you insubordinate brats, because *neither* of you are moving up after *this* fiasco."

Dean scowled up at the man—obviously his superior in some way—and said, "But is it *really* a fiasco, sir? We put an end to Bratva's merger with the cartel, helped eliminate two assassins without actually killing them ourselves, and took out a paramilitary installation with zero casualties. I mean… nobody's government is complaining, am I right?"

His boss turned purple, and the other man had to guide him out by his elbow, talking soothingly to him about his blood pressure and how maybe he should stop by the blood-pressure station and have it monitored because this level of stress *couldn't* be good for him, and how Bakersfield might be the best thing that ever happened to the Bureau regarding Cabrillo and Royal, so maybe they could call this a win.

Chance and Bailey exchanged glances and then walked quietly into the room, where the nurses fussed and lowered the lights again and pumped all three patients full of more painkillers.

"I don't know why *I* had to endure that," muttered their tiny pilot. "I'm not even part of your stupid organization."

"Sorry, Bird," Dean said, sounding drained. "He did offer you reimbursement for the plane, though."

"Yeah. Thanks, Dean. You came through like a champ." And with that Birdie grunted and fell asleep, leaving a groggy Marcus.

"You know what I hate about Bakersfield?" he asked, sounding stoned.

"Your parents," Dean said promptly.

"You know what I *love* about Bakersfield?" Marcus persevered.

"*My* parents," Dean said, a dry smile on his face.

"Think they'll let me live there secretly?"

"Sure, Marcus. But first I need an apartment so Bailey can move out."

"Good," Marcus said, sounding surly. "You'd better move in together after this last fucking week. Goddammit, that was close."

And then he saw Chance, his eyes widened, and he *pretended* to sleep, while Chance sat next to his bed and opened his phone, a cat-and-canary smile on his face.

Bailey sank into a chair next to Dean's bed, shaking his head.

"Whatcha thinking?" Dean asked, sounding not quite as stoned as Marcus. "And, uhm, no yelling." He winced. "'Bout done with that today."

"You did it," Bailey said, still stunned. "You're flat on your back, and you asked to be transferred home."

"It was your only stipulation, right?" Dean asked, narrowing his eyes on Bailey's face. "I mean, your dad, his dog, your cat, and my family—that's all you need, right? I know you can find another job easy, but you don't need anything else, right?"

Bailey laughed softly, restored almost completely by his sleep, by hearing Dean keep yet one more promise to him, by realizing how deeply enmeshed he really was into the lives of all the people Dean loved best.

Four years ago he'd lost a lover, and he'd been alone in a desert of grief. A week ago his lover had gotten lost in an actual desert—and had given Bailey an entire cavalry with which to retrieve him.

Dean wasn't going to stop being brave and crazy anytime soon, but Bailey was pretty sure he'd never be alone again.

"You're okay," he said. "That's all I need. Now get some sleep, and we can transport you guys to Bakersfield in a couple of days."

Dean grunted, sounding happy. "You know what sounds *great*? My mother's curry salad sandwiches. I am *dying* for one of those. She makes them in the summer, you know?"

Bailey felt tears starting in his eyes, the joyful kind that came when a person's heart was amazingly full. "They're *delicious*," he said. "And she makes a mean iced tea and lemonade."

Dean sighed. "Marcus has his own place in the basement. Think my dad could build a ramp for him?"

"With my dad to help? They'll probably have it done before we get there."

"Still afraid I'm holding back?" Dean asked, and Bailey realized he was using the last of his energy to search Bailey's face for signs of remorse, or dissembling, or fear.

"I think you fell in love with me the same way I fell in love with you," Bailey said, reaching up to skim Dean's cheekbone with his fingertips. "Full throttle, no turning back, no fear, jumping right off the crazy cliff like jumping out of an airplane."

Dean smiled and closed his eyes. "You get me," he said happily. "It'll be fine."

Plans Like Diamond Stars

Marcus was released to another hospital in Bakersfield, which was hard on everybody, but Dean was a little relieved. The ramp to the basement was well underway but wasn't finished yet, and Marcus was going to have a lot of gear down there until he was fully recovered.

Dean and Bailey said goodbye to him in the Bakersfield hospital after he was admitted there and before they took Birdie to the Royal home for a good week of sleep before returning the pilot to El Paso. Glen Echo had offered Birdie a job in Glen's Napa-based search and rescue crew, and Birdie had accepted for a limited duration, but there was business back at home to deal with first. Birdie still wanted a plane—that hadn't changed—but apparently the idea of working with a crew had its appeal.

As did being the pilot who was "too mean to die" in a crash in the desert.

"You sure?" Dean said to Marcus before he and Bailey turned to go. He was still headachey and mildly concussed, but cleared to recover at home. It was absurdly difficult to leave his partner, his *friend*, at the hospital while he got to go home.

"Oh my God, please," Marcus muttered. "Please don't tell my parents. I… you know my dad. He hated that I joined the Bureau in the first place. My head hurts, my leg's a *war zone*, and if I have to hear one more fucking time about how I'm needed in the family business, I'll give in and spend the next seven days throwing up."

Dean nodded gently, because the now-familiar throbbing between his ears told him that was a real possibility.

"I hear you," he said softly, gripping Marcus's hand. "I just don't want you here alone."

Marcus squeezed and gave a grim smile. "I'll be spending most of my time sleeping," he confessed. "But I expect your family will keep me eyeballs deep in company."

It was true. Dean had always, in a rather peripheral way, known his family was glorious, but now, when they'd already started a schedule for who was going to visit Marcus when, he felt that awesomeness keenly.

He'd lied a little when he'd told Bailey Sacramento had been Marcus's idea. In fact it had been both of them—they'd wanted to stay in the state, but fresh out of school with degrees in law enforcement, and then out of Quantico, they'd both been so full of themselves, wanting to be "away from family—my God, they're suffocating!" That had been six years ago, and Dean hadn't gone a day—sometimes an hour—without being pulled into his siblings' lives. Sometimes it was annoying, but even when it was, it was still….

Home.

Bailey was willing to give up the place he'd lived most of his life to be near Dean and his family.

Dean—and maybe Marcus—were both ready to come home.

"You're okay with moving to Bakersfield?" Dean asked, because although Marcus seemed to have gone along with it, he wanted to make sure.

Marcus grunted. "I'm not giving up my partner because some poor doctor had the bad luck to fall in love with him. I mean, Bailey needs somebody who can bail him out if he blinks twice."

Bailey snorted. "Thanks," he said. "That's code now, locked into stone. I'll hold you to it." He grasped Marcus's hand and shook gently.

Marcus closed his eyes. "Go," he said softly. "I've got a while still here. Dean, you need to go sleep and then deal with the fam and then sleep some more."

Dean was suddenly, absurdly protective of his partner. He bent and kissed his forehead. "Get well," he ordered. "We've got adventures."

Marcus looked mostly asleep as they left, but the corners of his mouth were turned up in the faintest of smiles.

HOME WAS… well, home.

Dean could never remember it looking bigger or smaller, more or less dusty, brighter or dimmer. While he would call himself the least sentimental of men—or, at the least, of his entire family—he knew beyond doubt that the way he saw his parents' house, on their dusty patch of yard with the carefully maintained pool and garden, was etched more on his heart than his vision.

The hardpan in front of the gate to the yard was full of vehicles, and he suppressed a groan.

"How's your head?" Bailey asked.

"Pounding," Dean admitted ruefully.

"I'm in the guest room, with some stuff Reg brought down from Sacramento," Bailey told him. "Let me go first, and you slip in there to sleep."

It worked—but the *only* reason it worked, he realized when he woke up in the long shadows of early evening, with Mr. Bumble slumbering quietly on his chest, was that Bailey had signaled to the family, and they had *let* him escape into the blissful quiet of the room.

Still, outside in the backyard, he could hear the babble of voices, the splashing of Laure's and Prock's children as they played in the pool, the low drone of his parents as they spoke in the kitchen. He'd find out later that Birdie was ensconced in Marcus's room, since the pilot would be long gone before Marcus was released, and Birdie told the same story.

Neither of them needed to be in the middle of all that babble to appreciate that there were people who were glad they were okay.

Just then he heard a gentle tap at the door, and his sister came in, her rich, dark hair pulled back from her pretty face, the lines at her eyes and her bold nose giving her character and kindness, which was so much more interesting than her beauty.

"Hey," she said, bringing in a tray of—oh thank God—chicken curry sandwiches and cantaloupe. "Bailey made us save some for you."

Dean tried to swing his feet over the edge of the bed, and the room started swimming. He pushed back so he could lean against the pillows and was humbled when Laure started shoving extra pillows behind his shoulders until he could sit up and eat. Mr. Bumble slid to the side and eyed them both with vague disapproval until he was settled.

"Thanks," he said humbly. "I *really* appreciate it."

"Course, little brother," she said, her lovely brown eyes lighting up with a smile. "You know this family—anytime." She offered Mr. Bumble her finger, and the cat rubbed up against it in a most dignified fashion. Dean figured his sister had charmed the cat, as she seemed to charm every other living creature, and was glad.

Like all the boys in the family, he sort of worshipped Laure.

And now he nodded and, to his mortification, felt his eyes burn as they hadn't in the hospital. "You all really came through for me and Bailey," he said. "I... I am so grateful."

"Well, Bailey and his dad are treasures. You know that, right?"

Dean managed a rather watery smile. "I do." He knew his cheeks turned red, but he had to say it anyway. "I really love him. We're getting an apartment together here."

She smiled like a teenager and kicked her feet. "Eeeeeee! He told us. And we're so excited. We miss you!"

Dean gave a soft laugh. "Well, as much as it pains me to admit it…."

She gave him a surprise kiss on the cheek. "You miss us too," she said simply, and something in her eyes flickered, and Dean knew who she was thinking about.

"He misses us too," he said mildly. "You know that's not why Sal moved to Grass Valley."

She sobered. "I know," she said. "I… I can't even blame him. But as much as he tries to be bitchy and campy and funny…."

They both shared a sympathetic look, and Dean knew, suddenly, what Laure and Val must go through as the oldest siblings. Their brother Sal's heartbreak was real and painful and unfixable, but that didn't mean Laure and Val hadn't wanted to try.

"He's still hurting," Dean said for her.

"Well, you or Val need to get married," she said practically.

"What?" he tried to straighten up more, but his head threatened to pop off his shoulders.

"One of those long, fancy affairs that gets him down here for two weeks instead of a couple of days." She nodded forcefully. "We could totally fix his life. Look at you there, your perfect doctor boyfriend in the yard, charming the parents and my teenage sons and Prock's adorable little monsters altogether. I mean, Chance says even Marcus approves, and you know how hard it is to slip one past the work wife."

Dean recalled that frantic first meeting between them, and how Bailey and Marcus had seemed to click. Not romantically—thank God—but as though they understood the pitfalls of their situation and needed to work in tandem to overcome them.

It occurred to him now, taking a bite of his mother's food, with his sister confiding in him like he was—*gasp!*—an adult, that *he* was both the pitfall *and* the situation.

"I think they'll plot a lot," he said, musing. "Try to manage me. You know…."

"Make you saner?" she said, that eye-crinkling smile in place.

"Yeah," he said, swallowing blissfully. He looked his sister in the eyes again. "He makes me better, Laureate."

She nodded. "Well, you used my full name. I guess it's locked in stone." She frowned then. "By the way, did he tell you Mom told *him* about the name thing?"

Dean blinked in surprise. Thanks to all seven children absolutely *begging* their parents to let the name thing be *their* secret, to be told only in strictest confidence and fudged on all school reports, he'd assumed that he might be able to keep his whole name to himself until he was forced to sign a wedding certificate or something.

"Really?" he asked.

She nodded soberly. "He hasn't used it against any of us, but he *did* tell me that Laureate Ivy was a godsend. I could have been Honorarium Vassar, and then I would have been *really* screwed."

Dean managed a chuckle. "Oh God. He's right." He gave his head the lightest of shakes. "His humor—it sneaks out and surprises you sometimes."

"Yeah." He'd finished his sandwich and the cantaloupe, and she snagged his empty plate from his fingers as she stood. "Get some more sleep," she said softly. "He'll come in when everybody's gone or settled. And then you two can plan to the moon and back." Her smile was sweet, nostalgic, remembering, he was sure, the husband who had been killed at war, thousands of miles away, when she'd been a young, heartbroken mother.

"Laure—" He wasn't sure what he wanted to say, but he felt like if Sal's pain had been recognized, hers must *surely* be spoken.

"The planning's the best part," she said, her voice not breaking at all. "Although watching the plans come true can be pretty awesome." She bent and kissed his cheek again, offered Mr. Bumble another whisker rub, and flitted away, and he slid down his stack of pillows and slept some more.

TRUE TO Laure's promise, he was awakened by Bailey's quiet entrance. Shivering, Bailey grabbed a clean T-shirt from the battered dresser that had once been Sal's, and a clean pair of sleep shorts from the pile on top of the boys' desk that each one of the boys had carved their initials on as they'd used it.

Seeing him there, amid his family's history, felt so right that Dean wondered why Bailey Dodge hadn't been in his life this entire time.

"You awake?" Bailey asked softly.

"Yeah," Dean said.

"Want to strip to your skivvies and we can cuddle?"

"Sure, but you need to pet your cat. He's been a neglected love sponge all day."

Bailey chuckled and slid into bed, pulling the covers to his shoulder in deference to the breeze now blowing in from Dean's window. Every night in the summer, if it got cool enough, somebody went around the house and opened the windows and turned on the fans before turning off the air conditioner.

Dean loved that feeling of breezes coming from other places, having seen other things, brushing up against his skin. He stood and stripped to his boxers before climbing back into bed and lying to face Bailey, Mr. Bumble between them.

"How's your head?" Bailey asked softly.

"Much better than this afternoon," Dean told him truthfully. "I think it was sleeping in my parents' home. Was everybody okay with me doing that?"

"Oh yeah," Bailey said, and then told him that Birdie had done the same thing. "By the way, did you know our fathers have completely refurbished the mother-in-law cottage?" He gave a partial shrug. "I think my dad is pretty close to negotiating rent on the place so he can move in. It'll take a trip to Manor with a stop in Fort Stockton for our stuff…." He grew sober.

"And then you both relocate your lives here, for me," Dean said, acknowledging what a giant thing this was.

"For me," Bailey said firmly. "I've been farther from my dad than I like for too long. This is good for both of us. But that's not the main reason. I know we've said this a couple of times, but it bears repeating. I love you, Stanford Dean Royal. We probably could have continued on like we were doing for a year before either one of us said it. But getting thrown out of an airplane and chartering a plane to the desert to bail you out didn't make me love you *more*, if that's what you're worried about. It showed me how much I loved you *already*."

Dean felt the words wash over him and knew that after a couple of repeats, they'd be a solid part of his soul, his identity, grounding him in himself as a man who was loved by Bailey Dodge.

He couldn't wait—but he had a question first.

"You never—*nobody* ever—explained how you all found us? You had to have been in the air before the plane went down or Marcus...." He didn't want to say it, but it was true. Marcus wouldn't have made it another eight hours, particularly not after sunrise when the plane would have become a convection oven.

"Oh." Bailey glanced away. "Uhm, your brother Reg. Uhm. How much schooling has he had in computers?"

"Junior college," Dean said. "He's got an IT degree, and he does a lot of work from home. It gets him his own apartment, but it's not... you know. Great."

"Mm...." And before Dean could ask what that had to do with anything, he added, "I... you know, you should maybe take a gander at the computer setup in your parents' den. I don't think a lot of it is legal."

Dean's eyes shot open, and he was fully awake and a little alarmed. "Like, legal *how*?"

"He... he has trackers on the entire family. Did you know that? Like, you and Marcus too. I think I saw Rory and Anthony in there. So when I told him I was worried...." Even under the covers, Dean could see Bailey's gesture of rubbing his stomach, and part of him warmed, because he'd seen that gesture before, but most of him was listening.

"He tracked my phone?" Dean's voice cracked. "Bailey, he's not supposed to be able to do that!"

"I know!" Bailey hissed, shaking his head. "I mean, it's a good thing you're moving back here, because I think this family really needs you."

"Oh." It wasn't a word so much as a sound, but Dean suddenly felt it, the tender place in his heart where his family lived. He needed them—but he'd always resented that until now. Until his conversation with Laure, with Bailey, about how much they needed him. Bailey too. Bailey had lost a lover once. Dean had almost made him lose another. Dean's family had saved them both, and it was Dean's job to return the favor.

It was the only job he'd ever wanted. The reason he and Val had fought so fiercely. Because Dean had always thought he'd *known* what his family needed.

But now he *felt* what they needed, much like Val and Laure had, and that was ever so much more important.

His heart rushed in his ears as his life seemed to come together in one moment, in one place, with this one man.

He needed Bailey closer, and while his head was still sore, and he was now keenly aware of his limits, he also knew about his needs. Human contact. Family.

This man.

He burrowed his hands under the covers and over Bailey's smooth, pool-washed skin, needing to touch him. Mr. Bumble—who had gotten used to such things in the past—gave a disgruntled meow and flounced off the bed and into his crate on the floor, which had a squishy cat bed inside as well as his favorite catnip mouse.

Bailey *hmm*ed happily and moved closer, until their bodies were tangled under the sheets and Dean could claim his mouth in a breathless kiss.

"What're we doing here?" Bailey asked, but not like he was hesitant. Like he was excited about what was to come.

"I haven't held you in two weeks," Dean murmured, kissing him again. He pulled back to say, "And now that you know all my secrets, I need to hold you some more."

Bailey's laughter was rich against his mouth, and then it faded as Dean let the kiss get hungry, and hungrier. After a breathless moment, Bailey pulled back, stern in the moonlight that washed in through the window.

"You have a concussion," he said. "No gymnastics, Stanford—"

"Use that sparingly," Dean cautioned.

"Okay, but you need to listen to me!"

"I am," Dean said smugly. He lay back, his hands laced behind his head. "No gymnastics. It's all you. I seduced you when we met. It's all your turn."

Bailey's mouth on his neck, his collarbone, his nipples, was all Dean could have asked for and more. And more. He wasn't simply being seduced—he was being *devoured*. While he lay still, his blood rushed under his skin, tingling, until his aching erection thrust forward under his boxers.

Bailey suckled on a nipple while palming his cock, and Dean almost forgot where they were. He barely silenced a groan and was left back against the bed, panting, while Bailey drove him quietly insane.

"I'm going to…." he began the threat, and then Bailey slid his boxers down his hips, leaving him dripping in the cool night breeze, and he forgot what he was going to say.

Bailey's mouth on his cockhead made him forget everything else.

He began to whisper, thinking he would give instructions—harder, faster, tongue around the head—but Bailey knew what he was doing. He squeezed the base, licked the slit, tongued his tight harp string, then stroked him, slowly, from bottom to top.

Dean let out a harsh breath, no words left, and he realized that Bailey's position on the bed, on his knees near Dean's head with his hips out as he ministered to Dean with his mouth, left his own body vulnerable.

Dean began to stroke Bailey's cock through his briefs, and Bailey's expert blowjob faltered before Bailey resumed it with renewed vigor.

Dean rolled the briefs down and sucked his own fingers into his mouth before stroking Bailey's cleft, looking for his sensitive, vulnerable entrance.

Bailey's moan around Dean's cock was one of the most erotic sounds he'd ever heard.

And then it was on, almost like a race, but slower, more sensual, tender. It was the dance of lovers who knew each other's bodies, who made love to care for each other's hearts.

Dean's climax rushed him out of nowhere, and he breached Bailey's backside with two fingers as he spurted into Bailey's mouth.

Bailey's cry was muffled, and then he moved his hand from Dean's cock to his own, stroking hard while Dean penetrated until he let out a mewl, still swallowing Dean's come. He collapsed on the bed, dislodging Dean's fingers and bucking against the sheets, undone from the simplest of lovemaking, and Dean caught his breath.

"This is awkward," Bailey said eventually, face against Dean's thigh.

"I'm sure I've looked prettier," Dean agreed, but seriously, he didn't care.

"How's your head?" Bailey asked, turning his own slightly, and Dean grimaced, pausing his long stroke of Bailey's backside, of his flank, of his shoulders, all of which he could reach from this position.

"Aches a little," he admitted. "But not as much as it would have if you'd let me do what I'd been planning."

Bailey chuckled and slid off the bed, headed for the small attached bathroom. He came out with a washcloth, and after cleaning them both up a bit and fetching Dean some painkillers, he resumed his place in the bed, but this time with his head on Dean's bare shoulder so Dean could hold him tight.

"So," he said, after some shifting and snuggling, some more kissing, and some hands in naughty places before settling down.

"Yeah?" Dean asked softly.

"We're going to live happy ever after, right? Get an apartment, I'll get a job, you and Marcus will go be superheroes. I'll get to play with your family on my time off, my dad will live here and be old with your parents and… and that's it. Happy ever after."

Dean thought of all that entailed, of all the changes Bailey was talking about, of all the joy that awaited them.

"Works for me," he said softly. "Do you mind?"

"Easy," Bailey murmured. "So easy. Easy as falling out of a plane."

Easier, Dean thought as they drifted off to sleep. But he really didn't want Bailey being pushed out of any more planes, so he kept that thought to himself.

Keep Reading for an Excerpt from
Devil and the Deep Blue Fish
Book #8 of the Fish Out of Water series
by Amy Lane

Fish Food for Thought

"Dammit, fuck, he's gonna get you, Henry, dodge!"

"To the left, to the left, get your gun—your gun, Jackson, not your grenade launch—oh."

"*Ha*! There we go! Die, motherfucker, *die*!"

"Whew, wow. Okay, yeah." Henry Worrall threw his X-box controller onto the arm of the leather couch with relief. "Well done, my brother. I'll believe you next time when you say you got it."

Jackson Rivers, Henry's PI mentor and friend, set the game to practice, but he didn't shut it off, and he studiously ignored Henry's sigh.

"You should always believe me when I say I've got your back," Jackson said, giving Henry what he hoped was an animated smile.

Henry wasn't fooled. "God, Jackson—have you slept at *all* this week?" he asked, sounding helpless.

"Have you?" Jackson shot back, and he felt a wave of petty satisfaction when Henry winced. But Henry'd had a year to learn how to be a real boy, and apparently he'd passed Jackson up on the emotional honesty scale in that time.

"I'm worried as fuck about Randy," he said dispiritedly.

Just *hearing* it said out loud helped ease the tightwire of stress between Jackson's shoulder blades.

"Burton says there's no sign of the guy," Jackson admitted with a sigh. Abruptly, he was tired, which was an improvement over the manic tired-not-tired that had possessed him since their friend had been spirited away by friends in the military after a close brush with a killer. And not just *any* killer, it turned out. A *special* nutcase, nicknamed "BJ" by the covert ops unit assigned to track him down. Apparently this guy got off on catching—and killing—people in the act. He loved to thrust a knife between the ribs of the person *giving* the blowjob, and then cut the throat of the person *receiving* the blowjob. So far, he'd killed at least five women and six men that they knew about— and he would have killed Randy but, well, Randy was *special*.

Jackson maintained that Randy's job as a *Johnnies* model in adult films made him particularly impervious to shame. Randy hadn't frozen when the 7-Eleven clerk, shamelessly taking advantage of Randy's naivete and love of a good Slurpee, had died in the act. Instead, he'd screamed in the killer's face and taken off running. Fortunately he lived in the flophouse—an apartment that housed a number of guys in the same line of work—and it was right across the street from the convenience store. As far as anybody could figure out, Randy had run fast enough to disappear into the apartment complex before the killer could even recover from what had to be a terrifying bray in his face as he was achieving his own climax, so to speak.

Henry, who admittedly knew Randy better, said that Randy was so loud and so spazzy and so pure of heart the gods simply stuck their hands from the heavens and took hold of the killer, proclaiming, "You shall not pass!"

Either theory held validity, as far as Jackson was concerned. Randy, for all his quirks, was a sweet kid. He needed to do some growing up (not physically, please, he was six five as it was) and get hold of his many neuroses, allergies, and divergences, but underneath all the noise was a gentle giant who wanted to do good *so badly*. He was the first in line to take over a roommate's chores or to go fetch a favorite treat or to lend a book or an article of clothing or an ampule of lube. (Life in an apartment full of young adults who had sex for a living had its own rules.) If anybody deserved to go hauling into the ether, pants around his ankles, to avoid the icy claw of death, it was Randy.

Which was why Jackson had called his contacts in the south with the serial-killer hunters to come take Randy somewhere safe. But getting Randy to safety and assuring themselves that the killer was out of the way and wouldn't track down Randy's brothers in the flophouse were two different things. Henry lived in the same building, and Jackson, Henry, and AJ, another law firm employee, had made sure the security setup from the *last* time something like this had happened was still securely in place. *Everybody* was wired for sound now—the kids who lived with Randy; Henry and his boyfriend, Lance, who lived in the same complex; Jackson; his fiancé, Ellery, a founding lawyer at the law firm; and Galen, Ellery's partner—*everybody* had a cell phone that would alert if a rabbit so much as sneezed in their area. And given that there was a cantankerous neighbor who lived upstairs and liked to stomp loudly on Henry's ceiling when she thought somebody was enjoying too much life, that had pretty much ensured Lance and Henry had enjoyed zero alone time since Randy had been taken away.

So that was one *very* good reason for Jackson's sleeplessness, but he and Henry both knew that wasn't it. Jackson was pretty good at danger—had gotten damned used to it in fact. This wasn't the first time somebody they knew and cared about was in trouble, and the fact that Jackson was on a first-name basis with a bunch of the serial-killer hunters in the covert ops unit probably said something uncomfortable about Jackson's personal life. But the most uncomfortable thing about his personal life, he thought irritably, was that for one reason or another, it had ceased to be personal.

Fact was, Jackson hadn't slept well in over a decade, for a lot of very good reasons, from betrayal to fear for his person to regret to terror for the people he loved. The hell of it was, Jackson had been working *really* hard to at least be functional, and Ellery had been on board with his efforts. He still spoke to a counselor of sorts every week, and he'd been opening up to his friends and family more since Ellery had come into his life. He wanted to be a real boy almost as much as Randy did, he thought sardonically. But Randy simply had some growing to do. For instance, maybe taking a blowjob in trade for his birthday Slurpee hadn't exactly been prudent. But for Jackson?

The answers were a little less simple.

"Jackson?" Henry asked gently. "Are you having second thoughts about the wedding?"

Jackson actually laughed. "No," he said. "When it gets really bad, I wake up and think, 'I'm getting married in June,' and that actually calms me down. I don't use it too much, though. I need something in my heavy-duty arsenal."

Henry made a sound—a pained sound—like he knew something Jackson didn't, and when Jackson glanced at him, he was massaging the bridge of his nose.

"Don't give me that shit," Jackson said bitterly. "We all play mind games with ourselves to function. You know that as well as I do. I'm sure you've got a list of yours."

This time Henry grunted and picked up his remote control, began scrolling through his character options for a new skin. "Very perceptive. Let's see. My ex-boyfriend will be released from custody in two months. That keeps me up at night."

"I'll add it to the list," Jackson said grimly. Henry's ex was an abusive toxic nightmare, and his role as Henry's brother-in-law had pretty much trapped Henry into an eleven-year stint as an unwilling mistress. Henry's effort to break away from the guy had resulted in a lot of torn knuckles on Henry's part and a stint in military prison on behalf of Henry's ex.

"Naw," Henry said, a twisted grin in place. "He's my boogeyman—let me fight him. Most of yours are *far* more colorful."

Jackson grunted again, but this time in appreciation. He and Henry had started out at odds, but when Henry had lost the chip on his shoulder and Jackson had learned to apply his fully functioning empathy to *everybody*, even rednecks with attitude as it turned out, they could be more than friends. They could be tighter than brothers; they could be *partners* who functioned so well together sometimes it was like Jackson loaned out his brain so Henry could take over.

Henry was giving him a way to talk, and Jackson needed to appreciate it.

"I've let people down in my life," Jackson said simply. "Not on purpose, and certainly not for lack of trying. But…." He swallowed. "When you're about to get married, that's the sort of thing that haunts you."

Henry nodded and kept sorting through the costumes on the screen. "Same," he said softly.

Henry looked young—sounded young most times as well—but he'd survived domestic abuse, and he'd been to war. Something about those experiences gave him weight when he confessed to feeling the same.

"It's… it's nothing I can do anything about," Jackson murmured. "It's not even anything I'd change if I could. But it scares me when I think of who I've failed and how badly I don't want to fail Ellery."

Henry let out a long sigh. "Help, I've been shot," he said without heat or passion—or truth, since his character on the screen wasn't engaged in anything remotely warlike at the time.

But probably with accuracy, Jackson reflected. Henry had betrayed his sister, and whether he'd done it willingly or had been blackmailed, bullied, and threatened into it, he wasn't going to let himself off the hook that easily. But he could make his peace with it.

Jackson had to do the same.

"You're a great kid," Jackson murmured, feeling—wonder of all wonders—tired.

"I'm almost thirty, moron," Henry muttered, prickly as always. He set his remote down and yawned, and Lucifer, who'd always loved Henry best, made an awkward leap into Henry's lap, crashing on his missing foreleg and doing a faceplant into Henry's thigh. Henry stroked the cat's smooth black fur and smiled, and Jackson felt a familiar prickle on his shoulder as Billy Bob, who had been lounging on the back of the couch, reached out and kneaded him some biscuits.

It was a brief, sleepy moment in the evening, not too long after dinner. One that said Henry might crash on their couch for a much-needed nap, and Jackson, maybe—just maybe—might retire to the bedroom and sleep. Ellery was working late at the office tonight, a thing he did rarely but offered to do *this* night because Jackson's insomnia had been so terribly acute.

"I don't care *when* you sleep, Jackson. If it's after dinner, it's after dinner, but fuck us both, you've got to get some sleep!" When he'd spoken next that afternoon, his voice had dropped, throbbing gently with worry. "Besides, baby, if you fall asleep after dinner, I'll get home just in time for your first nightmare. Timing is everything." He'd given a twisted smile then, and Jackson had been terribly, terribly aware that what hurt *him* hurt Ellery too. Ellery would probably like to sleep uninterrupted as well, and while the first nightmare was almost a guarantee these days, the second, as long as Jackson had Ellery in his bed, was often not. A compromise of sorts, and Jackson understood.

Jackson found himself giving in to it, laying his head on the back of the couch, letting his cat's steady kneading lull him into a sort of somnolence. He was there, almost asleep, when Henry shifted on the couch.

Jackson popped awake in an instant at Henry's muttered oath, his heart pounding with the urgency in Henry's voice.

"I'm up!" he said, struggling for breath. "What do we need to do?"

"Nothing," Henry said firmly, although he was already on his feet and heading for where his shoes sat and his jacket hung in the foyer. "This is a me thing, not a you thing."

"But you don't *have* you things," Jackson complained. "Me, your boyfriend, the law firm—we're the beginning and end of your existence!"

Henry's laugh was warm and rich, and Jackson had a moment to reflect that he was glad Henry had gotten to the point where he really *could* laugh like that. And also that Henry had a full life—he wasn't only liked, he was *beloved*—by his brother, his brother's family, Galen, Galen's husband, John, all the boys he helped to mentor in the flophouse, and by Lance, his boyfriend, who thought Henry was the best man he'd ever known.

"No, seriously," Jackson said on a yawn. "Tell me where you're going. I'll fuss if I don't know."

Henry grimaced. "Actually you'll probably get called in on it too, so I may as well tell you. You know how half the kids who ended up at the flophouse got there because they hit on John or Galen?"

Jackson nodded, because he talked to the kids. "A lot of them were cruising for business," he said frankly. "They hit on John and end up with the world's most ethical porn director, who tries to give them any job but the one they asked for."

Henry inclined his head. "And he only gives them that one if they're over eighteen and are still interested after they've been cleaned up, evaluated, and spent some time off the streets."

From what Jackson understood, John ended up with one porn model in twenty or thirty offers, but he *never* took advantage of his own employees, and he'd helped a *lot* of kids find a way to a different home.

"Did he get another one?" Jackson asked, curious. He knew that sometimes Henry was called in when the kids ended up at John's receptionist's house so he could make sure Isabelle Roberts was safe when she had a stranger sleeping in her guest room.

"Fourteen," Henry said grimly, and Jackson winced.

"Dear God."

"Yeah. So I'm on to help talk to the kid, but I think Ellery's going to be called in too."

Jackson frowned. "He's fourteen. Has he been accused of something besides solicitation?"

Henry shook his head. "No, I think he witnessed something. John and Galen got the story out of him. I think they're headed here."

"Aw shit," Jackson muttered. "Your gig sounds more fun."

Henry chuckled, but it was a strained sound, and Jackson understood the cost that must be involved with taking care of a kid who'd been out on the streets the way this one had been.

"I'm sorry," he said quickly. "I know it's gotta hurt."

Henry shrugged again. "It's hard. I mean, I'm glad we can get them to someplace good—a shelter, a foster home, someplace *not* the street, but...." He sighed. "My old man was a piece of work," he said. "There was a reason Davy and I had such fucked-up lives before we came out. But we always had food and a place to sleep. Can't say that would have been the story if Dad had known about either of us, but...."

"You're going to see yourself in them," Jackson said softly. "I was one good friend and his mom away from being one. Don't think I don't see that too."

Henry shook his head. "See, *that's* why you don't sleep," he said, blowing out a breath. "Because you know these things—you've already thought about them, and you see them going on in the world, and they scare you shitless. Some of us get surprised every single time."

Jackson chuckled weakly. "Yeah, but you also get to sleep." As he spoke, his back pocket buzzed, and he answered it as he stood and stretched.

Galen and John will be by in an hour or so. Maybe prep them some food.

"And you were right, sensei," he said, bowing in Henry's direction. "Go. Do good things. I'll stay here and make your bosses soup."

Henry grinned. "The wonton soup you fed me was *outstanding*!" he said before heading for the door. He paused, his hand on the knob, and turned. "Jackson?"

"Yeah?"

"Whatever it is you think you failed at, whatever it is you think you didn't do, you gotta find a way to let it go, man. You're a good friend—a good man. Get some fuckin' sleep."

And with that he was gone, and Jackson was fishing the ingredients for homemade wontons out of the fridge again.

JOHN AND Galen arrived in less than an hour, making Jackson glad he'd gotten a move on with the soup. The two of them blew in with a fierce March wind that drifted a few leaves in on their coattails, and Jackson could tell Galen, who used a cane to help him walk, was moving more stiffly than usual tonight, probably thanks to the surprising cold.

"If this is blowing in like a lion," he said acidly, accepting John's help to shed his coat, "I am against it. In fact I think we should boycott lions of every sort."

"We can't," John said practically, hanging both their coats up on the pegs by the door. "Lions are cheerfully homosexual in the wild and possess the world's most amazingly proportioned balls. I think we owe it to our people to give lions a chance."

Galen stared at him. "I don't owe my people the right to freeze my own generously proportioned balls off!" he argued, and John snorted.

"I'm just saying, maybe we shouldn't blame the lions. They didn't make the expression."

"I'll blame whomever I damned well—oh Lord, thank you, Jackson," Galen said, sinking down at the dining room table and accepting the steaming mug of the cocoa Jackson had put on when he was throwing the soup together. Under Galen's planned scruff and the curly hair he grew long to mask the scars from the same accident that injured his leg, Jackson could see white lines around his mouth.

"Would you like to eat?" Jackson asked. "Wonton soup and warm french bread." He grimaced. "Probably an affront to both Asian and European culture, but—"

"Who *cares*." John laughed. He had bright ginger hair and tanned freckled skin, and his green eyes almost disappeared into the lines at the corners when he smiled, which was often. "It smells awesome! Here, you grab your laptop, and I'll dish everything up."

"I already ate—" Jackson began, but Galen overrode him.

"I have strict instructions from Henry to take that for the excrement it is," he said in his acid Southern drawl. "You will eat twice, and you will eat a lot. I for one am *tired* of listening to Ellery worry about you. You will eat to accommodate *me* and for no other reason."

Jackson smiled slightly. Ellery had not been looking for friends when Galen had insisted he be hired at the firm, but he'd found a good one. Galen's dry sense of humor and carefully understated kindness was a good match for Ellery's constant insistence on reason.

As in it was only *reasonable* that they all make sure Jackson was doing well, since Ellery refused to even contemplate a future without him.

"Understood," he said wryly. "He's the boss."

Galen snorted, but Jackson had already busied himself fetching his laptop from the bedroom and trying not to trip on Lucifer, who had a tendency to sprawl any-old-where just to make Jackson's life more interesting.

After swearing at the cat, Jackson returned and set it up at his place at the table, workstation at the ready.

"Okay, guys," he said, trusting John in the kitchen the way you trusted a good friend who'd been over a lot, "tell me what's up."

Galen let out a breath. "Tell *me*," he said, making eye contact with John even as John was fetching bowls from the cupboard, "what you know about the Moms for Clean Living."

Jackson sucked in a breath. "You mean the Stepford Dragons?"

John snorted, and Galen arched a sardonic brow. "Of course. I had no idea they'd rebranded."

"You're talking about those super right-wing scary women who go from town to town ripping books off shelves and screaming, 'Keep those horrible queers away from my babies!' right?" Jackson asked, and while he was going off with his own brand of honesty, his fingers were also walking the talk by pulling up what he knew about the group on his computer.

"We are indeed," John said, and the grin he gave was truly manic. "I'm a soulless ginger porno-making queer—I'm, like, their devil!" He held a hand to his heart. "My nana would be proud."

Galen chuckled fondly. "From what you've told me, she would have been."

"My nana," John told Jackson, "was the most genteel whore you have ever met. She literally told me that's how she met my grandfather, while putting away enough hooch to kill a regiment. But after she married, she rocked a twinset and pearls, scandalized the PTA with her swearing, and—" He swallowed, and Jackson could see genuine fondness for the woman. "—told her entire neighborhood to go to hell after she took me in when my father caught me having sex and beat the shit out of me."

Jackson's mouth fell open, because he had not been expecting that much real emotion.

John shook him off. "No… no. I'm sorry. I'm a little too honest after Galen and I attend our NA meetings. I didn't mean to burden you with that." He straightened his spine, and Jackson could see the genuine strength in somebody with an admittedly odd, albeit altruistic, approach to life. "I *wanted* to say that my nana would have *abhorred* these women, and when my political rage gets acute, I like to imagine her telling them all that she hasn't seen this many twats since she stopped pulling trains in her old brothel." He let out a happy sigh. "God rest her soul. I hope she's teaching the other whores in hell how to cheat at poker and give blowjobs worth a fortune. She was, legit, a hero."

"I'll pour one out for her, next time I'm drinking…?" Jackson let John fill in the blank.

"Irish whiskey!" John said with a grin, indicating his red hair. "What else?"

"Fair enough," Jackson agreed, inclining his head. "To grand old dames." He glanced down at what he'd pulled up on his laptop. "We need more of them," he said with a sigh. White women, most of them with coifed blond hair, many of them with blue eyes, stared back at him.

Galen grimaced. "I don't even need to look," he muttered. "Scary Stepford Dragons?"

"Yep," Jackson said. "And hey, last year they started a chapter in… you guessed it—"

"Sacramento," John said grimly. "I know. They have a small office about two blocks from the church where Galen and I attend our NA meeting."

Jackson frowned at him. "Wait… correct me if I'm wrong, but isn't that only a couple of blocks from Lavender Heights?"

Sacramento's nightlife had made great strides in the past ten years—lots of small businesses, bars, restaurants, and streets people felt safe enough to walk late at night on pub crawls. Lavender Heights was in the heart of all that positive energy and activity, with an LGBTQIA library on one block and a couple of nightclubs three blocks away. It was the kind of place people—any people—could walk hand in hand after dark and mostly only be afraid of traffic.

Putting the office of a bunch of people with an anti-gay or -trans agenda within the proximity of Lavender Heights was like putting nitro and glycerin on the same block.

"It is indeed," Galen said, his mouth tightening. "And this evening, we met a young man who has… well, seen things."

Jackson's eyebrows rose. "Like what?"

John let out a frustrated breath as he brought bowls and such forward to set the table. "That's the hard part. He… well, first he propositioned us—"

"You," Galen said dryly. "He propositioned you. You were standing by the car, waiting for me to catch up, and the young man stuck his head out of the bushes at crotch level and said—"

John gave a pained grimace, and Jackson realized he was embarrassed. "Don't repeat it," he muttered. "Please, Galen. It's so embarrassing. He's a *child*."

Galen's droll smile faded, replaced by gentleness. "I'm sorry," he said softly. "I guess it's only funny to me because I know you're a decent man." He glanced at Jackson and finished the story. "Anyway, he stuck his head out of the bushes, suggested a convenient way John could receive his sexual favors, and then disappeared again as I walked up. John told him he didn't want favors, but we were lost and he'd give the kid a twenty for directions."

"Did it work?" Jackson asked, because it was a good idea.

"Like that," John said, snapping his fingers. "I asked him the way to a hamburger place, and the kid gave me one in two blocks. I said he could have the twenty and I'd feed him if he drove there with us."

Jackson smiled. "Another good idea," he praised.

John rolled his eyes. "Hey, just because the kids I work with are well over eighteen doesn't mean I don't understand what makes them tick."

"Sex and food," Galen said promptly.

"*Money* and food," John retorted. "Street kids really don't want to be doing the sex thing in the first place."

"Or," Galen added, "a place to sleep and food. And sometimes"—the play left his voice, because he too was a decent man—"a place to bathe and sleep and get clean clothes. And a kind voice. And food. Which is why we left him with John's receptionist and called Henry over. I do hope you don't mind."

"Of course not," Jackson said. "I didn't need the car anyway. It's fine."

Henry had driven their shared custody minivan that day when he'd dropped Jackson off at home. Originally the plan had been that Lance, Henry's boyfriend, would come get Henry after Ellery got home, but Lance had been forced to work late—he was a resident at UC Davis Med Center—so Henry got to keep Jennifer, the persnickety crap-brown minivan that only responded to Jackson and Henry and frequently showed her distaste for anybody else at the wheel by doing things like stalling out at intersections or throwing her doors open dramatically. Her previous owner, a perfectly lovely schoolteacher with three kids, told him that once the car had protested a family trip by throwing open her back hatch and vomiting luggage all over the highway—no mechanic on earth could figure out how the latch had opened since it was supposed to be electronically controlled. "Not needing the car" was frequently code for, "Oh God, at least someone else is dealing with her," but not in this case.

In this case, Jackson couldn't think of a more comforting vehicle with which to deal with a kid off the streets in all his probable suspicion and skittishness. Jennifer would feel very real to a kid like that.

"So back to the street kid," Jackson said as John leaned over his shoulder and frowned at the screen.

"I don't see her," he said briefly to Galen, who grimaced.

"Well, fixers aren't usually on the company website," he said acidly, and John stuck out his tongue.

"See *who*?" Jackson prodded, both amused and frustrated. It was fun to see the usually unflappable Galen be cheerfully "flapped" by his significant other, but he was also curious to get to the bottom of this case.

John and Galen exchanged glances, and John was the one who spoke.

"We got the kid a hamburger and a shake," he said after a moment. "And we told him we could get him a place to sleep and a line on a shelter, which was sort of a lie because I'd already texted Mrs. Bobby's Mom. I mean Isabelle." He grimaced. Bobby was one of his models, and the kid had made a lot of sacrifices to get his mom out of the tiny town that had been strangling them both. While she initially had *hated* that her son was in porn, she'd softened when she'd met his friends and they'd all been, well, kind. Sweet young men. And so many of them had been *so* deferential to her as a mother. She still probably disapproved of the porn, but she'd taken the job offer as a receptionist and had become a surrogate mother to the kids. And she'd also helped John and Galen with their effort to help place the young people who most assuredly did *not* belong in sex work, and to find them a shelter, a home, or a system that would keep them safe until they got their feet under them.

"And she, being made of awesome, took him in," Jackson filled in. "And you stole my gaming buddy for the night, and yes, I forgive you too." Jackson made a circling motion with his hands and then stood and placed the laptop on the end table so he could finish helping with the table.

John waved him down. "C'mon," he said with a laugh, bringing a basket of freshly heated bread to set in the middle. "Give me some credit. Galen, who cooks at our house? And don't say DoorDash."

Galen snickered, almost like a kid. "Well, since you've limited my options, you *do* prepare a mighty tasty chicken and rice."

"Thank you," John said. "I'm also hell on a grill, and I have my nana's steak marinade, so there." He sighed and went back to the kitchen. "Anyway, once we got the kid in the car, we started talking to him to make him feel like he wasn't being kidnapped—I always give them street coordinates and bus coordinates, because if they flee, I want them to feel like they can get back to their old spot."

"You would be surprised how many kids don't even know where they *are*," Galen muttered, sounding bitter. "It's like a bus dropped them off and boom! They were suddenly expected to feed themselves. Anyway, John is doing the schtick—'This street is 24th and K, and we're going to stay in midtown. There's some apartment buildings on 30th and L. Can you remember that?' and the kid goes, 'My mom lives on Watt and Whitney, so thanks. I didn't know this part of town until I ran away.'"

Jackson swallowed. "From his mom?"

"That's what we asked," Galen said, "mostly to clarify, and then the kid says, 'No, from the lady who came by to fix me.'"

Jackson shook his head like he'd been shocked. "Say that again?"

John and Galen met eyes, and Galen nodded. John spoke next. "He said, 'The lady who came by to fix me.' And Galen and I were, well, *very* confused to say the least. At that moment we drove by…." He held out his hands in a "gimme-gimme" gesture.

And Jackson got it. "Moms for Clean Living," he said in surprise. "Home of the Stepford Dragons."

John nodded grimly. "The very same. And Cowboy—"

"The kid?" Jackson asked, smiling slightly.

"Swore up and down it was his real name," Galen said, his voice ringing with fondness. "Anyway, Cowboy said, 'She had on one of those jackets.'"

Jackson nodded slowly. "And now we're here, looking up the Stepford Dragons. I get it. Did the kid say anything else?"

Galen shook his head and then sighed. "Well, yes. He was taken in and put in a room with four other boys, one of whom still had makeup on. He said they were… well, sad. He and another boy broke out, climbed out the window and down the trellis, and, well, that's part of the story. But the end of the story is that Cowboy ended up at a shelter—one of the church ones that made a big deal out of homosexuality, and about a week later…." John shuddered.

"Turned his first trick," Jackson guessed sadly.

"Sometimes I'm so angry," John said, sounding tired. "I feel like we've been fighting this battle my entire life, and then I realize how many people we've lost or almost lost to it and…." He shook his head again and gave a weak-tea version of his usual manic grin. "I'm sorry. I'm… you'd think with my job history I'd be jaded now. That I would have learned that sex was a commodity in my teens and gotten over it. But I remember such *joy* in the discovery, you know? Such excitement learning 'What does this button do?' And the kids that walk through our doors? Some of them discover such *power* when they discover themselves. To see that destroyed so horribly by the people who are supposed to protect kids. It's… it's infuriating."

"I can't argue," Jackson agreed, thinking about the way his nightmares chased him down. He and Ellery saw a lot of innocence squandered or destroyed in their jobs. Even the guilty—and not everybody who crossed their threshold was going to be innocent—were often caught by surprise. The eighteen-year-old who went to a party and got busted for party drugs suddenly realizing that he might be kissing goodbye a promising future, not to mention five years of his life. The young mother who did a favor for her boyfriend and got caught up in a trafficking sting. The bodybuilder who threw a hard punch in self-defense and is suddenly wanted for manslaughter. Or the person collecting welfare who got a job and didn't return their next check because it was the only reason they could make rent.

The week before, they'd taken on the case of a fifteen-year-old who had defended his mother from her abusive boyfriend and was being tried as an adult for assault. Jackson and Henry had spent a week listening to report after report of how the boyfriend had been about to kill both the mother and the boy and the police hadn't been able to keep him away. Ellery had brought the boy in for arraignment, face full of bruises and a cast on his arm, and begged a judge not to send him to adult jail while he awaited trial.

Ellery had won, and the boy and his mother were in protective custody—and he was well on his way to getting the case dismissed. But the fact that the small family had been put in this position had been tough on the entire office.

John was right. It sure did feel as though joy was being systematically vacuumed out of their lives sometimes.

A fourteen-year-old kid named Cowboy had needed to run away to defend his right to exist.

"What did you need us to do?" he found himself asking, and at that moment, Jackson heard the garage door open.

"Go greet Ellery," John said gently. "Let's have some of this delicious soup and bread. There's more to tell."

Scan the QR code below to order

Writer, knitter, mother, wife, award-winning author AMY LANE shows her love in knitwear, is frequently seen in the company of tiny homicidal dogs, and can't believe all the kids haven't left the house yet. She lives in a crumbling crapmansion in the least romantic area of California, has a long-winded explanation for everything, and writes to silence the voices in her head. There are a lot of voices—she's written over 120 books.

Website: www.greenshill.com
Blog: www.writerslane.blogspot.com
Email: amylane@greenshill.com
Facebook: www.facebook.com/amy.lane.167
Twitter: @amymaclane
Patreon: https://www.patreon.com/AmyHEALane

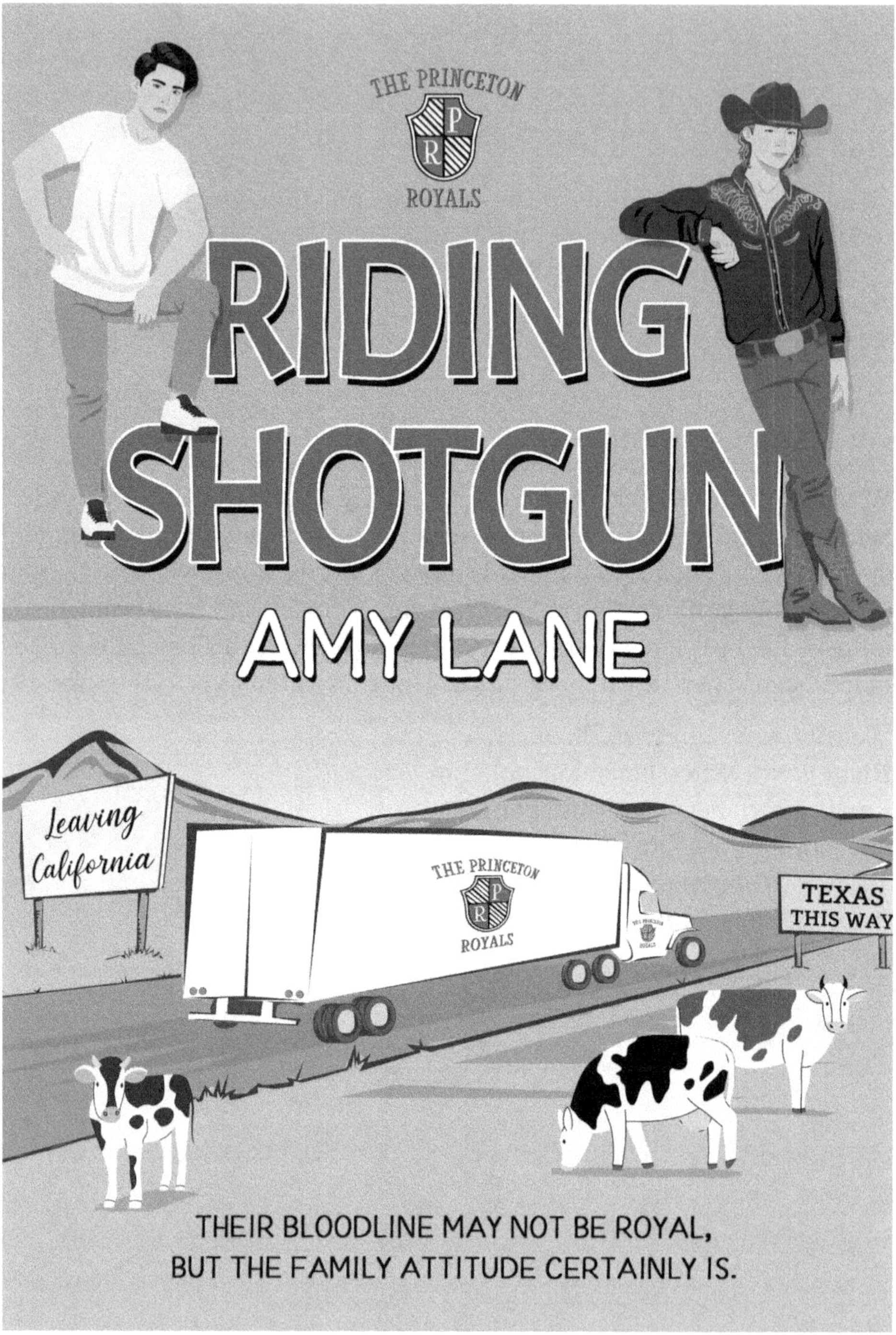

THE PRINCETON
P R
ROYALS

RIDING
SHOTGUN

AMY LANE

Leaving
California

THE PRINCETON
P R
ROYALS

TEXAS
THIS WAY

THEIR BLOODLINE MAY NOT BE ROYAL,
BUT THE FAMILY ATTITUDE CERTAINLY IS.

Princeton Royals: Book One

Val Royal's tight family has always had his back, but they love to interfere in his life. That interference almost sends him over the edge when they arrange for Rory McCauley, security specialist, marksman, and hound-dog smartass, to ride shotgun as security on his latest run.

Hot, bossy, and sharp as a tack, Val ticks all Rory's boxes, but Val's looking for something real, and Rory's allergic to intimacy. Besides, their gig running refrigerated bull semen from Bakersfield to Austin could make or break Val's buddy's ranch, so Val's understandably pretty focused on the job. Rory still wishes Val would let him help Val, uh, relax.

As Val and Rory work to keep their payload safe from a couple of determined saboteurs and they get to know each other as smart, competent, fearless professionals, sparks fly, and Val starts to fall for Rory's roguish charm. But can he convince Rory their romance would be worth more than a straight shot to Austin—that it would be a love worth coming home to?

Scan the QR code below to order

BOWLING for TURKEYS

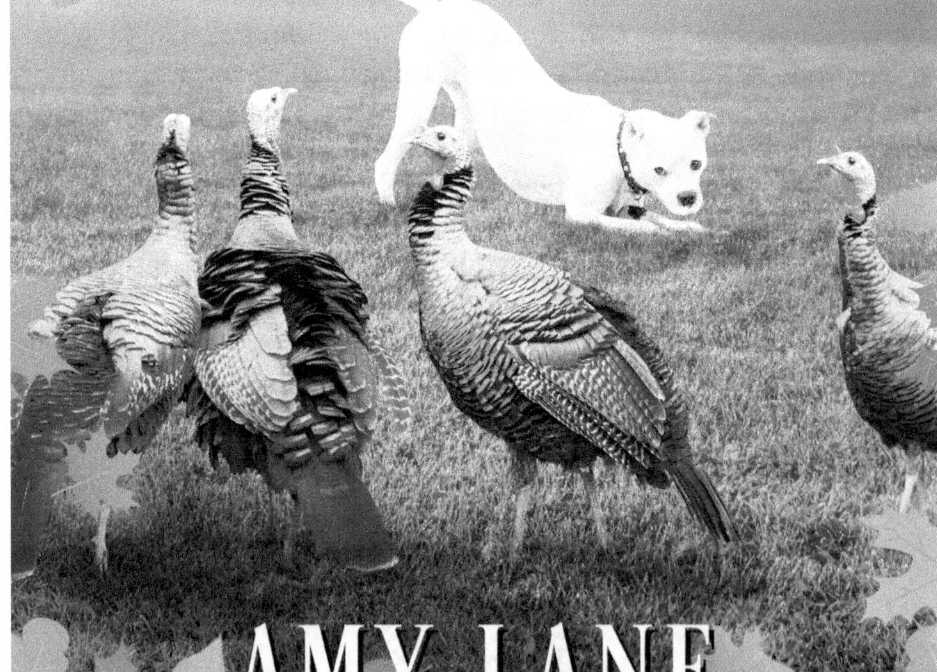

AMY LANE

Milo Tanaka was not recovering from the mother of all breakups when his best friend barged into his home and gave him a dog. While Julia the dog doesn't like squirrels, cats, turkeys, other dogs, or most humans, at least she gets him out of bed.

When a tiny blond dog rockets out of nowhere to bark ferociously at Garth Potter's enormous Daniff, "the Chad," Garth is annoyed, but Chad simply woofs in Julia's face. But when Garth looks around for her irresponsible owner, he finds a fey panicky disaster desperately trying to keep his dog from getting eaten, and realizes Milo is simply new to dog ownership, not neglectful or cruel.

In fact, Milo is a truly decent guy, and he and his best friend have been struggling to find their footing in adulthood and relationships. As Garth befriends Milo and the irascible Julia, he finds himself entangled in Milo's broken heart and fractured life. As much as Garth wants to fix it, he knows that Milo has to fix it himself. With the holidays approaching, Milo realizes that a good relationship won't leave him isolated and afraid, but surrounded with friends, and that the key to thriving isn't just chasing the turkeys out of his life—it's letting a good man in.

Scan the QR code below to order

AMY LANE

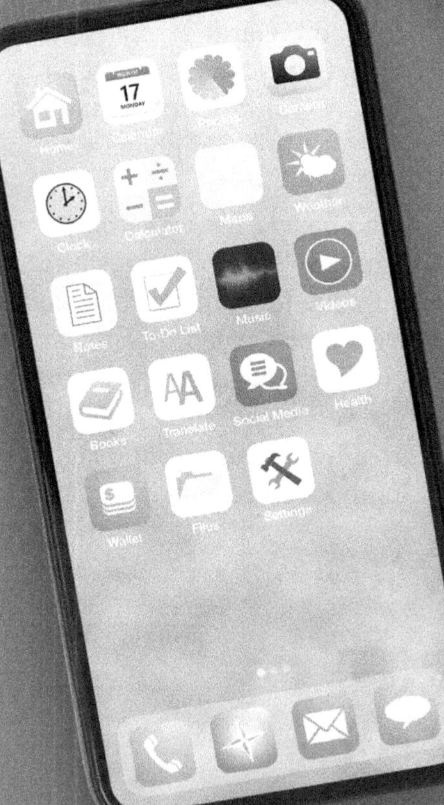

SWIPE LEFT, POWER DOWN, LOOK UP

Busy soccer coach Trey Novak doesn't have time for the awkwardness and upheaval dating can cause, but when his cousin stands him up for a lunch date, he meets someone who changes his mind.

Dewey Saunders is dying to get a real job in his field and start the rest of his life, but a guy's got to pay rent, and the coffee shop is where it's at. When the handsome customer in the coach's sweats gets stood up, Dewey is right there to commiserate—and maybe make some time with a cute guy.

Trey's making hopeful plans with Dewey when his professional life explodes. He and Dewey aren't in a serious place yet, and suddenly he's promising to make sports a welcoming place for all people. When Dewey puts himself out to comfort Trey after an awful day, Trey realizes that they might not be in a serious place, but Dewey has serious promise for their future. If someone as loyal and as kind and funny as Dewey is what's offered, Trey would gladly swipe right for love.

Scan the QR code below to order

FOR **MORE** OF THE **BEST GAY ROMANCE**

www.ingramcontent.com/pod-product-compliance
Lightning Source LLC
Chambersburg PA
CBHW070541100726
47907CB00004B/1209